LAWS OF PHYSICS BOOK 2: SPACE

PENNY REID

HTTP://WWW.PENNYREID.NINJA/NEWSLETTER/

Caped Publishing

Made in the United States of America

1st Edition, February 2019

PRINT EDITION

ISBN 9781635763409

PROLOGUE: LINEAR MOMENTUM AND COLLISIONS

Mona

L isa was there . . . *here.*
At the house.
In her room.
And so was I.

We were sitting on her bed and she was talking about the arrest, explaining what happened, how Tyler had known she was calling things off for good, so he set her up to make it look like she'd been selling drugs to kids, but that—though she'd been arrested—the charges were dropped when the witnesses changed their stories. She used expletives and insults to describe Tyler, her voice growing quieter and quieter with rage.

Now she was thanking me, and her eyes were wide and open, and she looked like a different version of herself, one I actually knew rather than the stranger she'd become. She was saying that she forgave me for what happened when we were younger, and that she'd been stupid to hold on to the grudge for so long, and that she missed me when she'd been sent away after I'd tattled on her and Gabby to our nanny, and that seeing media images of Leo and me with our parents at events and movie premieres and award shows while she was at boarding school alone made her feel like she was trash, unwanted, forgotten.

But she realized now that I had nothing to do with that, she realized I was just as trapped as she had been. And she was so sorry. So sorry. She'd expected Leo and me to protect her, but she knew we'd been powerless, and she was working on accepting being abandoned and wanted to move on.

Now she was saying it was all in the past, and I'd protected her now. I'd protected her and she would never forget it. I'd protected her and it meant the world to her. I'd protected her and now she felt like she had another chance at life and I was responsible for changing her life.

Now she was next to me on the bed, hugging me, apologizing for hugging me because she knew I didn't like it, but saying she couldn't help it, and thanking me, and telling me how much she owed me and saying that, if there was ever anything she could ever do to help me, I should ask. I should always ask. She promised that all the bad choices were at an end and that she was going back to school, she was done being selfish, she was done being destructive.

Now she was staring at me like she was confused, or she was worried, and then glancing at Gabby. Gabby shrugged, shaking her head quickly, wearing an identical frown to Lisa's, her eyes coming back to me.

Now they were both looking at me like they expected me to say something.

But I didn't know what to say. I didn't know what to do.

I didn't know . . . *I don't know.*

"Mona!"

My name sounded faraway, as though it had been spoken through a tunnel, or underwater. I felt a small shake. Someone was shaking me. I heard a sudden snap, like the crack of a whip. I blinked, abruptly surfacing to the present, the last half hour and all of Lisa's words rushing over me, flooding my brain.

Lisa.

"Hey, snap out of it." My sister was here, kneeling in front of me, snapping her fingers in front of my face, sounding frightened. She turned over her shoulder. "What is wrong with her? Did something happen? Oh my God, he didn't—did he hurt her?" Lisa appealed to Gabby, who shook her head.

"No, no, of course not. Not all guys are like Tyler, Lisa." Gabby was sitting on the desk, watching me with a worry-rimmed stare. "They got along really well. When I went downstairs, they were—"

"I can't do this." My hoarse voice brought Lisa's attention back to me. Her eyes darted between mine. I gripped her forearms. "Lisa, I can't do this. I can't leave."

"What?" My sister whispered. "What are you talking about? Are you okay? Did something happen?"

I shook my head, my thoughts a mess. "Yes. I mean, no. Not like that, not something bad. But it's-it's terrible."

Tightening my hold on my twin, I didn't get a chance to explain further because Gabby gasped.

"Oh my God! Oh no. Mona! I swear to God, Mona DaVinci. Did you fall for him?" Gabby had straightened from the desk, her eyes now a little crazy, rimmed with panic and accusation.

I sighed helplessly.

She groaned and covered her face. "No! No, no, no, no! I told you to stay away if you liked him! Why didn't you listen to me?"

"What is going on?" Lisa was glancing frantically between Gabby and I, looking completely perplexed.

Gabby abruptly dropped her hands from her face, setting them on her waist and shaking her head at me, her look one of intense frustration. "You are so smart, and yet so impossibly stupid. What are you thinking? That you're going to tell him the truth? Tell him about Lisa? If you do, you're *insane*. Insane!"

"What?" Now Lisa's eyes returned to me and she looked completely lost. "What is going on? Will someone tell me what's going on?"

I licked my lips, skootching forward on the bed, desperate to make her understand. "Listen, he won't tell Mom and Dad, okay? I really think he and I—"

Gabby's hard laugh interrupted me. "No, Mona. Abram *will* tell your parents. That'll be the first thing he does. Then he'll call his sister and give her a good scoop. Then he'll tell you to get lost."

"You don't know that!" I whisper-yelled.

"I do know it!" Gabby yell-yelled. She took a few rushing steps forward, causing me to lean back. "You think he has feelings for you? Well, guess what? That doesn't make you special. I tried to warn you, this is what he does! Everyone is in love with him. He doesn't care about you. You're just another one to him. But, I can guarantee you, he'll definitely care about being lied to. He'll be super pissed about that. And if you think he'll ever forgive you, you're out of your mind. He'll hate you forever."

My heart was beating out of my chest, each thump enormously painful, and I was breathing like I'd just run a race. It was on the tip of my tongue to reject her words, because I knew Abram. He wasn't like that. He'd forgive me. He'd keep—

"And for what? To clear your conscience?" Gabby asked shrilly, laughing again. "Typical Mona Mary Sue bullshit. You think you're doing the right thing? Well, you're not. You're doing what you think is the right thing *for you*. You couldn't care less about what will happen to Lisa, but it's going to blow up in your face. You've known him for six days. Six days! And you're choosing him over your twin sister? You're the one who is selfish. You're the reason Lisa was sent to boarding school when we were kids, and you'll be the reason she's banished now!"

"Okay, enough!" Lisa had stood at some point and she paired this proclamation with a double hand swipe, cutting her arms through the air and sending Gabby a fierce look. "That's enough, Gabby. I know you're trying to help, but you're not."

I blinked against hot tears, berating myself for all this confounded crying. I'd cried—or wanted to cry—more in the last twenty-four hours than I had in the previous ten years.

Something is wrong with me. I don't know who I am, but I'm not myself.

"Just . . ." I heard Lisa sigh and I looked at her, she was shaking her head tiredly. "Be quiet for a minute and let me talk to Mona, okay?"

Gabby nodded stiffly, and then sent me a cutting look, turning and pacing to the other side of the room. Meanwhile, Lisa sat next to me on the bed and pinched the bridge of her nose. I took a moment to look at my sister, to really look at her.

Her hair was dull, lifeless. She wore eye makeup, but more concealer than liner. Even with all the concealer, I could still make out the dark circles under her eyes. Her lips were thinned, pale. She looked exhausted, overwhelmed, and my thumping heart twinged painfully.

Was Gabby right? Was I being selfish? And why was I so sure of Abram? *You've known him for six days, and you're choosing him over your sister.*

I couldn't think. Everything was a mess. *This is why I hate messes!*

Lisa was taking deep breaths, frowning at whatever internal thoughts she was having.

"Lisa," I said unthinkingly, wanting to explain before she made up her mind about anything. But when she lifted her eyes, all I could think to say was, "I'm sorry."

Her shoulders sagged and the side of her mouth tugged upward in a sad smile. "Don't apologize, Mona. God, don't ever apologize to me. I —" She sighed, a full body sigh, her eyes glassy. "Listen, I don't know what happened, or what's going on with you. I'm tired. I'm so tired, I'm trying to think. But I do know one thing: I hate the person I've become."

She blurred in my vision until I blinked, two fat tears rolling down my face.

She shook her head at me. "Don't be sad, and please don't be sorry. I'm sorry I put you in this position, and I'm sorry you're upset now. This is my fault, not yours."

"Lisa—"

"No, listen. If you want to tell him—Abram—the truth, that's up to you. I've done a lot of thinking over the last week and I can't keep living like this, being like this. I trust your judgment a hell of a lot more than I trust my own. I just want you to know, I won't be upset. I won't blame you, no matter what happens. This is my fault, these were my choices, and you shouldn't have to pay for them."

I heard Gabby make a scoffing noise, like a growl, and Lisa turned to frown at her friend. "Gabby!" Her voice held a warning. "You need to let it go too."

Gabby crossed her arms and shook her head in a quick, jerky movement. "No. This is bullshit, and you know it!" And then she turned to me. "I don't trust your judgment. Your judgment is why the three of us were separated and Lisa was sent away." Her tone wavered, had turned quiet and earnest, her eyes were watery with unshed tears and her nose had turned red, her skin splotchy. "You think Lisa is the only one who lost her family after that? What do you think happened to me? I lost you both. I lost everything. Just . . . don't. Please don't do this again."

A sudden pain seized my chest and I winced at the raw helplessness in her voice, at the pleading I heard in her words.

But she wasn't finished. "Your judgment is telling you that Abram will forgive you when I'm telling you—since I actually know him—that he will not. He. Will. Not. He is the most unforgiving person I've ever met. I have been trying to tell you from the start not to trust him, and—"

"That's it, Gabby." Lisa cut in, standing and walking to the door. "You know I love you, but you can't put this on Mona." My sister opened the door and gestured to the hall. "Can you wait downstairs?"

"Yes—" Gabby sniffed, swiping at her eyes "—if Mona keeps her promise and I'm taking her to the airport, I'll wait for her." Walking to the door, she said to Lisa, "But if she tells Abram the truth, then I'll wait for you and I'll take you home with me. I don't know how my parents will react, but I don't care."

Maybe Gabby didn't think her words made an impact on me, but they did. She was willing to do whatever it took to keep Lisa safe, whereas I was not. Fact.

And I believed her about Abram. Rather, I believed she believed what she was saying. Also fact.

But I didn't know what to do. I didn't know what to think. I was lost. So lost. The logical path forward had been erased by my stupidity. Now, no matter what I did, I was making the wrong decision.

Did I tell Abram the truth? How could I? Even if I was convinced he wouldn't hate me, that what was happening between us was real, Gabby believed he would tell our parents the truth.

Did I leave now, like Gabby wanted? I would never see him again. But this was not a shock. I'd been preparing for this all week.

So why does it feel like the end of the world?

"Mona." Lisa had claimed her seat on the bed again and only hesitated for a second before grabbing my hands and cradling them; her fingers were freezing. "It's clear you've been through a lot this week."

I huffed a bitter laugh, abruptly angry with myself. "I've been through a lot? Lisa, you've been in jail."

"Yes. But that was my fault."

"That wasn't your fault." I gripped her hands tighter, willing them to be warmer. "That was Tyler."

"I chose Tyler. I lied about being with him. That was my decision. This, none of this, is your fault. And you—" She took a deep breath, her eyes dropping to our hands, like she couldn't look at me and say this next part. "You need to do what you think is right. But you also need to know that, no matter what, I won't be mad. You are my sister and I love you. I can't lose you again, and . . . I'm sorry. I'm so sorry."

This last part she said brokenly, tears finally falling. My imperturbable sister was crying. And not just quiet weeping. Massive, body-wracking sobs. My heart bled for her, for she was the other part of myself.

Pulling Lisa into my arms, I held her. I rocked her. I told her how much I loved her. I pet her hair and promised to always take care of her, because the path had revealed itself and I knew the answer.

I knew what I had to do.

* * *

Abram

Reaching for Lisa, my hand encountered only a cold, vacant couch. I'd hoped to find her next to me, to curl myself around her. But she wasn't there.

Opening my eyes, blinking at the darkness, I listened for a sign of her presence. A ballooning disappointment deflated hope. When it was clear she wasn't anywhere close, I flexed my jaw, stood from the sofa, and stretched while yawning. Discontented. Frustrated. She was gone, she'd taken her sweet softness, and—

Gone, and she took all softness with her.

Gone, and emptiness takes shape.

Gone, and summer is winter.

Gone, and... And?

Cassette tape? Fate? Concord grape?

Scowling for many reasons, I pushed the hair out of my eyes and left the dark theater in search of my lyric book, a toothbrush, and the exceptional woman constantly on my mind.

I wouldn't use "fate" to end the fourth line of this new stanza, and obviously not "concord grape." The first part was useable—her/winter wasn't a textbook rhyme, but that only made it more perfect—yet I couldn't work out what word to use with *shape.*

Gone, and I browse the internet using Netscape? No.

Gone, and where did I put that videotape? No, but it made me grin.

Gone, and something about a great ape? Ha ha!

Great ape. Funny. Perhaps I was the ape? . . . *worth considering.*

Stopping by the basement bathroom, I brushed my teeth and splashed my face with water. This was my usual waking-up routine, whenever I might wake up: absentmindedly going through the motions while words played musical chairs in my mind. Since agreeing to house-sit for Leo's parents, I'd been sleeping mostly in the recording studio on the couch. That's where all my lyric notebooks were as well as my guitars.

Before Lisa came, I'd found it was easier to write while in the studio, trying and testing lyrics with background accompaniment via the soundboard. But now that she was here, writing music, poetry, lyrics had been just like sharing her company: effortless.

Gone, and she took all softness with her.

Gone, and empty (or emptiness?) takes a shape. . .

Shape. What else rhymes with shape? My priority was to capture this feeling, that moment upon waking, discovered loss or whatever it was.

I wouldn't force it. If I had to force the words, then they were a lie. Studying words had been a compulsion of mine from a young age. I collected and hoarded them. I thought about how to assemble and arrange them to communicate the most truth in the least amount of syllables. I treasured them when they were real just as much as I reviled them when they were false.

Because of this, I wouldn't force the missing line, and I was certain I wouldn't need to. With Lisa here, the right ones would come to me.

I miss her.

Yes. That was it. I missed her. And missing someone is not just the absence of the person. Distance exists. Separation is real. It is a measurable construct, but also intangible.

This space between us is what? This space of separation is what?

Distracted, I left the bathroom and crossed the hall to the studio, flipping on the light and moving to my pile of notebooks. They weren't organized by anything other than the approximate date, and so I picked up the only one that was neither full nor empty and wrote those first three lines of a stanza that might become a song.

Then, when I reached the fourth line, I frowned at my reflection in the studio glass. I shook my head.

Gone, and . . . what do I miss about Lisa when she is gone?

Potential answers immediately and effortlessly piled upon each other: her eyes when she laughed; her smile; her body in that white bikini; smooth, hot skin; her strength; a silk waterfall of dark hair spread over my chest while she slept; her humor; her eyes when she was angry; her kindness; the color of embarrassment on her cheeks; her voice; her surprising cleverness; her equally surprising awkwardness; how, with each breath last night, the rise and fall of her breasts pressed against my side; her eyes when she was surprised; the weight of her, the warmth, and the awareness where every inch of her touched every inch of me; her mouth; her softness.

Her softness.

Yes.

I don't think women understand how much decent men appreciate softness, not just in the woman they admire and desire, but in the world. I'd had conversations with Leo about this a few times.

"What is it about her?" I'd asked the last time he'd gone crazy for a woman.

We'd been sitting in a VIP room at a club called Outrageous. He liked it because they changed the interior often. This made it feel like we were going to a new place but without the hassle of learning the names of new waitstaff, bartenders, bouncers, and managers.

"She's soft, you know? Like, she's not jaded. Man, my parents and everyone I know are so fucking jaded. It's just nice to be around someone who still has *the wonder*." He took a drink from his beer, smiling an uncertain little smile, his knee bouncing in time with the bass. "That's why I keep you around, Abram."

"Oh yeah? Do I have the wonder?" I didn't smile. I wasn't convinced.

"You so do, man. Yeah, you're also an abyss of deep thoughts and depressing shit, but—" he leaned forward, hit my shoulder "—you still make me feel my age, not . . ." His eyes drifted to the crowd beyond the wall of glass separating our VIP box from the club. "You don't make me feel like I'm ninety years old all the damn time."

I'd smiled. I knew he was referring to Charlie, our other good friend, drummer, and frequent co-conspirator. Where Leo was an optimist, Charlie was an eternal pessimist. I fell somewhere in the middle. They were both good guys, and unlike many of our mutual acquaintances, neither Charlie nor Leo needed to be high or drunk to have a real conversation.

"You have the wonder too, Leo." I returned the compliment, because I thought maybe he needed to hear it.

"Thanks." His eyes grew big, solemn. "Seriously, thank you, man. I try. I try to stay soft, but the world makes it hard."

I try to stay soft, but the world makes it hard.

I'd written down Leo's words about softness because they were true. It was maybe the truest thing I'd ever heard. What he'd said was brave and a difficult thing to live. I respected Leo for trying to be soft, but I respected him even more for never forcing it.

Presently, staring at the studio glass, I didn't sit on the stool by the soundboard. But I did flip through the last few pages of my notebook, letting my eyes skate over the iterative versions of a poem I knew would eventually be a song entitled, *Hold a Grudge.*

I wasn't finished. *Hold a Grudge* needed a chorus and structured stanzas, I still needed to figure out where to put the bridge, how often to repeat the chorus, and how to end it. But first, it needed the right melody. I was a much better lyricist than a composer. I found myself nodding at the accuracy of the poem, and then I flipped back to the new lines I'd just written.

Gone, and . . . What sounds like shape? Manscape? *God, no.*

I rolled my eyes at myself, and then read the three lines of this new poem again. I repeated them silently until they were fully memorized. And then I closed the book and returned it to the pile, certain the last line would come to me sooner rather than later. But right now, I was anxious to see Lisa, so I left the studio in search of her.

The longer I was awake, the more urgent the need to be in her company. This had been the case since the morning we drove to Michigan. At the time, I'd assumed it was because I was worried about her, because of how shaken she'd been that night before we drove to my parents' house. But now there was no mistaking it or explaining it away.

I was in love with her.

I didn't lie, not even to myself, not even when the truth felt impossible to explain. I could almost hear my friend Charlie and his jaded view on everything, "Don't be a dumbass. People don't fall in love in a week."

To which I would say, "Fuck people."

Over the last six days, Lisa and I had clicked seamlessly into place. I'd considered fighting, resisting the enormity of giving into wanting her so completely. But even when she'd pushed me away with talk of 'appropriateness' and 'power dynamics,' giving into the potentially impossible daydream of her felt better—so much better—than the idea of anyone else.

I'd fallen in love with Lisa, and all her contradictions, and all her beauty and character and strength and softness. She'd become my place. With her, I never had to force the wonder, and being soft hadn't seemed so hard.

Now, ascending the final step to the kitchen level, I spotted Lisa and it was like my body and mind finally became fully awake. She was on a stool at the island, her lovely profile to me, her waterfall hair sweeping the center of her back, and the whole stanza came to me at once:

Gone, and she took all her sweet softness with her.
Gone, and emptiness takes a shape.
Gone, and summer is winter.
Gone, and I sleep.
But when she's here, I'm finally awake.
A barren landscape,
Now beauty in her wake.

With Lisa, vibrancy. Without her, emptiness took shape, a barren landscape.

I filled my lungs with the sight of her, energized by the deprivation of desire—to see her, touch her, listen to her, engage with her—and reminding myself to take it slow. Wait. Tread carefully. I was certain of what I wanted, how I felt, but she wasn't someone to rush. The truth was, I had no idea when or if she'd get there. Though that was somewhat terrifying, it didn't stress me. Especially when she made the waiting and anticipation so much fun.

Lisa's eyes were on a magazine spread flat on the kitchen island and she was hunched over a bowl of something, distractedly eating spoonfuls while reading.

I loved that she read so much. I loved, even though she'd dropped out of school, that her brain was obviously hungry for knowledge, debate, and philosophy. I loved that she'd been kicked out of school but seemed to be an unbending rule follower. I loved that once you knew her, nothing about her past made any sense.

Leo had been worried about his youngest sister for a while, specifically that their parents had "fucking ruined her." According to Leo, Mona, the older twin, had never needed much from anyone and automatically knew what to do and how to behave in all situations.

I'd never met Lisa's sister, but there were pictures of her in the front room. From what I'd seen, Mona and Lisa didn't resemble each other much. In the family photos Leo had pointed out to me from

Mona DaVinci's recent college graduation, I never would have guessed that the two women were twins if I didn't already know. She was shorter than Lisa in all the pictures of them together, and seemed smaller, fading into the background, always smiling with a closed mouth, and definitely lacking Lisa's vibrancy. To be blunt, the older twin looked like she'd stopped aging at twelve.

"Mona is smarter than all of us combined," he'd said when he asked me to keep an eye on Lisa over a week ago. Leo didn't usually talk about his sisters, but he'd wanted to prepare me for her arrival. "I'm Mona's older brother, but I go to *her* for advice. She's like a superhero, I swear. Doesn't need or take shit from anyone, doesn't care what anyone thinks, not even me, not even my parents. But Lisa . . ." Leo had sounded worried. "I know you don't like her, man. And I'm sorry for what she did last year, but she needs people, you know? She needs community. She needs someone to take care of, someone to take care of her. Some people don't need that, but Lisa does."

Presently, I stuffed my hands in my back pockets so I wouldn't reach for her. I wanted to. I always wanted to touch her. But something had happened to Lisa since last year, something she didn't yet feel comfortable confiding, something that made every first touch difficult. Maybe more time together would fix it for her. Maybe not.

Whatever she needed, because I knew exactly what Leo had meant about Lisa needing people.

My sister and I had been born with this same curse: *Someone to take care of, someone to take care of me, an inescapable desire for codependency.* Another song lyric. I wasn't happy with it, it needed work, but that was basically the gist of why I didn't fuck around with my time or with people.

Lisa didn't look up as I approached, so I said, "Hey," not hiding my smile.

From now on, all my smiles belonged to her.

Her eyes flickered up, and then dropped just as fast to the bowl of what I now saw was cereal. She straightened her back, closing the magazine and clearing her throat while I studied the bowl. *Note to self, she likes Lucky Charms.*

"Abram," she said, swallowing, tucking hair behind both her ears. "Good morning."

Immediately, I heard the guarded, distant, and particular quality to her voice. But it was the *particular* that resonated like an out of tune piano. I ignored it, eager to remove that barren landscape between us.

"Good morning, Lisa." I leaned my elbows on the island, making my tone ironically formal and bending at the waist to bring us eye level. "And how did you sleep last night?" I hoped this would make her blush. She was so very exquisite when she blushed.

She didn't blush but she still wouldn't look at me. "I, uh, didn't sleep very well, honestly." Lisa lifted her chin but not her eyes. "We should talk."

I frowned at the persisting particular quality to her voice, my eyes moving over her. It was at least eighty-five degrees outside and she was dressed in a baggy black hoddie and yoga pants. On her feet she wore socks and she'd stuffed her hands into the pockets of her sweat-shirt. She was also wearing a lot of makeup, darker than usual, like the day she'd come home last week.

"Are you okay?" I dipped my head to one side, hoping that would encourage her to meet my eyes, hoping she'd let me take care of her.

Someone to take care of, someone to take care of me.

I couldn't shake those words. Spending time with Lisa, they resonated in a new way, one that was 3-D and in color, with softness and wonder and not just black ink written on a white notebook page.

She didn't meet my eyes, instead speaking to my forearms. "You have been very nice to me. Thank you. This is a difficult time, and I'm going through a lot, so I'm sorry if I've been acting weird."

As she spoke, I felt a chill. Something was . . . wrong. Her voice continued to hit the wrong note over and over.

Mystified, I said, "No need to apologize. You haven't been acting weird until just now."

Her eyes cut to mine and I started, flinching back and standing. *What the hell?* The chill became a sense of freezing dread I couldn't explain. Something was most definitely wrong. I couldn't identify the problem, but there was a problem.

". . . Lisa?" I asked like a fool, but—seriously—what the hell? This wasn't her. Her eyes were different. Not the shape or color or size, and yet unquestionably different. Lisa was there, but she also wasn't, like she'd been possessed. Or she was absent. It was freaky as hell.

Her eyes widened for the briefest of seconds, and then her lips flattened, her gaze moving to the closed magazine. She picked it up. She stood from the stool, glaring at the wall behind me, looking irritated and therefore the closest to acting like herself since I'd walked in.

"Look." Her voice was hard but also soft, quiet; I prepared myself for a whisper since she was visibly upset; an odd quirk I'd noticed about her, when she was upset, she always whispered. "Why are you doing this?"

"Doing what?"

"Pretending like you care about me." Her gaze fell to the floor and she sounded angry, but not at all hurt.

Were we playing this game again? The Push Abram Away Game? I didn't like games. I had a low tolerance and I'd never put up with them. Maybe it wasn't true for everyone, but I couldn't keep the wonder while also fucking around and playing games.

I made too much of things, I gave words too much weight, I searched for meaning where none existed. For me, there was no such thing as casual friends; you were my good friend, or you were an acquaintance. Likewise, there was no such thing as a meaningless hookup. An action, a touch was sacred, or it wasn't. Maybe that's why Leo thought I wasn't jaded? Because I didn't play games?

But with Lisa, I seemed to have an infinite reserve of patience that extended to game playing. Even when she was sour, she was still so intoxicatingly sweet, it was like being caught in a web of cotton candy.

So instead of giving into the building apprehension—even though she did sound off—I said, "Pretending."

She needed to push me away again? Okay. I could give her space. As long as later today, when she came to her senses, she also came to the pool, wearing that white bikini.

"Yes, pretending," Lisa said, her tone hard. "Gabby is my best friend, remember? She has my back."

"What are you talking about?" I needed to keep my head, but it wasn't just her words that unsettled me, or how she wasn't meeting my eyes. She was speaking to me like we were strangers.

Lisa gave her eyes a half roll. "You're a player, Abram. So whatever act this is, drop it."

The accusation angered me, and therefore distracted me from the discordant tone in her voice. Needing space was one thing. But believing and then spouting lies was another.

"This isn't an act." I tried to conceal the spike of temper by lowering my voice.

"Yeah. Right."

"And I don't know what Gabby told you, but she is misinformed." But obviously Lisa trusted her, and that had a shot of adrenaline clouding my vision.

"Okay. Sure. She just imagined the depth and breadth of your harem at gigs?"

Is that what this is about? I relaxed a little, breathing out. "Come on Lisa, this is nuts. I have female fans, yes. But I'm not dating any of them. Do you honestly think—"

"You don't date *anyone*. You just flirt with everyone and lead them on."

"I absolutely do not." *Fucking Gabby.* I could strangle her for filling Lisa's head with this shit.

She crossed her arms and shrugged. "I don't, for one minute, think that I'm special to you. Sure, whatever, we'll be friends, fine. But can you be cool and cut the act?"

She doesn't think . . . ? Was I hearing her correctly? How could she possibly think that?

The adrenaline returned, full force. "Then you're wrong, because you are special to me. And what happened last night was special, and dammit Lisa—would you listen?"

She'd turned and marched away. I reached for her arm, which she shook off. I let go immediately and stepped back. I shouldn't have touched her. Shit, I knew that. But I couldn't just let her believe Gabby's lies.

Knowing I'd fucked up, I pushed my fingers through my hair and tried to calm down. "Here is the truth: I have all sorts of fans, both male and female. They like my music, they come to my shows, maybe they like me. I don't know, I haven't asked them. I don't hang out with my fans and I don't lead people on, I don't flirt. The only thing Gabby told you that's true is this: I do not date. If you don't believe me, ask Leo."

Her eyes remained steadfastly on the floor and she mumbled, "You don't date because you're a player."

"No," I ground out. "I don't date because I don't believe in wasting time treading water. When I know, I know."

"What does that mean?"

"That means, I'm in love with you."

Finally, finally her eyes came back to me. They widened, her jaw slackened, and she stood silent like a statue. I couldn't believe this news stunned her as much as it seemed to. Maybe I could allow for some surprise, but she looked completely shell-shocked.

Hesitating only a second—partly because I wondered if it would be taking advantage, but also because she was acting so strangely—I closed the distance between us. Everything was wrong, but this might be my only chance to make things right. I slid my hands around her back. I held her. I kissed her.

She flinched and didn't respond at all, at first. But then she responded by twisting her face from mine.

"No, no, no!" She pushed me.

I let her go and grabbed fistfuls of my hair, turning away and pacing the length of the kitchen. Fire in my chest. My thoughts in disorder. *What the fuck was happening?*

I glanced at her. She'd covered her face and was shaking her head. And then she sniffled, the unmistakable sound of a sob rending from her chest that tore at mine.

Please don't cry. "I'm sorry. I shouldn't have—"

"Goddammit! You don't love me! I hate—" She cut herself off, shaking her head harder.

I watched her, helpless and so fucking confused, my mind all over the place, unable to see straight. *What is happening?*

"Lisa—"

"Just fucking listen," she shouted, surprising me, her hands dropping and revealing a face that looked like a stranger's. "I'm not who you think I am, okay?"

Despite hearing these words from her before, this time I believed her. I didn't argue, just watched her and waited for . . . I had no idea. A sign? A glimmer of my Lisa? The woman I couldn't get enough of? The woman I'd written twenty poems about in six days?

"But before I say anything else—" she swiped at her eyes leaving dark smudges on her cheeks, sucking in a deep breath "—I have to ask you something."

I waited, promising myself I wouldn't cross to her or try to touch her until invited. Strangely, this promise didn't seem as big as it had yesterday when we were in the pool, or when we were on the couch. Last night I'd promised myself not to touch her, and it had been torture.

Today? It was self-preservation.

When she didn't say anything, I prompted with forced calm, "Fine. What do you want to ask?"

She licked her lips, shifting her weight from one foot to the other, a nervous habit I hadn't noticed before. "If I lied to you, would you forgive me?" she finally blurted, shutting her eyes.

Lied to me? I straightened my back.

"About what?" The question slipped out, unplanned.

"No. I'm not—it could be about anything, okay?" Her eyes opened again and she stared forward at my neck. "If I lied to you at any point this week, would you be able to forgive me?"

My mind was racing with worst-case scenarios, my stomach sinking. "Did you sell those drugs? To those kids?" More unplanned questions, but what could I do? She was acting so crazy.

"No." She was back to whispering again, giving me a clue that the question had upset her. "I didn't do that. I would never do that."

I believed her. But the next obvious choice made my throat tighten with the urge to rage.

"Are you back with Tyler?" I asked roughly, determined not to raise my voice, but I was already so jealous. I didn't want to be jealous. I'd never been jealous. But I was so fucking jealous in that moment, the cloud around my vision turned red.

Fuck.

I'd never experienced anything like this before.

I hated it. *Hated it.* It felt like being branded with a million tiny hot pokers.

"No." Her glare turned distracted. "But it's something like that—" her eyes came to mine, still guarded, still off, still wrong "—something just as bad as that. A lie that big."

I'd never been so frantic before to recall previous conversations. I went through every day, every interaction, every word that I could remember. I came up empty.

"What is it?"

"Would you forgive me?"

I nodded but didn't answer out loud, trying to convince myself while also dealing with this insane jealousy. I would. I would forgive her anything. I would—

"Hypothetically, what if I told you that I've been lying to you every day, this whole week, about something important. You say you love me, but would you forgive me?"

I stopped nodding. "Have you?"

She remained silent, her eyes now narrowed, searching. "You wouldn't forgive me, would you?"

"I don't know!" I exploded, not understanding her or why she was doing this. "You haven't told me what it is. Fuck, Lisa. I don't even know what we're talking about."

"Forget it." She gave her head a small shake, her eyes dropping to the kitchen floor.

She looked exhausted and sad, and seeing her this way should've made me want to break all her unspoken rules about touching. I should've wanted to hold her, but I didn't. If this had been yesterday, I would've promised to forgive her anything and everything, and I would've meant it.

But now? I had no clarity. Making promises now would be a lie, and I never lied. If she'd been seeing Tyler this whole week while spending time with me, falling for her, I wouldn't forgive her. It wasn't in me. I would despise her.

Clearing my throat, I grit my teeth to keep from yelling again. "Forget what? What should I forget?"

"Forget me. You don't love me. You might think you do, but you don't." She sounded tired, but also as though she were trying her best to be compassionate, gentle. "Believe me, you'll get over this—whatever it is—so fast, I'll be a blip, a nothing. Seriously, forget it. You don't want to know me. I promise you, you don't."

"So you keep saying." I pushed back against a creeping numbness climbing up my ribs, stalling, needing a way to fix this.

"Then what's the problem? Why don't you believe me? I'm messed up, okay? I don't know who I am." Like a switch, her mood and manner turned exasperated. "I don't know what I want. I'm all fucked up. I am telling you the truth, but you refuse to believe me!"

In a huff, she turned and stomped to the back stairs.

"I don't understand what's happening," I called after her, another unplanned statement of my thoughts.

She stopped on the third step, turning halfway, giving me just her profile.

I walked to the bottom of the stairs, not seeing her or anything else, but wading through a general sense of everything crumbling to dust, a barren landscape.

"What changed? Between last night and this morning, what changed? What did I do wrong?"

Lisa swallowed, shaking her head. "I'm two different people, Abram." She pulled her sleeves down to cover her hands, turning completely away and crossing her arms. "I'm the person I want to be and the person I currently am, and if my parents disown me, I feel like I'll sink to the bottom of the ocean and drown. I feel like it'll be the end of the world." Initially her voice had been strong and steady, but it grew quieter and quieter as she spoke.

I stared at the back of her head, working through my own bitterness and this trail of crumbs she was leaving. I couldn't believe what she was saying. I couldn't believe this was the same person I'd spent the last week with. But there she was, looking just the same.

I'd thought her trust was a beautiful thing. I thought her values unbendable. But now? I couldn't see what had been right in front of me the whole time, I'd been blind to the truth: she had no trust in me, maybe not in anyone.

Swallowing around the vice tightening my throat, I glanced up at the ceiling. "Let me see if I have this right: you lied to me, about something big, and you think I'll tell your parents if I find out. Is that right?" The bitterness snuck into my voice.

We were now broken. This wasn't like before, where she'd used logic and ethics and temperance to push me away. I could forgive that. In retrospect, it had almost been cute.

But this?

Maybe it's for the best.

No. Fuck that. It wasn't for the best. Us together was for the best.

Eying her back, her stiff shoulders bunched around her neck, I felt myself soften.

What happened to make her this way?

I couldn't let her go without trying one more time.

"Lisa." I placed a hand on her arm, keeping my touch light.

She tensed and I swallowed fear. I ignored my drumming heart, the taste of sand, the uncomfortable tightness in my chest that made taking a complete breath unbearable, and I reminded myself of Leo's truest words: *I try to stay soft, but the world makes it hard.*

Be open. Be brave. Be soft, for Lisa.

"I told you yesterday, I just want to make you happy. Do you believe me?"

I watched her back rise and fall with a deep breath, and the barest glimmer of hope had me curling my fingers around her forearm.

But then she shook off my hand. "You can't *make me* happy, Abram. People can't *make* other people happy. I've tried that. It doesn't work. The truth is, I'm still—I'm still in love with Tyler and —" She took another deep breath, and when she spoke next, I could barely hear her, "And sorry for dicking you around but nothing is ever going to happen with us, so just give me some fucking space."

[1]

ELECTRIC CHARGE AND ELECTRIC FIELD
TWO AND A HALF YEARS LATER.

Mona

"You left."

Shifting my eyes from the computer screen to the doorway of my office, I blinked at Poe's sudden appearance. "Pardon?"

"The reception." He pushed his hands into his pockets, strolling to the chair in front of my desk and helping himself to a seat. "You left before the speech." Poe smiled at his own statement, though it was clear my leaving the reception was what he found amusing.

"I guess I did." I leaned back in my chair and returned his smile. "She always gives the same speech."

"You mean, she always brings up that she's mentoring the infamous genius, Mona DaVinci, and you find that irritating." Poe said this as he studied his nails, still smiling.

Stinker. He knew me too well.

Lifting my eyes to the ceiling, I shrugged. "Irritating is such a strong word. But yes. It feels a little condescending."

"Because your mentor doesn't actually mentor you, or why?" Poe leaned his elbow on the arm of the leather chair, stretching his legs in front of him as though getting comfortable, his brown eyes still bright with amusement.

He already knew the answer to this question, so why was he asking? I folded my hands over my stomach and inspected him, deciding that he was just in a teasing mood.

Therefore, I made myself sound lofty. "You know I would never say my mentor doesn't mentor me."

That made him laugh, a good, deep, belly laugh, and he shook his head. "You would never say it, even though it's the truth."

We stared across the length of my desk, smiling at each other, good feelings and trust and respect between us, and I couldn't help but wonder—

A moment flashed behind my mind's eye, a dark room, my cheek pressed to a soft T-shirt, the sound of a heart beating beneath my ear. Arms—Abram's arms—were around me. Reality and time felt fuzzy around the edges, as though I might be able to touch the past . . .

Sigh.

In the present, my hand reflexively moved to the folded envelope in my front pocket and I felt my smile fall, likely due to the ache in my chest. Despite my attempts to be rational about the short—*extremely* short—time I'd spent with Abram, memories of him used to cause a brutal, violent stabbing sensation in the vicinity of my heart, scatter my brain, and send a burst of heat up my neck and over my cheeks.

I'd written him a letter a month after returning from Chicago, hoping to dispel some of the near-constant torment; I'd placed it in an envelope; I'd addressed the envelope to his parents' house in Michigan and I carried it with me every day, folded in my front pocket. Writing the letter hadn't helped dispel anything, but it had given me something to hold, to touch when I felt like I couldn't breathe in those early days.

The ache I experienced now—over two years later—was a huge improvement. I hoped soon it would be a mere small twinge. Yet, I still carried the letter in my pocket, every day, though I was unsure why. Habit maybe?

Despite the nonsensical and lingering physical symptoms and resultant mental quirks, I didn't regret my decision to help my sister.

How could I? She'd kept her word, I'd kept mine, we were so much closer than before, and she was flourishing. Even Gabby and I were friendly more often than at odds. Her latest birthday card to me sat on a bookshelf at my right, proudly inscribed, *Donuts before bronuts. Love you forever, Gabster.*

Work, my research was good. Great even.

Things with my sister were good. Great even.

I had good friends. Great even.

However . . . *however.*

Taking a deep breath, working to disperse the ache and the image of Abram, I brought Poe back into focus. His smile had turned wry and he shook his head, a faint movement. We never spoke about it, about how I wasn't over a guy who I'd known for a blink of an eye, but I was almost certain my friend knew what—or who—I'd been remembering just now.

Poe, his smile slowly giving way to a thoughtful frown, reached forward and picked up the snow globe on my desk, shaking it. "Don't worry, I covered for you at the reception. I told everyone you had a flight and couldn't stay."

I knew he'd cover for me. We always covered for each other, which was why I'd left the reception. When I returned from my memorable one-week trip to Chicago, Poe Payton had been the shoulder I'd cried on the *one* night I'd allowed myself to cry.

It happened two weeks before the fall semester. I'd been nineteen and drunk at a grad school mixer. He'd told everyone I was on flu meds. I'd bawled in his car, telling him the entire story on the drive back to my condo between self-recriminating sobs and rants. He stayed over, spending the night on the couch. He also made me breakfast in the morning, told me a story about his oldest sister's disastrous love life that made me feel better about mine, and then we went for a silent, oddly cathartic walk on the beach.

I shoved the ghost of Abram from my brain and allowed myself to be distracted by the floating bits of white swirling around the snow globe Poe had just given another shake.

"Are you sure you don't want to go with us? To the cabin?" I asked, hoping he would change his mind. "It's not too late to get you a ticket."

"Nah," he said, bringing my attention back to his face. "Who wants to spend a week surrounded by snow, skiing in Aspen when one could be here, surrounded by ocean and sunshine, surfing in Southern California?"

I made a face. He'd tried to give me a surfing lesson once and it hadn't gone well.

"You know I don't ski. Or surf," I added quickly, just in case he offered to teach me again. "And the allure of being surrounded by snow has more to do with the beverages and hermit life than the activities."

"The beverages?"

I began ticking off my fingers. "Hot cider. Hot chocolate. Hot, mulled wine. Hot—"

"I get it. You like it hot."

"Yes. But only in the snow." I didn't mention that the other main attraction was the snow itself.

Hushed, gently falling snow was the closest I would get to the quiet of space without visiting a sensory deprivation chamber. I'd tried that once and had something like a panic attack after two minutes. The walls had been too close, claustrophobic. It had felt oppressive, suffocating.

But I'd grown a bit preoccupied with the concept of complete silence, a recent occurrence after testifying before Congress on climate change last summer. There'd been subsequent interviews on cable news outlets during the fall and everyone had been so loud. Why did reporters shout on TV? Didn't they know viewers could turn the volume up if needed?

Stressful.

Summary: The quiet isolation of the mountains, cut off from the world by distance and snow, felt like the only place I could draw a complete breath these days. Whenever I had free time, I went to Aspen.

"So noted." Poe reached forward again, arranging the snow globe on the desk so that the front of the little model cabin within faced me. "Does the cabin actually look like this?"

"Not exactly." My attention flickered to the rustic little log structure encased in water and glass, a memento I'd picked up on my previous return trip from Aspen. "And I don't think 'cabin' is really the right word for it. It's more like a—"

"Mansion?" he asked dryly, making me smile.

"Uh, lodge?"

"A mansion lodge?" His voice was still dry, likely because he knew he was right. All of my parents' properties were mansion-like.

But I didn't like to admit it, not even to myself. I suggested instead, "A small estate."

"A huge estate compound mansion lodge? Something like that?"

I laughed. "It's not like that."

It was totally like that.

"Really? How many bedrooms does it have?"

"Um . . ." I moved my eyes up and to the right, counting silently. "Twenty?"

He made a choking sound and I looked at him just as he'd placed his hand flat on his sternum, like the number upset his delicate sensibilities. "Twenty?"

His expression was priceless. I laughed again.

"You could sleep in a different room every night, and still not sleep in them all."

My cellphone, face down on the desk, started to buzz. "Why would I do that?"

"Because you live your life like the princess in that story, where the bed is never right."

"You mean Goldilocks? She wasn't a princess. And I don't like cereal, not even oatmeal." Glancing at the phone, I saw it was Allyn.

"No. The other story, the one with the pea." He sounded oddly stern.

I swiped my thumb across the screen, whispering just before I brought the phone to my ear. "Don't be ludicrous."

He quickly whispered back, "Ludicrous is awesome, everyone wants to be him."

I gave Poe a glare that was ruined by a traitorous smile, and suffused my voice with friendliness as I answered the phone. "Allyn! Hey! Are you all packed? Is there a problem with the itinerary?"

"No, everything is great! I'm just calling to let you know I'm on my way to the airport and I'm SO EXCITED!" She yelled this last part necessitating that I hold the phone away from my ear.

Poe chuckled, shaking his head at Allyn's exuberance. They'd met a few times and got along wonderfully, almost better than she and I did.

His gaze was warm as it settled on the cell in my hand. It was also full of mischief. "Tell Allyn I say hi," he whispered loudly, clearly hoping she would hear him.

"Wait. Is that Poe?" Allyn asked. "Did you convince him to come?"

He shook his head, but he smiled. "I'm not going."

"Did you hear that?" I asked Allyn, not returning his grin. "He said he's not going because he doesn't like all-expense paid trips to Aspen."

"But if y'all were going to Hawaii . . ." he sucked in a breath between his teeth, moving his head back and forth in a considering motion, making me laugh again. Even though Poe was from Tennessee, he had almost no accent. However, the occasional *y'all* did slip out from time to time.

Allyn asked, "Do your parents have a place in Hawaii?"

"No! I mean, yes. But we're not going to Hawaii. We're going to Aspen to drink hot beverages while wrapping ourselves in warm blankets, avoiding people, luxuriating in silence, and that's that." Once again I tried to glare at Poe. Once again I ultimately failed.

He stood. "I'm just saying, if you wanted me to come, you'd go to Hawaii. That's all I'm saying."

"Next time go to Hawaii!" Allyn urged. "And tell him we're holding him to his promise."

Poe captured my gaze, one of his eyebrows raised in a slight challenge, his lips faintly curved. I felt my stomach flutter.

Another topic we never broached: the possibility that—if we gave it a good try, and if I'd ever get myself together and move on from the impossibility of Abram—there might be something worth exploring between me and Poe.

Unthinkingly, I touched the outside of my front pocket again, my finger tracing the outline of the folded envelope. *Move on, Mona.* How many times had I told myself that? The X-axis was now approaching infinity.

I'd followed every mention of Abram for over a year after leaving Chicago, obsessively checking sources for music news, hunting through social media for information from his shows, pictures, videos, snippets of stories. An interesting byproduct of my investigations was that I'd learned a great deal about him, things I didn't know, most of it definitional in nature.

Where he'd gone to school: Melvil Dewey High School, where he'd been voted most talented his senior year even though he'd dropped out before graduating.

Why he'd dropped out of high school the last half of his senior year: To pursue music full-time after receiving an offer to play bass guitar on tour for an (at the time) up and coming indie rock band named Cyclops Ulysses.

What jobs he'd had: Dishwasher at fourteen for his uncle's restaurant; construction jobs at sixteen and every summer with his dad's old company (which explained his lean yet broad build); bass guitarist for Cyclops Ulysses at eighteen until they'd disbanded; bass guitarist for another, equally promising band named Ink Revolution at twenty-one; bass guitar for hire and solo artist at twenty-three.

His self-professed musical influences: Victor Wooten, Marcus Miller, Carol Kaye, Eddie Van Halen, Tal Wilkenfeld, John Lennon, Tupac Shakur, Tom Waits, Bob Dylan, and Kendrick Lamar.

Shortly after I left, right after I'd written the letter, he'd been photographed with a remarkably beautiful woman. His arm was around her shoulders. In one photo he was kissing her neck while she grinned at the camera, a cigarette held aloft. Seeing that photo had hurt. A lot. It had hurt like being punched hard in the stomach. I'd lost my breath. Admittedly, breathing had been difficult for a while after that.

But I got over it. Or rather, I kept telling myself there was nothing to "get over." *Move on, Mona.*

And yet, I'd still searched for news about him, nightly, religiously, obsessively. His first arrest caught me by surprise, but by the third I almost mailed the letter. All the charges had eventually been dropped as far as I could tell, he'd never been arraigned, but—and I didn't feel this was a controversial statement—Abram seemed to be in a downward spiral. I almost mailed the letter because I couldn't help but wonder if I'd been the cause even as I rolled my eyes at myself.

No, Mona. Abram is not getting himself arrested and into fights and losing weight and taking up smoking because of you. Six days. People change. Don't give yourself so much credit. Move on.

Mentions of him began to taper off around the one-year anniversary of my trip to Chicago. He wasn't playing the club scene, he wasn't signed with or subbing for any bands, he wasn't out publicly for any gigs. I simmered in my uneasiness until finally, sixteen months ago, he'd disappeared. From everywhere. No stories. No bookings. No performances. No arrests.

After three weeks, frantic for news, I'd called my sister and made some bogus excuse for why I was curious. The excuse hadn't been a lie, but it also hadn't been the whole truth. Lisa then called Leo, and Leo explained that he and Abram had lost touch, but he was aware that Abram had changed his last name. After his latest night in lock-up, Abram had told Leo he was worried about tarnishing his sister's journalistic name and reputation. Leo told Lisa he thought it more likely that Abram didn't want to keep embarrassing his parents.

Lisa didn't give me his new last name.

I hadn't asked.

I'd tried to take it as a sign from the universe: move on.

Move. Stay in motion. Keep moving. Move on, Mona.

So that's what I'd done. I moved. I worked. I read. I wrote a paper about the age of the universe, it had been called groundbreaking. I testified before Congress. I gave interviews. I worked some more.

Constantly moving hadn't yet yielded moving on, but it had made me tired. So very, very tired. Sometimes I was even too tired to fret about Abram—what he was doing, who he was with—before falling asleep. Sometimes I even forgot to fret.

But back to Poe and us staring at each other, and all the unspoken 'what ifs' heavy between us. No, we never talked about it. But what if we did? What if I put Hawaii on the table? *What if I actually moved on?*

After a protracted moment—during which indecision refereed a tug-of-war between my irrational longing for the impossibility of Abram and my rational desire to stop being a pathetic lunatic—Poe sighed, dropping his chin to his chest and licking his lips. The flutter in my stomach was abruptly overshadowed by a hint of guilt.

I liked him. What was there not to like? We wanted the same things: kids who we could fuss over and adore, a house in a nice neighborhood with neighbors and neighbor kids and a lawn to mow, a big library, work that was meaningful and interesting, a car payment and retirement accounts and more savings than debt. A normal, quiet life of exceptionalism.

Poe was loyal, wickedly funny, brilliant, kind, and so very, very handsome. I liked him.

But do you deserve someone like him?

I was attracted to Poe, *really* attracted. Maybe I could become someone who would deserve him? How long did I expect him to be single? It was a miracle he wasn't already married.

"What's going on?" Allyn whispered in my ear. "Why aren't you promising him a trip to Hawaii? You know he's crazy about you. Promise him!"

Crazy about me?

Studying him now, the dark glitter of hope in his gaze tempered by the stark line of his mouth and jaw, I felt jarring certainty that Poe Payton had remained single for a reason. He'd been waiting. For me. And that was hugely unfair. To him. He shouldn't be waiting for anyone. People should be waiting for him! He—like Abram—deserved better. Much, much better.

Abruptly, the spark in his eyes extinguished and he gave me a polite smile. "I'll be thinking of you while you're snowed in. Have a good time with Allyn." His words were also polite. So polite.

My stomach sank.

"Gaw! You're infuriating!" Allyn huffed.

Poe, seemingly nodding at his own thoughts, pressed his lips together and turned for the door, stuffing his hands in his pockets as he left.

"Say something!" my friend urged. "Don't just let him go!"

Another flash of Abram clouded my vision, this time he was kneeling in front of me in the dark, his hands on my knees, worry etched into his forehead. *Are you okay?*

Before I could fully experience the ache, I shoved the image away and cleared my throat, calling out without allowing myself to think, "Hey Poe."

I stopped tracing the envelope in my pocket. It was time to move on. In fact, it was past time. Really and truly. Abram had disappeared over a year ago. I needed to let him go.

Poe paused, his hand on the door frame, and then turned. His expression was free of everything but mild curiosity.

"How about Hawaii for spring break?" I asked, the question sounding awkward and amiss to my ears. And my heart.

His eyes narrowed. "You're in Europe all next semester."

"Yes."

"You're going to fly back from Europe? All the way to Hawaii, just for spring break?"

I hesitated, because he had a point. I hadn't considered whether going to Hawaii for a week would even be possible, given my commitments in Geneva. Poe's gaze moved over my face, like he was searching for something, a sign, a tell. I held my breath, clearing my features of expression.

Eventually, he bestowed upon me one of his small, patient smiles. "Okay, Mona. Whatever you say. See you in a week."

"See you in a week," I croaked, managing a smile for him in return, even though I felt embarrassed by my clumsy, sudden, and logistically unsound suggestion. Embarrassed and wrong and sad and anxious.

Giving me a slight nod, Poe turned and left. Reaching my hand in my pocket, I gripped the envelope, squeezing it, and breathed out, or at least I tried to. The ache in my chest had returned full force. Yes, I needed to move on. Yes, I'd been behaving irrationally for over two years, holding on to the possibility of an impossibility. But no, I shouldn't use Poe to move on.

I felt like an ass.

Meanwhile, Allyn squealed in my ear, "Yay! Hawaii with Poe! Of course, I'll find a reason not to go so you two can—"

"Calm down, Allyn. It's probably not going to happen." Releasing the letter, I lifted my fingers and rubbed my sternum, so ready for this vacation. So ready for quiet and calm and peace.

So ready for less motion.

[2]
ELECTRIC CURRENT, RESISTANCE, AND OHM'S LAW

Mona

My parents' McMansion was built into the side of a mountain. Reaching the property during winter required the traveler to have a certain degree of flexible ambivalence for their own safety. I'd explained the situation to Allyn months ago, perhaps even exaggerating the danger, just to be sure she was fully informed prior to giving her consent. She'd readily agreed.

As soon as my plane touched down, I powered up my cell to message Allyn. The screen told me that my brother had called and left a voicemail while I'd been airborne. Making a mental note to check his message later, I sent Allyn a text, letting her know I'd finally arrived.

The plane had been delayed leaving LAX by an hour and a half, therefore our flights arrived within a half hour of each other instead of mine landing first. After grabbing my carry-ons, darting off the plane and through the gate area to baggage claim, I discovered Melvin—one half of the caretaker team for the Aspen property—had already found Allyn and her bags.

As soon as she spotted me, Allyn—as usual—didn't say hi. She began talking as though we were in the middle of a conversation. "I was hoping to get a good view of the mountains as we touched down, but it was too cloudy and dark. I didn't get to see anything."

Pulling me into an embrace once I was within arm's reach, she didn't seem to notice how I tensed. Allyn never did notice my reticence about being touched, but that was fine. I'd been working on my "touching issues" for a while now and I appreciated her ignorance of my struggles. I didn't want anyone walking on eggshells or making it into their problem.

"You couldn't see the mountains because of the snow," Melvin said, stepping forward to reach for my bag. "This is it? Did you check anything?"

I shook my head, lifting my shoulder to indicate that I'd be fine carrying my backpack. "Just the two carry-ons."

"Good. Let's go." He turned and began power-walking to the exit.

It took me a second to react to his swift departure. I'd expected to hear all the local news, as Melvin was typically the chatty sort. He and his daughter Lila were Aspen natives. He seemed to think of the place as a small hamlet rather than the opulent resort town it had become. The last time I'd visited—just two months ago—he'd told me all about the latest issues with sanitation management and how the mayor's son had been escorted out of Big Ben's Bear Shack after dancing on the bar.

But instead of chatting, Melvin—now ten feet away—twisted his head to see if we were following, and then waved us forward urgently. Following his lead, we were wordlessly and hurriedly ushered out of the airport and into the waiting car.

Once we were packed in, on the road and on our way, I lowered the glass separating Allyn and I from Melvin.

"Can we stop at the store?" I'd been assured via email by Lila— Melvin's daughter, the other half of the caretaker team all year round, and the chef when my parents were present—that the house had been appropriately stocked for our arrival. Even so, I'd wanted to make a stop in downtown Aspen to pick up a few supplies.

Melvin clicked his tongue, not sparing me a glance in the rearview mirror. "We can, but the forecast has another two feet by midnight. If we stop now, there's no guarantee we'll be able to access 82 at all, or reach the house for the next several days. It's a good thing you girls arrived when you did. Lila's been fretting all week. If your plane had been further delayed, you might've been staying the week at one of the lodges instead."

"Does that mean we won't be able to leave once we get there?" Allyn addressed this question equally to both me and Melvin.

"Forecast has snow slowing by week's end, and they plow on Fridays. You should be fine to fly out, assuming the forecast is on target."

"But we can't leave for the whole week?" She didn't sound upset or worried, merely curious.

"That's right. Once we get there, you two will be stuck for the week with the rest of us. But don't worry, we do this all the time, it's not unusual. And Lila has a menu planned. We'll do our best to make it bearable for you."

By 'rest of us' I assumed he meant Lila, me, and himself, but I was surprised that Lila was planning to cook.

"I told Lila she doesn't need to cook," I reminded him, leaning forward in my seat. When it was just me, I made sure she never felt pressured to make anything.

"Mona, don't you make a big deal out of it." Now Melvin did spare me a glance in the mirror, narrowing his eyes. "Just let her be. She likes cooking when there's company. She is a pro chef, after all. And if she's not making her fancy dishes, her talents just go to waste. Think of it that way."

I didn't argue, but I still wasn't convinced. I didn't like to inconvenience people. I could take care of myself.

After driving through downtown Aspen, we took several precarious off-shoots from State Road 82. I tried not to look out the window, but Allyn seemed fascinated by the near whiteout conditions. At one point, Melvin must've been going five miles per hour, it was fully dark by the time we arrived. Even so, I barely noticed the length of the car ride. Allyn had talked non-stop, her pretty, melodic voice filling the car with stories about her difficult last semester, all of which seemed hilarious to her in retrospect.

The three parking garages near the base of the peak served only as a pitstop and storage. A funicular, which was just as fancy as it was functional, had been installed well before my parents purchased the Mountain McMansion. It was the only way to actually access the main house October through April, give or take a month depending on the snowfall.

Melvin pulled as close to the funicular structure as he could, knocking on the back door of the Jeep before opening it for Allyn. "Okay, ladies. Time to get out. You go up first while I clear a path to the garage, must be two feet of snow up here since I left this morning. I'll come after with your bags and the supplies I picked up on my way to the airport. Hurry, it's cold."

White flakes of frost swirled around him, but nothing much else was visible. Happy to do as we were told, my friend and I gathered our backpacks and left the warmth of the SUV. Melvin had been right. The snow came up to my knee, my boots disappearing into two or more decimeters of fresh powder.

Glancing back, I smiled at Allyn's huge grin and laugh, her eyes on where her feet should be. "Follow me," I said. "The funicular is just through here."

"Funicular is a fun word to say." She held her hands out to keep her balance. "It sounds like fun and particular had a word baby."

"Well, this funicular is particular, but I don't know how fun it is."

"Everything can be fun. You just have to want it to be fun," she said, the combination of her bright eyes and wide smile a sunbeam in the cold darkness, laughing as she added, "And, you know, the habit of constantly laughing at yourself."

That made me laugh, though I wasn't sure why. When Allyn was around, I always seemed to be laughing. And, in truth, taking the fancy funicular used to be fun. As a kid, it was my favorite part of visiting the mountain house. I would hang out inside, reading books, breathing against the paned window and drawing designs into the puff of condensation with the tip of my finger.

The benches were a gold-ish velvet and there was space for four comfortably, six if absolutely needed. Our ride up the mountain was uneventful despite the snowfall, but I felt a little badly about the inclement weather.

"I was snowed in here twice last year, but only for about three days. After that, it cleared up. We should have some nice views, assuming the snow stops." I motioned to the darkness beyond the glass. The flakes were so big, they made tapping sounds against the window reminiscent of light rain.

"That'll be nice. Can we do any hiking? Is it safe?"

"If you want exercise, there's an indoor pool and gym. But if you really want to go for a walk outside, you can go snowshoeing through the trails."

"I've never gone snowshoeing."

"It's just very slow walking, with funny shoes. Though it'll feel like you've covered a hundred miles by the time you finish. There's a few Jacuzzis for warming up after, and a sauna near the gym as well as one on the top floor."

Allyn's eyebrows pulled together even as she smiled. "A few jacuzzis? Two saunas? Are you sure this isn't a hotel?"

I rolled my eyes good-naturedly, but didn't respond. I didn't come here for the Jacuzzis and saunas and huge fireplaces and the music room and the sound studio and movie theater. My parents had houses all over the world, and they put money into a travel account for me (and one for each of my siblings) every year, mostly because they never wanted us to have an excuse if they requested our presence at some event. I rarely used the travel account and the mountain house was the only one I ever asked to visit.

"I'll go snowshoeing with you if you really want to go." I breathed on the glass, making a rough oval of condensation, and drew two smiley faces. "But mostly, I'd like to get some reading done."

"Work stuff?" Allyn asked, making her own condensation canvas in the glass and drawing a flower. It looked like a thistle. She was a good artist.

"No, actually. A few novels I've been saving."

"Really? Which ones?"

The funicular car began to slow, and I twisted my neck to peer out the window behind me. The house was now fully in view and all lit up. It looked warm and inviting, though I frowned at how many windows were illuminated. I usually stuck to the main floor, eschewing the larger rooms on the upper levels. *Why would Lila turn on all the lights in every room?* Strange.

"Uh, Lisa Kleypas. Her most recent two," I answered distractedly.

"Oh, you haven't read her latest book?" Allyn sounded anxious, which brought my attention back to her.

"No. Not yet. You know me, I've been saving them."

"When you finish, I need to talk about it. I have feelings!" My friend did jazz hands, wiggling her fingers in the air.

Laughing, I stood as the car came to a stop in the top-side structure. "Okay. Sounds good. I'll probably have feelings too. We can compare feelings notes."

"Yes!" She jumped up and turned to grab her bag.

I unfastened the door and slid it to the side, and then I paused because I spotted a dark figure approaching the funicular structure, silhouetted by the lights of the house. The size of the outline made the person too big to be Lila, and the wrong chromosomal arrangement. Meaning, it was a man. And he was carrying what looked like a shovel over his shoulder.

"Who is . . . ?" I narrowed my eyes, stepping off the car, leaving my bag for the moment, and opened the structure door.

"Mona!"

I stood straighter at the sound of my brother's greeting, ignoring the blast of cold wind. "Leo? What are you doing here?" I had to raise my voice over the gust. It hadn't been nearly as blustery at the parking structures. I gripped my hat to my head, just in case it decided to fly off.

Fully materializing, he grinned down at me, his dark eyes moving over my face. "It's good to see you! Do you need help with bags?" Leo made no move to hug me, not that I expected him to. After putting up with my stiff, detached hugs for several years, he'd stopped trying.

I shook my head, confused by his presence, and also by the uncomfortable prickling at the back of my neck. "It's good to see you too. I didn't know you were coming."

"Did you get my voicemail?" he asked, but then glanced over my shoulder, obviously spotting Allyn. "Oh, hey. Alan, right?" He extended his hand automatically, but then chuckled at himself when he seemed to suddenly remember the work gloves covering his fingers.

"It's pronounced Al-lean," I corrected.

"Oh, sorry." Leo seemed to be apologizing for both his inability to shake her hand and mispronouncing her name.

"That's okay. You can call me Al if you like. And I can wave," she offered cheerfully, coming to stand fully beside me. "I can also salute, but that might be weird."

Her comment made Leo laugh, and he gave her another look, his eyes narrowing slightly as they moved down and then up. "I guess we're saluting," he said, smiling, saluting, his eyes still suspiciously squinty.

I say *suspiciously* because they were sparkly as well as squinty, and I knew that face: Leo had decided she was worth a second look. Allyn and Leo had met just once, separated by many people and meters, and very briefly, at my graduation from undergrad almost three years ago. It had been so short, I don't think he even heard her name correctly and had called her "Alan." Before I could correct his error then, he was pulled elsewhere, and Allyn had disappeared into the crowd.

Presently, they were still smiling at each other, almost like I wasn't there, and the exchange was exponential levels of cute. Under normal circumstances, it would've initiated my innate scheming proclivities (arranging an accidental half-naked interaction, planning their wedding, sending out save-the-date cards, and prepping for her bachelorette party) because who wouldn't want a best friend to marry an awesome sibling? But I was still perplexed by his presence and the sense of being suddenly and inexplicably *on edge*.

I also saluted and stepped in front of Allyn once again. "Hey, what's going on? Why are you here?"

"I called you and left a message. I invited a few—" A gust of wind filled the small structure, pushing Leo forward such that he had to use his free hand to brace himself against the door.

Just before he righted himself, I noticed movement behind him. Another man—a big one by the looks of him—was walking toward us along the path. My stomach tensed. A shivery—yet hot—spike of awareness shot up my spine to my neck. And my heart . . . *my heart.*

I licked my lips, my eyes wide on my brother. "Leo. Is there—is there someone here with you?"

"Why don't you come inside? I'll explain everything."

I grabbed his arm. "Explain now." *Why is my heart beating so hard?*

It was like that moment in the sensory deprivation chamber, I was hot and cold and clammy everywhere.

Leo shook his head, giving me a look of mild exasperation. "Mona, it's freezing and you're doing that whispering thing. I can barely hear you. Let's go."

He easily pulled out of my grip, turning for the house and lowering the shovel, and I reached for him again. But before I could grab my brother, the new person emerged from the dark and snow, and entered the little halo spilling from the funicular structure's overhead lights.

I stopped.

I think even my heart stopped.

I know my forebrain stopped, or was—at the very least—broken.

It was . . .

He was . . .

He looked . . .

How . . .?

"Abram."

[3]

MAGNETISM

Abram

"Abram." Leo stopped upon catching sight of me. Most of his face was in shadow, but what I could see looked relieved. "Good. Hey, so I guess I will need you to take the funicular down to the garage level after all."

I nodded, my attention moving beyond him to the two women. The one on the left must've been Mona's friend, Alan. My eyes sought the one on the right.

Huh.

She was shorter than I remembered. Memories are tricky that way, always trying to make the past bigger, more important, more interesting and relevant and meaningful. But memories were so seldom reflective of reality.

And yet, I had to concede that she was just as beautiful as I remembered, even though all the color had leached from her skin. Mona looked like she'd just seen a ghost. This filled me with a perverse kind of satisfaction, because she was staring right at me. I was the ghost.

Even wan, she was still extraordinary. Those honey colored eyes of hers were wide with surprise and her pretty pink heart-shaped lips were parted slightly. The delicate line of her jaw, the gentle point of her chin, the subtle indent just beneath her cheekbones, it all made me want to hold her face in my palms, push her hat off, thread my fingers into her dark hair, tilt her head back, and—

"My sister didn't get the messages I left earlier. Thanks for your help. I know it's freezing." Leo lifted his voice over the howling wind. "I want to get the girls settled, make introductions, you know."

"Not a problem." I shoved my hands into my pockets, lest they get any ideas, and gave Leo another nod. But my attention remained fastened to the genius astrophysicist who continued to gape at me. I didn't remember her looking at me that way during our week together, nor during any of her interviews, and I wondered if this was a new expression for Ms. Mona DaVinci.

Had she ever been unpleasantly surprised before? Had she ever come face-to-face with a mistake? Leo had once told me Mona never made mistakes. What did that make me?

The opposite of a mistake is intentional action.

I felt my lips curve into a bitter smile at the thought and blinked, moving my carefully bored glare from Mona to her friend. Leo had said the friend's name was Alan, so I'd been expecting a man. Obviously, this Alan wasn't a man. For some reason, the discovery relaxed the tension around my ribs somewhat. I wouldn't think too much about that, if I could help it.

Alan was also staring at me, her lips also parted, but she wasn't looking at me like I was a ghost. She was looking at me like she knew who I was, and she was a fan. *Great.*

Sighing, I dropped my attention to the pathway and moved toward the ski lift house, or whatever it was called. Despite Leo's shoveling, the large slate path was quickly refilling with snow. The old guy down at the garage level would definitely need help. That's what I would think about.

Eyeballing the doorway blocked by the two women, I hesitated before walking slowly forward. Mona's friend wasn't a big person, but I was. Unless she wanted to press herself flat against the wall, there was no way we'd both fit in the tight hallway. Thus, it was no surprise when, at my approach, Alan scrambled out of the way, stepping around Mona and onto the much broader path.

The friend wore a wide, shy smile as my gaze flickered to her. I gave her a single head nod in acknowledgement. I'd learned the value of keeping an air of detachment. Fans preferred the myth that I was inherently aloof to any version of truly knowing me. Who was it who'd said, "Better to shut your mouth and be thought a fool than open it and remove all doubt"? These days, that was basically my mantra.

Unlike her friend, Mona's feet did not move at my approach. Her body still blocked most of the door. But she did lift her chin as I closed the distance between us. Except, I wasn't closing the distance between *us*. She was in my way, and I needed to move past her in order to continue forward.

Given her inconvenient location, I was forced to slow, stop, and then wait. Clearing my throat, I kept my eyes fastened on the ski lift behind her and waited for her to get out of my way.

"Let me show you the house." Leo lifted his voice behind me, presumably speaking to Alan. "Abram will help Melvin with the bags. We saved the top floor for you and Mona, so it'll be quiet, just like she likes. Do you . . ." His voice drifted off, swallowed by the wind and increasing distance.

I wasn't close to Mona, allowing her plenty of space to walk past me. If memory served, and in this case I trusted memory, Mona didn't like people getting too close. *Unless, that part was a lie too.*

"Hi—hello," she said, stepping forward but not out of the way, drawing my attention.

She was still staring at me, her face still pale, but her eyes had turned searching instead of stunned.

"I—" She stopped herself, swallowing, her gaze dropping to the front of my coat, a cute little frown furrowing her eyebrows. In the next moment, she was pulling off the glove of her right hand. Abruptly, she shoved the ungloved fingers toward me, returning her eyes to mine. "I'm Mona."

I suppressed my disbelief at her small action before it could break my outward mask of calm. I wasn't calm. Just to be clear, I was the opposite of calm.

The fact that she was introducing herself to me now meant that she thought I was too stupid to figure out her lies over the last two-and-a-half-fucking years. She was arguably one of the smartest people in the world, after all. To her, people like me must seem like housebroken pets. So it shouldn't have surprised me. But it did. The tension and tightness around my ribs reappeared, squeezing uncomfortably.

Dropping my attention to her bare hand, I pressed my lips into a tighter line, dismissing the way my pulse jumped at the sight of her wrist, the olive tone of her skin under the yellow string lights overhead. Glaring at her outstretched offering, I considered telling her to go to hell.

I considered it, but I wouldn't.

I didn't trust myself to speak, that was reason number one.

The other reason was harder to explain, or use as a justification, or admit to myself. Staring at her hand, I braced against a sudden flare of hunger. She might consider me a lower life-form, but that didn't change the fact that I wanted to touch her. I wanted to touch her more than I wanted to tell her to go to hell, and that was fucking pitiful.

But there it was.

Acting on the compulsion, I lifted my right hand and tugged off the ski glove, sliding my warm palm against her much colder one. Her hand felt good in my hand, the right weight, the right size, the right texture, and I inhaled freezing air.

Mona also seemed to suck in a slow but expansive breath as our hands touched, held. This brought my eyes back to hers in time to see her lashes flutter. Pink colored her previously pale cheeks. The sound of the wailing wind, the sting of the air and frost momentarily melted away, leaving just her, her soft skin warming against mine, her beautiful face filling my vision.

So beautiful.

She really was. She was stunning. I hated that she was still so beautiful to me.

She looks just like her sister.

I blinked, stopping myself before I shook my head at the bitter thought.

Except, no. She doesn't. Not at all.

About two years ago, when I'd begun to suspect the truth, I'd compared countless images of the twins. The pictures were more contemporary than my fuzzy memories of the photos at the house in Chicago, the ones where Mona had looked twelve, and Lisa hadn't.

I decided they looked identical, especially in pictures taken this last year. Side by side, they looked like the same person. When the suspicion became growing certainty, their similarity in photos made me feel a little better about the possibility of being so completely fooled.

But now, looking at Mona *now*, seeing the physical differences in sharp focus, I felt sick.

I should have known immediately. God, I should have known.

The way she'd looked at me then, the way she was looking at me now, so completely different than her sister. The last question I'd struggled with—the final puzzle piece—snapped resoundingly into place. *She left after the movie.*

I'd suspected, but now I knew with absolute certainty. It had been Mona during *The Blues Brothers,* and Lisa in the morning. That's when they'd switched places.

Riding the wave of nausea, I pulled my fingers from hers and shifted my attention to the interior of the ski lift, no longer wanting to touch her or look at her or breathe the same air as her.

"You're Abram," she said, moving closer, too close.

I sidestepped her, brushing past into the small building. My tongue felt thick and dry, and a pulse of heat radiated from my skin outward, but also pushing back at me, just like the sensation when a rollercoaster takes a dive. *How could I have been so fucking stupid?*

Behind me, I heard the door close, cutting off the sound of the wind, and she said, "You and Leo are—uh—good friends."

Not answering, I closed my eyes against the spike of anger. I took a deep breath. Her boots made noise on the tile floor as she drew near. She was trailing me.

"I didn't know anyone would be here. We thought it would be just us. I . . ." She cleared her throat, then continued, "I hope we didn't interrupt you guys or that us being here is an inconvenience to—to—to —uh, to anything. If you need us to go, we can leave." Her voice had grown quieter as she spoke, sounding like *her*. Even at a near whisper, I heard every word as I stepped onto the little car.

Grinding my teeth, I spotted a backpack through the haze of red tinting my vision. I lifted it. I turned. "This yours?"

She shifted back a half step, her eyes still wide and searching. "Uh. Yes. Mine."

I shoved the bag at her chest. Not hard, just enough to force her to retreat another step, clearing the doorway of the car so I could slide it shut, which I did.

She flinched, blinking at me through the glass, visibly astonished by my closing of the door so abruptly, and she either whispered or mouthed, "Abram."

Didn't matter. I gave her my back and started the car's descent, though she was still visible in the reflection of the glass in front of me. But I couldn't hear her with the closed door between us, and soon I wouldn't be able to see her either.

So fucking stupid.

I shook my head at myself, exhaling slowly, lead in my chest, but relieved to have made it through this initial encounter without making an idiot of myself. Biting the inside of my lower lip, I stared at the snow beyond her reflection until she disappeared, feeling and welcoming the cold.

I'd caught Mona DaVinci's testimony to Congress a few months ago. She'd been as eloquent as she'd been brutally brilliant, passing off cutting remarks as polite responses. Strangely, after watching her make fools of the most powerful people in the country, I felt like I'd also been torn to shreds. She was magnificent. She'd also been completely without emotion.

Still, even then, I doubted. I bargained with myself, I reasoned against the likelihood of such a scheme. Who would do that? And how dumb would I have to be to fall for it? Between the two possibilities of crazy or stupid, crazy seemed like the lesser of two evils. In pictures, Lisa looked like my Lisa. Yet, so did Mona.

But then, during an interview on the news several days after the testimony—I'll never forget—Mona said, "I disagree. Senator Nevelson's question was irrelevant and lacked a fundamental understanding of the scientific method, and then the wolves came."

And then the wolves came.

Sometimes reality feels like a dream. Something happens, and it makes you question everything you know to be true, everything you take for granted about the world, about yourself. When that happens, your surroundings and interactions become likewise warped, like you're watching those around you through a magnifying glass, or in high saturation color, and you can't stop. You can't make the world normal again, you know too much.

I'd spent two years doubting my sanity. Instead, I should have been doubting the fundamental goodness of people, my willingness to trust, and my intelligence.

And. Then. The. Wolves. Came.

So. Fucking. Stupid.

I stopped lying to myself, wishing for a different explanation, wishing *my Lisa* would somehow reappear and miraculously want to be with me. I stopped assuming people had good intentions. I stopped looking for the good. I stopped assuming the best, of anyone.

In that moment, I knew without a shadow of a doubt what they'd done. Nothing about that week had been real. Everything had been a lie.

But shame on me.

I should've listened to her the first time she told me to hold a grudge.

[4]

ELECTROMAGNETIC INDUCTION

Abram

M elvin reminded me of my uncle. They both gossiped. A lot.
No complaints. Melvin's gossip served as a welcome
distraction, as was the biting cold. It's hard to remain focused on being
pissed when your appendages are freezing.

Even better, Melvin didn't seem to require any response from me. I
let him talk, mostly about Aspen politics and recent local scandals,
while we shoveled snow. Apparently, the garage closest to the main
road, if you could call a one-lane mountain road a "main road," housed
a small snow plow and he liked keeping the area in front of it clear.

"It's for emergencies," he said. "It's good to be ready, just in case
we need to use it. And this path between the funicular house and the
snow plow gets shoveled too."

"Why don't you just use the plow now? Clear this area?"

"Well, I wouldn't use the plow at night." He lifted the rim of his ski
cap to scratch his head. "Yeah, I got those lights up there." Melvin
gestured to the high intensity work lamps on each of the garages, illu-
minating the clearing where we stood and the area around the three
garages. "They're bright, but I might not see a big branch or something

like it. Plus, it uses diesel, which I don't have an unlimited supply of, and I like the exercise." His eyelashes were frosty, but he was grinning as he said this, his gloved hands resting on the pole of the shovel. "You ever want to come down and help shovel, just let me know. Think about it."

I didn't need to think about it, any excuse to leave over the next few days would come in handy. "I will. You come down here every day?"

"Yes. Sometimes twice, sometimes three times. Snow is easier to shovel if you move it within six hours of falling."

I nodded, knowing this already. Michigan winters were why I never wanted to live someplace where daily snow shoveling in the winter was a requirement for leaving the house.

My dad would wake me up before school with a shovel in hand, saying, "God gave you those shoulders for a reason, son. And today that reason is shoveling snow."

"Hey, we'll clear this here together, and then you got this area?" Melvin gestured to the last few feet before the ski lift. "I'll go get the bags and we can ride up together."

"Bags?" I blinked as freezing flakes fell on my face near my eyes.

"Mona's. And her friend, Alan, or All-lean, or Al-lena, or something like that. These names, I can't pronounce them without practicing."

Glancing away, the white cloud of my exhales following me, I studied the pile of snow near my boots. "Sure. I got it."

"Thanks. You know, if it were just Mona, like last time, she could have taken it all up in one trip." Melvin began shoveling again. "Never met a person who packs as light as our Mona."

I said nothing, but that hot pulse of energy radiated outward again, pushing back, my stomach dropping, a tight band around my throat.

"She's something else." Melvin paired this statement with a chuckle and a headshake. "You know, she never lets Lila cook for her. Says she doesn't want to inconvenience anyone. And she'd be out here shoveling if I'd let her. One time, she got up before me, at the butt crack of dawn. Snow was coming down like a waterfall and she shoveled half the path before I arrived. Reamed her a new one for being so reckless."

I lifted an eyebrow at that. "You reamed Mona 'a new one'?"

"Yep. Gave it to her, good and hard."

I swallowed, internally stiffening and growing hot at the word choice.

But he wasn't finished. "She said she liked the exertion or some such nonsense. Something about never being worn out, since she sits at a desk all day." Melvin rolled his eyes heavenward. "That Mona, she needs a firm hand, doesn't like to take no for an answer. I've had to lay the law down with her a few times."

A spike of something both pleasant and unpleasant had me shaking my head to clear it. "About shoveling snow?"

"About all manner of things. She wants to do her own laundry. She cleans her own room, vacuums and dusts, even. She likes to stop by the store in town before coming up here, every time, and usually eats only what she brings. Drives Lila bonkers."

"You mean she's picky."

"Nope. No. Not that. Not that at all. She doesn't want to be a bother. Between you and me and this snow here, I like Leo a lot. The parents, I could take or leave, and Lisa hasn't been here in ages, she was a sweet kid when I knew her. But Mona is my favorite."

"Because she doesn't want to be a bother?" I decided Melvin talked too much, and one day his gossiping was going to get him in trouble.

"No. Because she goes out of her way to treat us like people instead of servants. Now, I know, I know." He paused shoveling to make a waving motion with his hand. "We work for them, we're their employees. But Mona checks in before she comes to make sure the dates work for us, since we live here and all. Who else does that? No one. We didn't even know Leo was coming until you people arrived. Don't get me wrong, I'm not complaining, but there's definitely a difference. As an example, one time Lila was sick, so Mona canceled her trip and sent a care package instead." Melvin pushed his shovel forward, resuming his work. "They're all nice people, but Mona is a different kind of nice. You know Mona?"

I was listening so intently, I almost didn't catch his question. It took me several seconds to figure out how I wanted to respond to it, and a few more before I trusted my voice to sound disinterested.

"She seems like she'd be judgmental."

"What?" He scrutinized me, sounding confused. "Mona?"

"Yeah. Isn't she supposed to be a genius?"

"Is she? You mean because of going to that Ivy League school when she was little?" Melvin laughed. "I guess that makes me a genius too. Because I beat her at poker every time we play. Or maybe she's just bad at bluffing."

I didn't respond, clamping my jaw together, taking my frustration out on the pile of snow instead.

"No, Mona isn't judgmental. She's a little quiet, but I think that's because she's . . . well, she's shy."

"Shy?" I asked without meaning to, and then snapped my mouth shut.

"Yeah. Shy. She never did have friends. Lisa was always bringing friends here, kids from those boarding schools she went to, and Mona would play by herself, mostly here, in the funicular, reading books. Leo would also bring friends, he still does." Melvin lifted his chin toward me. "That's why I was surprised to see all you guys when you arrived, since Mona was coming."

I found I needed to clear my throat before asking, "She's always alone?"

He nodded. "Yep. Always alone. Every time she comes, and she comes up here a lot. Which is why we take pity on her and play poker, or Scrabble. She also likes Trivial Pursuit—the one from the eighties, when USSR was still a country—but we just read the cards back and forth to see who knows the most answers. She tried to get us to play this new thing called Punderdome or Punundrum, but it needs an even number of people."

Punderdome? That sounds—

I interrupted the rhythm of my thoughts. Gripping the shovel tighter at the realization we'd just spent the last ten minutes talking about the one person I least wanted to talk about, I shook my head, scowling at the snow.

Stop asking about her.

I'd spent over two years trying to forget about one week. Nothing Melvin said, or was going to say, would help me move on. Clearly, he liked her, respected her. Fine.

Stop talking about her.

"Mona is real good at chess though, never have beat her at that game. But she—"

Enough.

"Hey, I'll move up here and get this taken care of. Why don't you get the bags?"

Melvin's perspective on Mona confused me, unsettled my mind. The man might talk all night about her if I let him, and part of me wanted to let him. But that would've been counterproductive.

Stop thinking about her.

I didn't want to like Mona, nor did I appreciate this urge I'd carried with me, this wanting to know her, the real her, all about her, sketch an accurate likeness of her character. What was the point?

She'd lied to me. She'd pretended to be someone else. Knowing Mona DaVinci better wasn't going to change that.

Melvin paused his shoveling at my abrupt suggestion, but then he chuckled. "Getting cold?"

Stop wanting her.

I forced a quick, tight smile and nodded. "Yeah. Something like that."

* * *

Melvin took me around to the side door of the house, which was much closer than the path Leo and I had shoveled earlier to the main entrance. We both removed our jackets, boots, gloves, and snow pants and hung them up in the mudroom closet.

"Here, I'll take the luggage up. Go get warm by the fire in the big room, go see your friends."

I hesitated, glancing at the small stairway behind him that led to the upper floors, struggling with the desire to seek her out. Bringing her luggage up would be a perfect excuse. Then again, not taking advantage of the opportunity to see her was an opportunity in and of itself.

Stop thinking about her.

"While you're there, do you mind checking on the fire? Might need more wood," Melvin called over his shoulder, already on the fifth stair.

Curling my hands into tight fists, I nodded and stepped back, removing myself from the temptation of the suitcases. Watching Melvin disappear up the flight of stairs felt both good—like I'd finally been successful in flexing that self-control muscle—and not good. I stared at the roller case he'd left behind, a hollow, restlessness in my stomach.

Turning toward the faint sound of a piano, I walked out of the mudroom and toward the music, not looking at the remaining bag despite feeling a pull to return, pick up the case, and take it to the third floor where Mona and her friend were staying.

Earlier, when I'd left the house under the guise of helping Leo and Melvin with the snow, the crowd Leo had gathered were in high spirits. I knew most of them, but not all. Leo had this magical superpower of bringing talented people together and making valuable connections within the community he'd built.

The only valuable connection I'd ever introduced to Leo, and not the other way around, was my songwriting partner, Kaitlyn Parker. Meanwhile, Leo had been the one to introduce me to our drummer when I was fifteen, our lead guitarist five years ago, and our producer three years ago. Our producer was the one who'd eventually helped sign us to the label.

My mind on suitcases and perfect excuses, I slowed as I approached the entrance to the main floor living room, a thought suddenly occurring to me. What if Mona was here, on the main level with everyone else? What if, by attempting to avoid her, I was actually achieving the opposite?

Mouth suddenly dry, I approached the wide doorframe and stopped, taking a moment to scan the room. Leo wasn't there, neither were Mona or her friend, but most everyone else seemed to be. The mood had shifted since I'd left over an hour earlier.

Instead of everyone gathering around the piano, playing music, talking in a haphazard circle, they'd separated themselves into smaller, two- or three-person clusters. They were talking quietly. No one looked especially happy. And the music wasn't helping.

My attention moved to Kaitlyn sitting at the piano, playing a technically brilliant and woefully ominous sounding piece on the instrument. I suspected it was improvised, something she was making up on the spot, as was her habit.

Rubbing my cold hands together, I entered the large living room—which looked more like a medium-sized hotel lobby than a living room—nodding at our drummer, Charlie, as I passed, and declining our guitarist's invitation to join her small group on my way to the piano. I did take the long way around to check on the fire. It wasn't low, but I added another two logs anyway.

Sitting next to Kaitlyn on the bench, I brought my folded fingers to my mouth, breathing hot air into my cupped hands, and bumping her shoulder lightly. "What's that?"

Without stopping her improvisation or looking at me, she said, "I'm providing the soundtrack."

"The soundtrack?"

"Yes. If we were in a movie, this would be the soundtrack for the moment," she whispered. "Earlier, before *the arrival*, everything was light and fun and fancy-free, like a Disney cartoon. C major."

I glanced between her profile and where she depressed the keys. A maudlin tune, with frequent dramatic pauses, reverberated from the grand piano.

"And now?" I prompted.

"And now, D-sharp." She said *D-sharp* in a very deep voice, sounding like Eeyore, pulling a smile from me. Her left hand moved lower down the bass clef, taking the mood from maudlin to morose.

Shaking my head, and despite myself, I chuckled. "You are so weird."

"Thank you," she said brightly, giving me a quick, bright smile.

"Why did the key change?" *The arrival* she referred to was obviously Mona and Alan's.

"Well, let's see. Where to start, where to start . . ." Kaitlyn leaned to the side, extremely close.

With anyone else I would've suspected she was trying to flirt, but not with her. Kaitlyn Parker wasn't a flirter. I doubted she had any idea how to flirt. One time after a gig, when we both played for the same for-hire live band, she did a robot-dance-off on a dare and won after twenty straight minutes of impressively stunted movement and seriously committed beeps and boops. But her lack of flirt-skills didn't matter. She was a brilliant composer, gorgeous, smart, and hilarious both accidentally and on purpose.

She was also engaged to be married, and the guy was a real asshole. A ridiculously rich asshole with an asshole name (Martin) who was a stockbroker or something equally asshole-like. Yeah, he worshipped her. Yeah, he treated her like a goddess as far as I could tell. But he was still an asshole.

"Did something happen?" I whispered close to her ear.

She nodded and lifted her rounded gray eyes to mine, saying in a hushed rush, "Yes. The first one came in and everything was fine— Allyn, very nice, kind of kooky but sweet—and then Leo noticed his sister wasn't anywhere. He opened the door, and then we all kind of heard this screaming sound, and—"

"Screaming?" I sat up, alert and alarmed. "Is she okay? Was she hurt?"

"No, no. Not hurt. Actually, it was more like yelling or growling, not screaming."

I frowned, confused. "What?"

"She was standing on the path to the house, yell-growling."

"At what?"

"Honestly, I don't know. A bear, maybe? No explanation was offered. Anyway, it kind of killed the mood and freaked everyone out. And then Leo went outside to get her."

My eyes drifted to the piano keys, trying to make sense of the story. "Did she stop yelling?"

"Yes. As soon as she saw Leo, she seemed to stop. And then she came inside with him and he introduced her to everyone. One by one. All twenty-one of us. And it was awkward, so awkward, because clearly everyone was still thinking about the loud yelling, she was very . . ." Kaitlyn paused here, now she was frowning, and she turned her attention back to the piano, switching to a new key, no longer the existential angst of D-sharp.

"What key is that?"

"D minor," she said, sounding thoughtful, pensive, just like the music she was playing. "It's actually Requiem in D minor by Mozart."

My eyes flickered between her and the room full of people quietly talking. Everyone seemed to be whispering, still on edge.

"Why D minor?" I asked.

"Because Mona DaVinci seems like a D minor kind of gal." Kaitlyn's response sounded distracted.

The piece she played was growing in intensity, louder but strangely restrained. The song frustrated me. It was like riding a rollercoaster that only went up, building anticipation with no foreseeable payoff.

Swallowing against the aggravation making my throat tight, I covered her treble clef hand, forcing her to stop playing. She glanced at me, giving me a questioning look.

"What?"

I swallowed again, and then cleared my throat, letting my hand drop from hers. "Leo introduced her to everyone?"

She nodded and, still looking at me, began softly playing "Chopsticks." She replied, "He did. And it was weird."

"Weird?"

Stop asking about her.

"Like, we all expected her to be hurt, or injured, or upset, or have slain a bear and painted herself with its blood—you know, because she was just moments prior literally yelling. When she came in though, she seemed fine. Frosty, but fine."

"Frosty?"

"She was about as warm and friendly as a polar vortex. *Super* frosty." Kaitlyn frowned, and then scrunched her face. "I've read that about her. Mona DaVinci, supergenius, personality of fifty below zero. But then, if I had her IQ, I might be the same way. We must all seem like single-cell organisms to her."

I bit the inside of my lip to keep my expression dispassionate and from asking another question, though many scrolled through my mind,

How long did she stay? Did she say anything to anyone? Did she say she'd be back down tonight?

"Anyway," Kaitlyn continued, "in that interview I read? The interviewer said she was a cold person. Perhaps she's the mythical Snow Queen. And that yelling was her speaking the snow language, giving orders to her minion snowflakes. *ATTACK THE BEARS!*"

Preoccupied and unsettled, I forced a smirk at Kaitlyn's silliness and scratched the back of my neck. I'd read every interview Mona DaVinci had given, or all the ones I could find online, and Kaitlyn was right. If Mona was described in an interview, they used words like cold, emotionless, blunt, and abrupt just as often as they used gifted, intelligent, smart, and brilliant. They'd also called her "the greatest mind of her generation," and, "this generation's Einstein."

The closest anyone had come to 'friendly' was when Rolling Stone had done a profile on the exceptional children of famous musicians. The journalist mentioned something about Mona DaVinci only being animated while she discussed advances in the field of physics with an audience of high school seniors.

According to the article, Mona donated some of her free time to a foundation dedicated to advancing women in STEM fields. Mona flew around the country a few times a year, giving speeches to assemblies in rural areas and underserved schools. Apparently, she was also a philanthropist. I didn't know why, but evidence of her good deeds aggravated me.

However, the rest of the article went on to describe her as single-mindedly focused on her research and the foundation, disinterested in questions about all other facets of life.

At one point they'd asked, "Do you think you'll ever get married?"

To which she'd responded, "Irrelevant. Next question."

Then they'd asked, "Anyone special in your life?"

To which she'd responded, "Yes. The Large Hadron Collider at CERN. Next question."

And that made me laugh. It also pissed me off when her responses in interviews made me laugh.

Kaitlyn pulled me out of my thoughts by bumping my shoulder.

"Hey there, Abram. What's going on in your brain? You are behaving in odd and uncharacteristic ways."

I lifted an eyebrow at her. "What do you mean?"

She studied me for a moment before asking, "Why are we here?"

"To write music." *And to assuage my . . . curiosity.*

Curiosity was not the right word, but it was definitely a part of why we were here now.

When Leo had suggested the trip three days ago, I thought he was nuts. I didn't see how I could drop everything for several days and go to Aspen for New Years, just two weeks before leaving for the tour. But then he mentioned we'd have to share the house with his sister. Mona.

We'd left New York for Aspen the next day.

Revenge was a construct I used to actively avoid, the idea of it both repulsive and tempting. Repulsive because my parents had raised me better, and tempting because . . . *Honestly?*

I'd always felt injustice on a visceral level. Fairness was a sore spot, a stumbling block, the wall I banged my head against instead of searching for a door or a window. When I was younger, I'd avoided the temptation of seeking vengeance, made better choices, been a better person, had more restraint and self-control.

Now? *Not so much.*

So, yeah. I was curious. Given what she'd done to me, what would revenge against Mona DaVinci look like? What could I possibly do to this generation's Einstein that would be a just settling of accounts between us? Maybe nothing. Maybe she was too frosty and couldn't be touched. Maybe I didn't want revenge at all. Maybe I didn't care.

I was on the fence, committed to nothing, not a place I spent much time.

Presently, Kaitlyn's eyes narrowed slightly. "You haven't written new lyrics in over a year."

I tilted my head to the side, avoiding her searching glare. "All the more reason for me to write now."

"You're being quiet," she accused.

"Am I?"

"Yep. You've been quiet since we left New York. And you've been pensive. I'm not used to pensive Abram. I'm used to salty, sarcastic Abram. What's going on? Is your manbun too tight?"

I shrugged, forcing another smirk. "Just tired."

"Falsehood. Untruth. Lie." She punctuated the triple accusation with chords, singing the words in a falsetto voice like an opera singer.

My grin this time was genuine. The only thing bigger than Kaitlyn's talent and her vocabulary was her personality.

"Let it go, Kaitlyn."

She removed her hands from the instrument, turned at the waist, and leaned away to inspect me. "Are you nervous? Worried? About the tour?"

I shook my head, my eyes dropping to my hands. "No."

"I would be, if I were you. It's okay to be nervous. You'll do great. It'll be great. You've been playing live for years."

"I'm not nervous."

"But you're not excited either?"

I shrugged again, movement by the big staircase drawing my attention. Leo was walking down the stairs, taking them slowly, a frown on his face.

I sat up straighter, wondering what had happened to make Mona yell and if she was truly okay, or hurt and hiding it, or what?

Stop thinking about her.

"I'm ambivalent about—" I paused, sighed, frowned "—about it," I finally answered.

Kaitlyn made a snorting noise, and then said, "Scoff."

I cut my eyes to her. "Did you just say, 'Scoff'?"

"Yes. Scoff-scoffety-scoff-scoff. You are crazypants, Abram Fletcher. I know what ambivalent means. How can you be uncertain about the tour? You have the number one song in the country—"

"No. *We* have the number one song in the country."

"You know what I mean, it's your song."

"No." I turned to face her. "It's our song."

"It's *our* musical composition, but they're all your words. It's seventy-five percent your song, at least. And the rules of scientific digits mean that it's your song. But that's beside the point. As I was saying, you have the number one song in the country, and two others climbing the charts. That's a BFD."

I let her claim—that it was seventy-five percent my song—go, even though it wasn't true. Most of the words were mine, true. But Kaitlyn had helped me fine-tune the lyrics. Her vocabulary was crazy, which made sense. She had this game, where she'd chant synonyms, when she was nervous.

"By BFD, you mean big fucking deal?" I smiled at my friend, lifting my eyebrows.

Kaitlyn hated curse words, which was why I usually never cussed in front of her. But I did enjoy teasing her for this peculiarity in her personality from time to time.

She wrinkled her nose, right on cue. "No. By BFD, I mean a beautiful fantastic delight."

"Suuure." I crossed my arms, my eyelids dropping.

She mimicked my pose and expression. "Look, all I'm saying is that you are winning at winning. You're in Aspen. At DJ Tang and Exotica's *mansion* with your awesome friends and bandmates. You're about to go on a world tour with said bandmates. Your songs are everywhere. You have everything you've ever wanted."

I frowned, dropping my eyes to the piano, the last words she'd spoken echoing within my mind, sounding lonely and untrue. A memory—*the* memory of Mona pretending to be Lisa I contemplated most frequently—materialized. It was the moment after she'd apologized for Lisa's behavior, standing on the second-floor landing outside Lisa's room, how horrified she'd been, shocked, remorseful.

I replayed it often, the way she'd sucked in a startled breath, the anguish—for me—plain on her features. Everything else, I questioned. Every other interaction, I'd easily convinced myself was false, a charade, part of her act.

But that moment—

Kaitlyn poked my shoulder, drawing my gaze back to hers which was now squinted, her lips a stern line.

"Is this about that woman?"

I stiffened, turning my face and glaring at her from the side. "What?"

"You know. That woman." She gave me a look like, *you know what I'm talking about.* "The one you've been trying to get over since forever?"

I tried to shush her.

She kept talking, "The one you wrote all those songs—awesome songs BTW—about? The someone worth hurting for? The woman—"

"God, shut up." I covered her mouth with my hand, glancing around, because her voice wasn't quiet. I swear, sometimes she was like an irritating little sister.

Arching her eyebrows, she waited, blinking slowly.

Dropping my voice to a whisper, I lowered my hand. "Don't . . . don't bring that up."

She shook her head at me, her mouth a flat line, and then turned her attention back to the piano, playing the theme to the movie *Love Story.* "Oh, the *angst! THE DRAMA!*"

"Shut up," I said, glaring at her, trying not to laugh.

"Come on, Abram. Cheer up." Kaitlyn nudged my elbow, switching to 'The Entertainer.' "Turn that frown upside down. Don't make me say something nice about you, you know I hate it," she teased.

I gave in to a small laugh, shaking my head. "Fine. I'm happy. This is me happy. I have everything I've ever wanted." Sarcasm wasn't technically a lie.

A genuine frown invaded her usually sunny expression while she inspected me. "Yes. You do. Maybe take a moment to recognize how far you've come. No more fistfights, no more arrests. No more gig weddings and corporate parties. Now you're six months without even a cigarette. And! No more playing Def Leppard covers."

"Those were dark days," I agreed with mock solemnity. "Except for the Def Leppard."

She ignored me, but she did crack a small smile. "You have it all. So maybe, possibly, perchance just . . . enjoy it?"

I nodded thoughtfully. My friend was right. I had everything I wanted.

Stop thinking about her.

Well, everything I wanted, almost.

[5]

ELECTROMAGNETIC WAVES

Mona

"**A**re you okay?"

I nodded, continuing to stare out the window at the flecks of white appearing, and then disappearing. We were in my room—the room I'd be staying in—which was the largest room in the house. It wasn't, oddly enough, the room my parents typically used. My parents preferred the master suite on the main level in this house. I wasn't sure why. I'd never given it much thought.

"Mona." Allyn placed her hand on my knee, and I flinched, my eyes darting to hers. She looked concerned. Really concerned. "You, uh, haven't said anything since Leo brought you inside."

Her statement was accurate, so I nodded. Again.

Allyn's expression grew pained and she did a squirmy little dance in the window seat where she sat facing me. I watched her, though it felt like she was behind some kind of filter, fuzzy, distant.

But then she blurted, "What happened? Why were you yelling? What is going on? Why aren't you talking? Are you sure you're okay?"

Abruptly, Allyn, the room, the cold, time, and my position relative to all four came into focus. Also in focus? The hot, leaden weight on my chest. It was an invisible weight, and I hypothesized that all dark matter were actually feelings, clustering and pressing upon hapless humans during the most inconvenient of times. Perhaps dark matter was attracted to heartache?

"I'm sorry," I croaked, even though I'd cleared my throat before speaking.

She sighed, her head tilting to one side as she examined me. "The yelling? You have to tell me what the deal is with the yelling."

I shook my head. "I wasn't yelling."

"What were you doing?"

Hesitating, I lifted my eyes to the tall, vaulted ceiling, and tried, "Growling?"

"Growling?"

"Yes?"

Allyn made a sound of confusion, and then asked, "Why do all your answers sound like questions?"

I brought my gaze back to hers. "Because they are?"

That made her laugh lightly, but she still looked concerned. Now, sitting here, looking at my behavior over the last hour or so, I understood why she was concerned.

After Abram left, unceremoniously shutting the door in my face, I'd watched the funicular until it disappeared down the mountain. I then stared at the darkness where the small car should (approximately) be for much longer, all the while arguing with myself.

He knows the truth. *He doesn't.*

He does. He definitely, definitely does. *He doesn't know. How could he know? And at this point, why would he care?*

The way he looked at me, like he *hates* me. He knows, and he hates me, and now I feel like becoming one with the snow. I want to make snow angels until every part of me is numb and I can't think, or feel my toes, or my heart. *He doesn't know and stop being so dramatic. If he knew, wouldn't he have reached out? Confronted you? Or told your parents? Or told Leo? Or a million other things?*

Then why did he look at me like that? *Maybe he still has feelings for Lisa? Maybe you remind him of her and that's why he was distant?*

But he wasn't just distant, he was aggressively aloof!

I'd rubbed my chest, wincing. It hurt. It hurt reminiscent of those early days after Chicago, with the searing intensity of sitting too close to a campfire, in a sauna, while severely sunburned, under a heat lamp, and sitting on coals. My brain was a mess—again—and I couldn't draw a full breath no matter how much I tried.

What are you going to do? *I don't know.*

I didn't know what to do. Standing there in the funicular structure, staring at black nothing, I hurt all over and I didn't know what to do.

DAMMIT ALL TO HECK!

Therefore, I'd growled. Glaring at the ceiling of the funicular house and foisting my free hand into the air while I gripped the backpack to my chest with the other, I turned and marched down the hallway, growling. Once I was outside, in the snow and wind, I growled again, raging. This time louder and longer, like maybe a tiger might do, or a mountain lioness. And then I did it again and again and again.

I wasn't thinking because I didn't know what to think. The truth was, I didn't want to think. But I also didn't want to feel, because it hurt, and it was an inescapable hurt. It hunted me relentlessly, except when I growled—or, I guess, yelled—all I felt was the cold beating against my face and the rawness of my throat and the constricting of my abdominal muscles. Yelling had been a relief, until I sucked in another breath and—

"Mo-naaaah!"

I'd stiffened, squinting at the snow around me, wondering at first if what sounded like my name was actually an echo of my growl/yell. But then I spotted movement on the path ahead and heard a second call, "Mo!"

It was my brother.

Exhausted, I'd exhaled a sigh, but then pressed my lips together when the sigh sounded dangerously like a sob. Stumbling forward, I pushed my arms into the straps of my backpack and attempted to gain control or administer some semblance of order over my chaotic thoughts:

I needed to go inside, because I was freezing. I needed a minute, or sixty, to come to terms with the sudden reality of seeing Abram. I needed to figure out whether Abram knew the truth. If he didn't know, I needed to figure out what to do next.

But if he did know? And he hated me?

I can't think about that. If I think about that, I'll start making snow angels and never go inside the house.

The several minutes that followed were a blur, mostly because I'd spent them in my happy planetarium, gazing at the stars, blanketing my awareness with the sparseness and peacefulness and darkness of space. I remembered walking into the house with my brother. I remembered there being a lot of people. I remembered making an effort to look at each of them as they were introduced, but I couldn't quite bring myself to shake anyone's hand.

And then we went up the stairs and I sat on the window seat while Leo and Allyn spoke in hushed tones. Sometime later, Leo left. Sometime after that, Melvin arrived with the bags, but he also left.

Now it was just Allyn, me, and all these horrible feelings. Horrible feelings were the third, fourth, and fifth beings in the room, making the large room feel crowded, suffocating, uninvited guests on what was supposed to be my vacation.

"Did something happen, between you and Abram Fletcher, after Leo and I left?" Allyn's question had me looking at her sharply.

"Fletcher? Who?"

Her gaze was steady, patient. "Abram Fletcher. The guy who went down to help Melvin?"

A strange buzzing sounded between my ears. Abram Fletcher. *Fletcher.* Why did that name sound so familiar?

"Mona?"

I squinted at her. "You know who he is?"

"Yes." She shook her head at me, a small movement. "Of course."

"Of course?"

"Don't you know who he is?"

I thought about how to answer that question and decided there was no right answer that would encapsulate the enormity of the truth, so I settled on, "Why don't you tell me who you think he is?"

"He's Abram Fletcher, lead singer and guitarist—bass guitar, I think—for Redburn."

"Redburn?" *Redburn?* As in Herman Melville's fourth book?

"Yes." Allyn laughed, making a face like she thought I was funny. "Redburn, the band? Haven't you heard 'Hold a Grudge'?"

"Hold a grudge?" The question arrived sounding more like a breath than words, and my right hand drifted to my chest.

"Yeah, Mona. Where have you been? It's been playing everywhere for weeks. You can't go into a coffee shop without hearing his album."

This was . . . this was terrible.

I swallowed around the rocks in my throat and was once more croaking my replies, "You don't say."

For some reason, a very specific teenage memory was summoned. My mother had invited me to lunch at a swanky hotel near my summer camp and I was excited. But when I arrived, she wasn't alone. She introduced me to a man, and when she left to use the lady's room, he told me that he was one of her lovers.

One of her lovers.

One of them.

I didn't believe him, but I'd been twelve at the time. But when I told my mother what he'd said, she confirmed it.

"Monogamy isn't for musicians, honey," she said. Her voice had been gentle, her expression compassionate. "I love your father, and he loves me. Love isn't supposed to be confining, it's about allowing the space for the other to fly. We both have many partners who feed our creativity in different ways. The soul of an artist is too needy. Once person could never be enough."

I knew this. This was fact. And Lisa also knew this, which was why—when Tyler hadn't been faithful to her—no one was surprised.

Presently, Allyn lifted her phone in the air above her, as though searching for a signal. "If you were on any social media at all, you would know this. Or watched TV other than those Turkish shows with the hot guys. Or listened to the song lists I send you. I've been following Redburn for seven months, before they released the studio album. I think their next single releases this week—their fifth—let me see . . ."

I was having too many thoughts. Too many. Way too many.

However, the logical path forward decided to do me a solid and reveal itself, a miraculous unveiling of crystal-clear obviousness. If I thought about it rather than bemoaning it, I wasn't surprised by Abram's success, just like I wasn't surprised by my ignorance of it.

"Shoot. I have no connection here and I didn't download the album." She frowned at her phone. "You should turn on the radio every so often, or check out the top ten once a month."

Allyn was right. I didn't listen to the radio. I didn't visit coffee shops. I didn't watch TV. I wasn't on social media and I didn't care to be. I no longer read articles written about me. Ever. Other than semi-stalking Abram's sister Marie's bylines and articles, I didn't read much other than scientific journals.

Popular culture was a world I'd purposefully and systematically eschewed.

It didn't matter if Abram knew who I was. It didn't matter if he'd figured everything out. It didn't even matter if he hated me. He was a wildly successful musician, living on the same planet as me, but now existing within a world firmly removed from mine.

The last two and a half years had been like waiting in a line with no guaranteed destination. It had been a line for the sake of lining up, for the sake of having a spot to stand. Then, abruptly and randomly, I was now at the front of the line. Standing in place and waiting were no longer options.

Abram and I, we were two circles in a Venn diagram that would never overlap.

We were two asteroids on opposite sides of the solar system, ensnared by Jupiter's gravity, destined to orbit the asteroid belt in the same direction, but never together.

We were two magnets with the same polarity.

Conclusion: If he didn't know about my deception, I would tell him the truth. It was the right thing to do. It was time. First, I'd call Lisa and inform her of my decision. And if he already knew, okay. That was fine.

But I knew now, reality being what it was, my logical path forward didn't include Abram Harris (Fletcher), it never really had. The past, our past, and this present random encounter were irrelevant to my future.

Just like my existence was irrelevant to his.

* * *

I slept horribly. But, no matter. That was the thing about sleep, there would always be more time to practice.

As soon as I opened my eyes, the events of the prior evening came back to me. But, again, no matter. I was prepared. The space suit of numbness, my recognition and swift acceptance of the futility of wanting Abram, saved me from a repeat of the searing pain.

Sitting up in bed, I checked the time on my phone, 6:14 AM, my hand knocking the letter I always carried to the floor. Leaning over the edge, I picked up the letter, my thumbs moving over the worn, smooth corners of the envelope, and gently returned it to the side table.

I needed to ready myself for the day. There was still the small matter of telling Abram the truth, assuming he didn't already know. And in order to accomplish that with a clear conscience, I would have to call my sister. And that's what I did.

Reaching for my phone again, I unlocked it, dialed her number, and waited. She'd become an early riser and our weekly phone calls typically took place before 7:00 AM, so I knew she'd be up now. The line rang on the other end, but the connection sounded spotty, broken, like a skipping record.

When she answered, I immediately asked, "Lisa? Lisa? Can you hear me?"

"Yes. Hey, Mo. I can hear you. Where are you? Aren't you supposed to be in—" the sound dropped off, replaced with clicks and scratching sounds, and then suddenly she was back "—thought you were going this week?"

"You're breaking up. Listen, I have to talk to you about something important." I pushed the covers back and strolled to the window seat where Allyn and I had taken up residence the previous evening until close to 2:00 AM. Without any prompting, I'd told Allyn the whole story about my week in Chicago before we'd gone to bed last night, and I do mean the *whole* story.

I figured, if I was really going to tell Abram the truth today—and despite the fact that any interaction with him was ultimately pointless to my future—I would still require some level of moral support after the task had been accomplished. I continued to have alarmingly nebulous and irrational feelings for the man. It would therefore make sense that my subsequent antiphon post-truth-telling would also be likewise irrational.

I wanted to be prepared, so I'd made preparations.

"What? Sorry, you're breaking up," Lisa's voice sounded from the other end of the phone.

"This is important. Can you hear me?"

"Yes. I can hear you now, but there's static on the line or something."

"Okay. I'll make it quick. Listen, Abram is here."

"What?"

"Abram." I whisper-yelled, stepping into a corner of the room, as though facing the corner would keep my voice from leaving the little triangle of secret shame I'd created with my body and the two walls. See? Already, just talking about him made me behave in strange and mysterious ways.

"Oh shit. Abram?"

"Yes. Listen." I clutched my forehead, squeezing my eyes shut. "Just listen."

"You want to tell him the truth," she said, surprising the heck out of me, but also relieved that she'd guessed.

Gripping the front of my shirt, I twisted the neckline of my sleep shirt around my middle and index finger. "Yes. I want to tell him. He's here, at the house, in Aspen, with Leo and other music people of an indeterminate number. It's snowing, and we're trapped. If he hasn't figured it out yet, he definitely will now that we're—"

"You're breaking up again. Before the call drops, if you're asking, my vote is to do it."

My eyes flew open. "What?"

"Do it. Tell him. Mom and Dad will never cut you off, so I think them finding out now won't hurt you. And they aren't looking for reasons to cut me off anymore. I mean, they don't talk to me, but I've let go of ever being a priority to—" She cut off for several seconds and

I frowned, willing the line to reconnect. It did midsentence, "—getting to the point where I don't even care. I have a good job, I have school, things are good, I can take care of myself. If that was keeping you from telling Abram, don't worry about me. At this point, it's not like the story would be interesting to his reporter sister. No one would care and it would just make him look idiotic. And if after all this time you still —" The line clicked and hissed, and I only caught skipped syllables of what she said for a few seconds, but then it picked back up, "—and it's still really bothering you, then I say do it. I never should have asked you to lie in the first place. You tell him, clear your conscience, and don't worry about me. I'm good, we're good, I understand why you want to do it. You have my support one hundred percent."

For some reason, my breathing was labored. Instead of feeling better upon receiving her blessing, I felt worse.

I said and thought at the same time, "How long have you felt this way?"

"What?"

"How long have you, I mean, how long ago could I have told him?"

She hesitated, and I thought for a second that the line had cut out, but then she asked, "Wait. Mona, have you had feelings for Abram all this time?" She sounded confused, like it hadn't occurred to her that this might've been a possibility.

I let my forehead fall to the junction of the two walls and confessed the truth. "Yes." As the prophesy foretold.

Yes, I'm not over him.

Yes, I think about him daily.

Yes, I've wanted to tell him the truth since I left and have lived in a state of readiness to do so, carrying that letter everywhere I go.

Yes, I'll never be able to mentally move on until he knows, until that equation is solved, that hypothesis proves null.

I had no choice now but to move on. He was a famous musician, a fact that was inescapable. I had no desire to live in that world ever again. Even if, by some cosmic miracle and warping of reality, he was eventually interested at some point—which he definitely *would never be*—we might as well have existed in different dimensions.

The line cracked, buzzed, but was otherwise silent for several seconds until finally she said, "You should have told me."

"Told you? I thought you knew."

"No! I had no idea!"

I had to press the phone closer to my ear because her voice was quiet, and I struggled to keep my voice loud enough to be heard on her side. "How could you have no idea?"

"You never said anything! I can't read your mind, Mona. You never say anything about how you're doing, how you're feeling, what you want. All you talk about is telescopes and—" she cut out again, and so I counted.

One, two, three, four, five, six—

"—we're all going to eventually use blackholes to power settled planets in different solar systems." She sounded exasperated. "The only time you mentioned him was that one time, when he changed his last name. I kept waiting for you to ask for his new name, but you didn't. And then, when I tried to get you to talk about Abram, you kept changing the subject. I kept expecting you to talk to me about him, about what happened after you left, but you didn't want to hear it and—God, honestly?—I didn't know how to tell you. I didn't want to make anything harder, after what you did for me. But Abram had been everywhere this year, his songs are everywhere, his face is everywhere, and still nothing from you until right now. Until he's there, in front of you, and you have no choice but to confront it."

Yikes.

She had a point. I'd never talked to her about Abram, or what happened the day after I'd left. I'd only told Poe about Abram because I'd been drunk—very sloppy of me—and Allyn knew nothing about my fateful trip to Chicago at all.

"Okay. Yes, it's my fault. You're right."

"That's not what I'm saying. It's not your fault. It's—"

Another break in the line. *One, two, three, four, five, six.*

"—but you have to stop pretending like you don't have any emotions." Her voice was steady now, louder. "If you have feelings for Abram, then tell him. Maybe he feels the same, maybe he doesn't, maybe he'll break your heart, maybe he'll disappoint you, but you can't expect him or anyone else to know what you're thinking if you keep quiet, or if you keep denying your feelings, or pretending they don't matter. You have to stop acting like you don't need anyone. You have to let people care about you, and I'm not just talking about this guy, or whatever guy or person you ultimately—"

One, two, three—I thought about interrupting her, explaining that telling Abram the truth now wasn't about hoping for a future with him, but rather giving our past closure. However, my sister was really on a roll with this rant and I doubted I'd be able to get a word in. At this point, I just wanted to get off the phone, tell Abram the truth, and finally place all this messiness behind me—*four, five, six.*

"—come visit me, you're always invited. I mean it. Okay?"

"Okay. Thank you. Sounds good. I appreciate you supporting me in this decision."

"Uh, no problem? I mean—uh—wait. Are you coming to visit me or what?"

"Sure. Yes. I can do that."

She huffed. "When?"

I closed my eyes again, scrunching them shut tighter. "When?"

"Mona!"

"I'll email you."

"Fine. I'll come to California. I'll visit you." It sounded like a threat.

"How about next week?"

"Next week?" I could tell I'd surprised her with the offer, but I was serious.

"Yes. Next week. I have nothing for the next two weeks but prepping my stuff for next semester in Europe, and everything is basically done. I can come next week."

"And we'll hang out?" She sounded so hopeful and—despite the blanket of numbness to protect me from the Abram-angstravaganza— my heart softened.

"Yes."

"Awesome! Okay. Well." Even with the static on the line, I heard her take a deep breath. "I guess I'll see you next week."

"See you next week." I opened my eyes, sighing, nodding resolutely, and turning away from the corner to face the room.

Step one, done. Step two, after a shower!

"And good luck with Abram," she added. "And though I've never believed he was actually in—"

One, two, three, four, five, six, seven, eight, nine, ten, and so forth. I waited until the count of twenty before the line made a definitive click-off sound, followed by a beeping dial tone.

Frowning, I reselected her number, wanting to ask Lisa to finish her sentence, but also end the call the right way, with *I love yous* and plans to talk about my trip to see her next week. But each time I tried to dial her number again, it wouldn't connect. Peeking out the window, seeing the blizzard-like, whiteout conditions, I understood why.

I gave up, for now. Gathering a steadying breath and placing my phone next to the letter on the side-table, I dragged myself into the bathroom to take a shower.

Soon, all of this choas would be set to order.

[6]
GEOMETRIC OPTICS

Mona

I concocted a plan in the shower.

First, I would write Abram a note, which—after drying off, dressing, and braiding my hair—I did. It went through several revisions.

~~Dearest Abram,~~

~~Dear Mr. Fletcher,~~

~~Abram,~~

Mr. Fletcher,

If you have the time and inclination, ~~I was hoping~~ I would be most appreciative if you would ~~meet with me~~ extend me the courtesy of meeting ~~today~~ sometime this week for a short conversation about ~~what happened in Chicago two summers ago~~ an important matter.

If you have neither the time nor inclination, I completely understand and wish you ~~nothing but the best, the happiest, and the most fulfilling everything, you deserve it~~ well.

~~Please don't hate me.~~

~~Love,~~

Sincerely,

~~*Wishing you the best,*~~

Best Regards, Mona DaVinci (Leo's sister)

Content with the final version, I placed the letter in an envelope, which I sealed and stuffed in the side pocket of my black cargo pants. Of note, I loved cargo pants. They were my favorite due to the plethora of pockets.

My work uniform consisted of a white button-down shirt and either black, brown, or navy cargo pants. If I needed to look more business casual, I'd wear a suit jacket of a coordinating color over the white shirt. No muss. No fuss. No making myself nuts, wondering what to wear.

In addition to my jacket, gloves, hat, etc., all I'd packed (other than utilitarian swim shorts and a swimming top for the pool, underwear, bras, and wool socks) were black leggings, black snoga pants—like yoga pants, but for the snow—black cargo pants, and black drywear long sleeve shirts. Therefore, picking out an outfit for *the truth telling* wasn't an issue.

Walking to the door, I turned and surveyed my room. The bed was a crazy mess, the comforter and blankets a twisted pile in the center as usual. But everything else was tidy. My attention snagged on the other note, the letter I always carried, laying on the side table.

On a whim I didn't bother examining too closely, I strolled to it, picked it up, and placed it in the pocket at my knee. I always carried the letter, why wouldn't I carry it now? Turning back to the door, I breathed in through my nose, told myself to be brave, and then slipped out of the room.

It was early enough that I hoped most of the house would still be asleep, but that Lila and Melvin would be up. Discovering which room Abram occupied should be easy, Lila always kept a chart of who was sleeping in which room, no matter the number of guests. Then it would only be a matter of interacting with the others, acting normal, and waiting.

My suspicions proved right. The corridors were quiet, but Lila was up and moving around the kitchen. After exchanging a bit of friendliness, where I asked after her sprained ankle and she asked about my work, Lila relayed the morning's gossip, like father like daughter, and informed me of a few critical facts:

Number one: I was the second person down for breakfast if you didn't count her or Melvin.

Number two: Melvin and the nice—but rough-looking—young man named Abram had left about forty-five minutes ago to go clear the slate path and the base area around the garages.

Number three: Leo had been expecting more than the twenty-three guests already present, but these extra people—spouses and significant others—were delayed due to the heavy snow.

Number four: She showed me the chart where she'd assigned everyone's rooms. Abram was on the main level, in the green room with teak paneling, as opposed to the green room with ash paneling or the blue room with teak paneling.

Thanking her, and even though I didn't like the idea of her cooking for me, I promised to return in a little bit for a Belgian waffle since she'd already made the batter.

The most direct path, even though it was the most public, took me through the main floor great room. Running into one of Leo's guests wouldn't be the worst thing in the word. I'd behaved oddly last night, I knew that, I regretted it, and the sooner I started smiling at people and making chit-chat, the better. These people were important to my brother, otherwise he wouldn't have invited them. Therefore, they were important to me. I would make an effort!

No one was encountered on my way to Abram's room. I knew he wasn't inside, but I knocked anyway, my heart in my throat. There was no answer. I tried the knob. It turned. I walked in. My plan was to leave the envelope on his pillow, where he'd certainly see it, and then leave. That was the plan.

Instead, I took a moment to stand just inside the doorway and stare like a lunatic at his things, cataloguing them: his phone appeared to have a cracked screen, unclear as to whether it was the screen cover or the screen itself that was cracked. It sat on the side table. Next to it were two quarters and a penny, and a book. I longed to read the cover of the book. I didn't.

Counting his change and noticing the fractured screen of his phone was one thing, but inspecting the title of his novel felt like an invasion of privacy, so I tore my eyes away, swallowing around my aching heart lodged in my throat, and rushed to his bed, endeavoring not to notice the contents of his suitcase open on the floor.

Do not look. Do not look. Do not look.

I looked. Clothes and more books and—

AH! STOP LOOKING!

Screwing my eyes shut, I withdrew the envelope. Peeking just one eye open, I placed the envelope on his side table, on top of his phone instead of on his pillow which I suddenly decided felt too intimate, and turned for the door. Breath held, I made it to the door without any more creeping on Abram's stuff, shut the door, and turned back toward the kitchen for a waffle.

And then he was there.

Startled, I froze.

Head down, he was strolling toward me, wearing a long-sleeved white shirt and green snow pants that did wonderful things for his chest and thighs, which did all kinds of wonderful and terrible things to my chest and thighs.

Regrouping my scattered wits, I drew myself up straighter, squared my shoulders, and faced him.

Okay. This is it. This is it. Be brave like Ahab.

What? No! Ahab was insane, not brave!

Well, honestly, if the shoe fits . . .

Frowning and mentally shaking a fist at my internal dialogue, I shook my head to clear it and allowed my gaze to move over Abram. I hadn't really looked at him last night. The lights of the funicular structure at night were dim compared to inside the house during the day, and I'd been somewhat blinded by shock. But I looked at—and saw—him now.

He looked so different. So astonishingly different. And yet, he was the same.

For one, he was bulkier, which made him seem taller. In the last images I'd seen of Abram, before he'd changed his last name and disappeared, he'd been thinner, not bulkier. Obviously, he'd made some changes. He looked like he'd been working out a lot. Like one of those people who took a healthy gym habit to the next level. Like lifting weights had become a source of mental health more than physical health. The added muscle suited him, looked extremely good on him, but it also gave Abram an air of power and strength that I found both flustering—because, *holy hot specimen of the male species, Batman*—and alarming.

Another change, his scruffy stubble had become a bountiful beard, trimmed and shaped neatly. Also, his hair was much, much longer. It was so long, he wore it in a manbun twisted near his crown. It wasn't a pithy manbun. No, no. This manbun restrained a quantity of thick, shiny brown hair. I wondered tangentially if he'd cut it since Chicago.

Of course, there was also the small matter of his face. He had scars where none had existed prior, presumably from the fights I already knew about—the ones where he'd been arrested but no charges had been filed—and perhaps from a few fights I didn't. Nothing major, just enough to give him an air of wickedness without verging into sinister territory.

But his nose, which had obviously been broken, was different. It looked more pronounced than before and . . . different. Again, I knew about his broken nose already, having internet-stalked him for over a year. Maybe that's why the change in his features from handsome to hardened—but still handsome—didn't faze me much, and maybe he didn't receive congratulations cards on his face anymore. But I hadn't been mooning over his external attractiveness for the last several years. Abram's nose hadn't been the star of my dreams. It was his heart I longed for.

Therefore, the most startling of the changes revealed itself as our eyes met. My heart did a double backflip but failed the dismount, splattering all over and making a mess, while his steps slowed. I held my breath again. No amount of numbing space suit technology, bracing rationality, or accepting the futility of the future prepared me for what I saw.

Gone were the warmth in the amber of his eyes, the knowing twinkle, the sensitive spark. In their places were cool aloofness, sharp intelligence, and stark asceticism. The difference suffused every corner of my being with sorrow, caused a deep, potent ache in my chest such that I dreaded my next breath. I was dizzy.

But Abram, other than slowing his approach, showed no outward sign of, well, anything. His features were wiped of expression, and he seemed to gaze upon my face like I might be a piece of furniture.

Oh. Ouch. Jeez. That hurts. Yikes. What's the temperature in here? Is it set to Venus-hellfire? Or is that just me?

But he did speak. "What are you doing?"

I swallowed my nerves, lifted my chin, and pointed to the door behind me with my thumb. "I was leaving something for you, in your room."

"You were in my room?" he asked, shifting closer.

And that's when I smelled the Abram smell. My pulse hammered against my neck and wrists, my blood somehow made thicker by the fragrance of him. I reminded my bones that they were not made of liquid, but they weren't so sure. Despite recognizing the madness of the impulse, I greedily inhaled through my nose. The memory, the nostalgia left me feeling an acute sense of wonder and subsequent calm.

Some things change completely. Even the rate of change changed, fluctuated. Change was the only true constant in the universe.

But, over short periods relative to the existence of time, some things changed not at all. In this instance, the lack of change, the consistency of how Abram smelled, was overwhelmingly comforting.

"Hello?"

I blinked at him, opening my mouth to respond, but I'd forgotten the question. "Could you repeat the question, please?"

His eyes flickered between mine and I perceived a crack there, a curiosity, a bit of ye-Abram-of-old peeking through. But his tone was flat as he asked again, "You were in my room?"

"Oh. Yes." Coming back to myself, I gripped the material of my cargo pants and nodded. "But, don't worry. I knew you were gone. I would never go in your room if I thought you were in it."

Abram stared at me, his eyes narrowing, his lips parted as though he wanted to ask a question, but my words were so confusing, he didn't know where to start.

Discerning the fact that he was confused, I reviewed my statements, and what might have been confusing about them. I'd spoken on instinct, my goal to assure him that he didn't need to worry about me sneaking in, in the middle of the night, and pulling a teenage-Lisa.

Clarification was in order. "I just mean, you are safe. From me."

He blinked once, slowly, shifting back on his feet and lifting his chin. While doing so, he tucked away his confusion and that sliver of his former self, leaving a half-lidded glare of hostility. "Oh. Really?"

"Yes." I nodded emphatically, experiencing the long dormant sensation of being discombobulated.

"What did you leave in my room?" The question sounded bored with an edge of the aforementioned hostility.

"A letter. Or, rather, a note. It's not long enough to be a letter."

"You left me a memo?"

So discombobulated was I, I didn't think before responding, "Uh, no. Memos usually have dates and subject lines, I didn't include either of those. But I can." I tossed my thumb over my shoulder again, indicating to his door. "If you want to wait here, I can go get. . ."

As I spoke, one of Abram's eyebrows slowly lifted, and I belatedly caught on.

Sarcasm. That was sarcasm.

Poe used sarcasm to tease me, and I used sarcasm to tease him. Our sarcasm-interactions were well-meaning and helped keep my sense of humor (and self) healthy. Without Poe, Allyn, Lisa, and to a certain extent, Gabby to tease me and keep me grounded, I shuddered to think how shuttered I might be.

Poe's sarcasm was friendly. But Abram's statement was the other kind of sarcasm, the unfriendly kind.

My unfriendly-sarcasm detection abilities were usually within one standard deviation of normal, a skill I honed for obvious reasons. Not many, but a sparse few of my colleagues enjoyed making the youngest person in the room feel inadequate and naïve.

Unfriendly sarcasm didn't usually faze me now. I used to visit my brain planetarium or mutter nonsensical phrases as a means of distraction. I still muttered those anytime phrases, but more as a joke with my friends than as a coping mechanism.

Twenty-one-year-old Mona believed the best policy was to ignore unfriendly sarcasm. Being the butt of someone's joke was only funny if I reacted. If I kept my head down, if I stayed focused, if I outperformed and outthought them, if my research was ultimately more relevant and necessary and important than theirs, no one laughed.

I cleared my throat, struggling with an uncomfortable rush of embarrassed heat, and gave Abram a thin smile.

"No. Not a memo. Just a note. It's—uh—on your dresser."

Every word out of my mouth arrived quieter than the last and my gaze settled on his chin covered in a baby wizard beard. I knew he still had the potential to grow one. I wondered if I would ever see it.

"You went into my room without my permission and put a note on my dresser," he summarized, sounding unfriendly and distracted.

I'd thought I'd be safe in my spacesuit of acceptance, but apparently, I wasn't. He was here. Real. Standing in front of me. Smelling like Abram. Looking like Abram, but not. He was Abram, but not. I asked myself a question that hadn't occurred to me before just now, *What do you hope to gain from this?*

The answer was an immediate and resounding, *Nothing.*

That made me feel better. I honestly didn't want anything from him. I wanted to tell him the truth, so he would know, because it was the right thing to do. That was it.

Taking a deep breath, I lifted my gaze to his and met his glare, an action made easier now that my specific aims had been clarified. He seemed to flinch this time as our eyes connected, a subtle wince I might've missed if we hadn't been standing so close.

Abram studied me, and I gave him a polite smile, gathering a breath in preparation for making an excuse to leave.

But then he asked, "What's in the note?"

"Uh . . ." My eyes moved up and to the right as I recalled the note's contents. "I asked—it's very short. I request a time to meet, if you have the time and inclination."

"You want to meet with me?"

"Y—yes."

"Why?"

"To talk to you," I answered honestly, meeting his gaze with equal frankness.

"What about?"

"An important matter," I quoted the note. Since we were standing in a hall with many bedrooms attached to it, I didn't think he'd want me to go into details here.

He lifted the eyebrow again, his lips twisting. "What's wrong with now?"

I swallowed reflexively, startled by the suggestion. "Now?"

"Yeah. Now."

"Okay. Sure. If you follow me, there's a study on the second floor we can use, and—"

He stepped closer, very close, necessitating that I take a step back if I didn't want him to bump into me. For the record, I had mixed feelings about being bumped into by Abram, and with mixed feelings, erring on the side of caution was always prudent.

He reached around my right side and apparently turned the knob, opening the door to his room. "Let's do it here."

"Here?" I squeaked.

"Yes," he said, staring down at me, taking more steps forward. Like before, I stepped back to avoid coming in contact with his advancing form, which had a by-product of carrying us both into his bedroom.

Once we were fully inside, he shut the door behind him without turning, his eyes never leaving mine. And then we stood like that, looking at each other, in his room with the door closed, for several seconds.

In his room.

With the door closed.

Wait.

How did I get here?

I felt suddenly winded, like I couldn't catch my breath, and I couldn't quite pinpoint why. On the one hand, this was how several of my amorous nighttime fantasies started: Abram, a room with a bed, us alone, many sexually explicit moments to follow.

On the other hand, I didn't feel particularly amorous at present.

I felt cold. My palms were clammy. A river of disquiet rushed down my spine. Instead of focusing on Abram, my eyes saw only a big man standing in front of a closed door, two barriers between me and the hall.

In the next moment, I sensed him move and I recoiled, stumbling backward and reaching for . . . something.

He stopped moving.

We stood in silence for another few seconds. I assumed he was looking at me, but I was too busy chasing the abruptly worn threads of lucidity, telling my galloping heart to *chill out*, and blinking against the loss of focus caused by adrenaline.

This is Abram. You are perfectly safe. He would never hurt you.

Before I could discover where my wits had scattered, and why, Abram opened the door again and stepped to the side.

Clearing his throat, he backed even further away. "You said there's a study on the second floor?"

"Yes." I breathed the word, a burst of wary relief radiating outward from my stomach to my fingertips at the sight of the hallway.

"Okay. Let's go there." Abram's voice was soft, even, calm, and he came back into focus for me.

I was mildly surprised to discover he was now leaning against the wall farthest from the door, his arms crossed, and he was watching me with a strange kind of intensity that felt significant. I couldn't deconstruct its meaning.

My mind automatically informed me—even though he was much bigger than me, and stronger, and probably fairly fast on his feet—at his present distance from the door, he wouldn't be able to catch me if I made a run for the exit.

Not that I was going to make a run for the exit.

Because making a run for the exit would be silly.

"Lead the way," Abram said, using that same soft voice and not moving from his spot, his gaze still watchful.

I nodded and unclenched my hands that had at some point balled themselves into fists. Taking a deep breath, I walked forward, my steps calm, normal, unhurried.

When I breached the doorway, I laughed lightly at myself, and continued down the hall. When I didn't immediately hear him follow, I glanced over my shoulder and our eyes met. His features had rearranged themselves into a mask of indifference, I was once again furniture. But he was behind me, and he was following.

Just, following from a distance.

[7]

SPECIAL RELATIVITY

Abram

I'd been wrong.

Not everything about Mona was a lie, and this made me want to murder someone.

I kept ten feet away from Mona DaVinci as she walked down the hall, and as she climbed the stairs to the second floor and walked down another hall. Her wild eyes, the way her skin had gone from flushed to waxy in the span of twenty seconds were responsible for my murderous thoughts, and reminded me of another time, when I'd stumbled across her in the dark.

Sitting in the large front room of her parents' Chicago house, pushing her dark hair from her beautiful face, she'd had the same wild look in her eyes. The intensity of her reaction at the time hadn't been part of the lie. *Unfortunately.*

Since her panic wasn't an act, then there was a reason for Mona's freak-outs, her dislike of being touched unexpectedly, closeness, and apparently closed doors. It didn't take a genius to connect the dots: the reason for her freak-outs was a person, and what that person had done to her. This knowledge made me as frustrated and irate now as it had then.

What happened to her?

I'd speculated often over the years. Initially, the mysterious incident was blamed for Lisa pushing me away. As time passed, especially once I'd realized the truth, I'd wondered whether it had been part of the pretense. Did she overreact to distract me? Gain my sympathy? Make me care for her?

No. It was real. She'd been harmed at some point.

Whether it was instinct or what, this knowledge turned my mind to vengeful thoughts, but not against her. Revenge for her, for her peace, for justice. Someone needed to suffer for making her suffer.

Mona reached a closed door in the hallway. I stopped, maintaining the careful distance, willing to do just about anything to avoid seeing her panic again, especially when the panic had been caused by something I'd done. She knocked on the door, paused, and then opened it. Just inside the room, she turned and motioned me forward, her eyes lifting no higher than my chest.

"If you still have time," she said, giving me a smile that touched only her lips.

At my approach she took a small step to the side, providing more space for me to enter. But once I was in, she surprised me by closing the door. My attention dropped to the handle as she moved further into the room. She hadn't locked it.

"Abram."

I lifted my eyes to hers and said, "Mona," before considering the impulse.

That made her swallow, revived the alluring blush she'd worn earlier. Her long lashes fluttered like I'd blown dust in them. I watched her, riveted. She seemed to be working hard to remain calm, but not like she'd been inside my room, not with a feral kind of panic.

This was like before, outside of my door, when I'd caught her. She wasn't freaked out, she was adorably agitated.

My instinct was to put Mona at ease. This instinct surprised me. I was determined to be uncompromising in my distrust of and disinterest in her. *That* was the goal. Thus, I didn't understand this instinct. Therefore, I said nothing. Instead taking advantage of the opportunity to look my fill.

She shoved her hands in her pockets, drawing my eyes down to her hips. Mona DaVinci did not dress like her sister. All black, her clothes were somewhat baggy, loose, definitely not tight, leaving much to the imagination. Unashamed of my imagination, I licked my lips, wondering if she was still as fast of a swimmer now as she had been then.

Yanking my mind back from maddening memories of a certain white bikini, I lifted my attention to her face, a move necessary for self-preservation. She wore no makeup that I could see, and her hair was pulled back into a long braid. It was longer than before, several inches longer, and made me think of shiny, thick rope.

Mona dropped her gaze to the vicinity of the floor, but her voice was steady as she said, "There's something you should know."

I stared at her, at this exquisite face, this face I'd dreamt of and hated and longed for, and knew at once what she was going to say. I felt it in the vibrations of tension coming from her body, the set of her jaw, the dazed but resolute look in her eyes. I felt it in the absence of sound, the stillness, how even the dust seemed to be suspended.

I felt it in myself, how my muscles tightened, my breathing slowed, as though she still had that kind of power over me.

So, I laughed.

Mona's gaze darted to mine, and I laughed harder at her obvious confusion, turning and finding a desk. I sat on the edge of it and faced her, clasping my hands together, one leg braced on the floor, the other dangling at the knee.

The bitterness returned and was powerful motivation, like last night when she'd offered her hand and introduced herself, assuming I'd been *too stupid* to discover her lies. Well, she'd been right about one thing. I *had* been stupid.

But I wasn't stupid anymore.

"I wonder," I said without thinking, still laughing lightly, my concern for her well-being overshadowed by the sour memory of her duplicity. I gave myself fully over to the anger. "I've always wanted to know, did she tell you I loved you?"

Mona flinched, her eyes bugging out of her head. "What?" she asked, the single word more breath than sound.

"When you two talked about it, after you switched places?" I waved my index and middle finger in front of me. "Did she tell you that I loved you? She tell you about that?"

She said nothing, her breaths coming faster, looking visibly stunned.

I laughed again, more of a light chuckle this time. "Was that part of the plan? Or why switch places for the week? I've always wondered."

Like last night, Mona's face was devoid of color. Staring at me, shell-shocked, eyes glassy.

"Abram—"

"You know, I thought I was crazy." I had to cut her off. The way she said my name caused a pulse of heat to press outward against every inch of my skin and behind my eyes. I didn't like it. "For a really long time, I thought I'd lost my mind. It was like . . ." Tearing my eyes from hers, I glanced over her head and finished my thought. "It was like, I woke up that morning and you—Lisa—were someone else. She broke my heart, but she did a good job of letting me down gently, everything considered." Smiling with mock-ruefulness, I shook my head. "See? I even sound crazy now."

Mona made a soft sound of distress. I ignored it. I'd trusted this woman blindly, after knowing some version of her for six days. Just six days. I'd fallen stupid in love with a fictional person, and now here we were.

"What I'm trying to say is: letting that Lisa go wasn't hard. I couldn't stand her voice. It was the same, but it wasn't. It grated, nails on a chalkboard, everything was wrong. But I couldn't stop thinking about *my Lisa*." I stopped here to laugh lightly again.

Moving just my eyes, I studied Mona DaVinci from my spot across the room. Anguish, sorrow, regret played in equal measure over her features. Her nose was red, and seveal tears had rolled down her cheeks. How much of it was real? Impossible to say. But it did succeed in wiping the smile from my face.

Swallowing, she closed her eyes, but then she clenched her jaw and opened them again. Lifting her chin with a stubborn tilt, Mona affixed her stare to mine, looking dejected but also determined, giving me the impression she was forcing herself to meet my gaze. An inconvenient suspicion, that she was trying to accept my spiteful words as some kind of punishment, as a way to take responsibility for past mistakes, infuriated me, because it also made me respect her.

It doesn't matter. It's too late now.

"When did you find out?" she asked, her voice hoarse and quiet.

"I suspected almost immediately, the month after you left, in fact. But, like I said, I thought I was crazy for a long time. But then, I saw your testimony in front of Congress this summer." I paused here, my attention moving over her face, reprimanding myself again for taking so long to accept the truth. "You were wearing glasses, and your hair was pulled back, like it is now, but in a bun. You didn't look like my Lisa, but your voice . . ."

Mona cleared her throat, sniffed, and pressed her lips together, continuing to hold my glare with admirable self-possession given the fact that tears were still leaking out of her eyes.

So beautiful.

Faking it or not, even sorrowful, even pale and tear streaked, this woman was unbelievably beautiful to me. Ethereal beauty, not of this world, inhuman in its hold over me. There was something else about her, devastating gentleness and strength, ruinous sweetness and vulnerability despite the severity of her intelligence. *Or maybe because of it?*

And a genuineness that was so convincing, despite everything I knew to be true, I believed it.

I knew *for a fact* that she was a fucking liar . . . and yet I believed her to be genuine. How was that possible? How did that make any sense?

Another pulsing wave of heat pushed me toward her, one that demanded action and urged me to go to her, grab her, and finally, finally fucking kiss her. I ignored it by telling myself that she wasn't really the one I wanted. She wasn't my Lisa.

She's not my anything.

Instead, I pulled my bottom lip between my teeth and bit it. Lowering my eyes to my hands, I held the lip in place until the impulse dwindled and I could trust myself to speak.

But when I did, I spoke to my palm because I didn't trust myself to look at her. Not yet. "I thought it was just more of me being crazy, grasping at something that didn't exist. But then, the next day, or maybe the day after, I caught an interview you gave on Fox News, or maybe CNN. You ended a sentence under your breath with, 'And then the wolves came.'" Another sound of amusement escaped my throat, and I admitted softly, "And that's when I accepted it."

She was quiet for several moments. I sensed she was looking at me, but I wasn't ready to look at her. The urge to kiss her hadn't yet fully passed. I waited for calm, for my heart to slow, for my chest to expand enough for me to breathe normally, but it—all of it—never happened.

Sitting there, unable to look at this woman, this *liar* without craving the feel of her in my arms, I confronted the pitiful truth: I still wanted her. Or maybe, I still wanted the idea of what she represented.

My muse. My inspiration. The desire in me to take care of her, and the hope that she'd take care of me in return hadn't diminished. It lived in me, a constant corrupting companion, a foolish optimism that refused to yield. It was the reason my mind drifted to her before falling asleep, the reason she'd appeared in my dreams and was on my mind when I awoke. The reason all my songs were ultimately about *her*.

But why? I shook my head, tracing the lines of one hand with the thumb of the other, asking myself for the millionth time, *Why her?*

Six days. It had been nothing. We'd barely touched. We'd never kissed. Why did the idea of this woman feel so essential? I thought we'd clicked seamlessly into place. Together. Counterweights that balanced a scale. I'd given myself over to the idea fully, without reservation. And she had been a lie.

"What do you want?" Mona asked softly, her voice steadier than before. "What can I do?"

Again, I spoke without thinking, "I don't want to be crazy."

"You're not crazy. You're right. I was . . . it was me. It is me."

No. It wasn't you. It's not you.

I readied myself, and then lifted my chin to level her with a glare. Mona swallowed, but otherwise she didn't move, and she didn't look away. The tears had dried on her face, but her nose was still red, and her eyes were still glassy.

God, how I wanted to touch her, to brush away her tears and whisper words of forgiveness. *Without reservation.* But I wouldn't, because that would make me actually crazy.

Suddenly, out of nowhere, I was exhausted. What was the point of this? Why keep asking questions? Nothing could change the past.

I'd fallen for the contradictions, the surprises, how she'd challenged my expectations. I'd felt the pull, the draw intrinsically, without searching for it, without giving it much thought. With "my Lisa," I'd never had to force the wonder, and being soft hadn't seemed so hard. But this person wasn't her. All of it had been imagined.

And yet, even knowing, I asked softly, "Why'd you do it?" Her reason didn't matter, but I wanted to know.

"She needed my help."

"Lisa? How so?"

"She'd been arrested."

I blinked at that, the puzzle I'd thought was finished suddenly had another piece. "Lisa was arrested?"

"Yes. She called from lock-up the night before I arrived. She asked me to help her, to be her, to take her place until she was released. She promised me it wouldn't take more than a week."

"And you did it." It wasn't a question. Obviously, I already knew the answer.

"She's my sister." Mona's voice broke on the last word and she finally looked away, her eyes moving to some point over my shoulder, her lips forming a stubborn line.

Unable to tear my eyes from those lips, I mentally filled in the rest of the story I hadn't realized were blanks, and it all made so much more sense: Gabby's hovering, the missing phone and wallet that "Lisa" didn't care about picking up from the post office, how exhausted real Lisa had looked the morning after Mona left, why real Lisa hadn't budged on telling me the truth. *She'd been in jail.*

"Abram."

The pleading edge in Mona's voice had me looking at her.

"I wanted to tell you."

A shock of something unidentifiable, but that felt dangerous, had me standing and pacing to the large window. It was the furthest spot from her.

I don't need to think about this.

This new information changed nothing. Mona had pretended to be someone else, and then she'd left. Lisa being in jail and Mona covering for her sister explained the initial lies, but it didn't justify the rest of it, and it didn't change the fact that the woman I'd fallen in love with didn't actually exist.

"Abram, I—"

"Why'd you do it?" I turned to face her. My feet were carrying me across the room while her confused stare moved over me. Again, nothing she could say would make me forgive her, so I wasn't sure why I asked the question.

"Like I said, she needed my help."

"No. Not that. I'm not asking why you stepped in for your sister. I get that. What I want to know is . . ." I needed to stop advancing, but my feet had a mind of their own. Soon I was upon her, inches away, and this time she didn't retreat. She lifted her chin to maintain eye contact and seemed to sway forward just as I asked, "Why did you pretend. With me?"

Mona shook her head, her attention dropping for a split second to my mouth and then darting back to my eyes. "I didn't."

"You did."

"I didn't."

"You left."

"I promised Lisa I would protect her! You don't know, you don't know what it's like to have parents who don't care about you except as an extension of their reputation. I wasn't going to be another person who let her down."

"I get that, *Mona.*" Her name came out sounding like an expletive. "That's not what I'm asking. Why talk to me at all if you knew you were just going to leave."

"I tried to avoid—I didn't—I don't know."

"You don't know."

"No. I don't know what I was—I didn't think—"

"Did you love me?"

Mona snapped her mouth shut, a hint of what looked like terror playing behind her eyes. Her lips parted, and she took several gulping breaths, making me think she was preparing herself to say something difficult.

I decided I didn't want to hear the answer, whatever it was, and guessed, "You regret it."

"I do," she agreed immediately.

My eyelids lowered and I flexed my jaw once, twice, absorbing the blunt force of her honesty, not understanding why her response had hurt as badly as it did. "Okay."

"No. Not okay. That's not what I—I mean, I do regret what happened. I regret so much, but I didn't have a choice, did I? I couldn't not—I couldn't let Lisa down."

"You could have told me."

"Really?" She sounded both curious and disbelieving. "Really? You would've forgiven me for lying to you? You wouldn't have told Leo, or my parents about Lisa? You would've lied too?"

"Yes! You ask for forgiveness, I give it!" I answered honestly, because such was the idiocy of my devotion to this woman at the time. Blind. Senseless. *Without reservation.* "I thought I loved you. I was crazy about you. I wanted nothing but to make you happy."

New tears sprang where the old ones had dried and she pressed her lips together more firmly, working to subdue the unsteadiness of her chin.

"I was an idiot," I said.

She flinched. And then she struggled to swallow, still wincing, like my latest words had a lasting, painful effect.

I wasn't finished. "*I* regret it. No one falls in love with another person in six days, that's stupid. I was stupid and naïve, trusting. *Soft.*" I spat this last word, despising her for not understanding the importance of it.

Mona reached out, as though she might touch me, so I backed

away. She used the hand she'd lifted to cover her mouth, her eyes following me, turning as I walked to the door.

I opened it, but I couldn't leave without making one more thing perfectly clear. "Don't worry, Mona. I have no more illusions. I'm not in love with you, because I never really was. I know now, you are no more that woman than your sister is."

[8]

INTRODUCTION TO QUANTUM PHYSICS

Abram

"Has anyone actually seen Mona? Since she and her friend arrived?" Charlie spun a drumstick between his fingers, the movement absentminded as he shifted his eyes from me to Kaitlyn, to Ruthie, and then back to me.

Ruthie shook her head and Kaitlyn reached for another of my lyric notebooks, setting it on her lap. Sitting in the large room on the main floor, we were going through my old notebooks with the band, looking for lyrics to pair with her recent compositions. Since the partners/husbands/wives/significant others were delayed—including Kaitlyn's fiancé Martin and Ruthie's girlfriend Maxine—we'd decided to make the best of it.

Or more correctly, I told everyone to meet me in the living room and so they did. I told them we were working on new music and so here we were. I told them to bring their instruments and so Charlie had drumsticks, Ruthie had her Martin D-28 acoustic, Kaitlyn sat at the piano and had a composition notebook on the music stand, and I'd brought a Fender Kingman acoustic bass and the lyric notebooks.

"I haven't seen Mona, unfortunately. But Leo said she's not very social, so maybe she just needs time to warm up to us?" Kaitlyn shrugged and turned her attention to the book of my half-finished poetry, as if being antisocial explained Mona's absence at every meal for the last few days, that she never left the third floor, went outside, or interacted with anyone in a house full of people.

Antisocial didn't quite cover it.

I'd read Mona's note, the one she'd left on my side table, the one where she'd asked me—*if I had the time and inclination*—to meet with her. It was impersonal and polite. It made me angry. I tore it up and tossed it into the big stone fireplace two days ago.

I glanced at the large fire there now, unable to see any trace of the burnt letter. It looked like Melvin made a habit of cleaning out the ashes every day. Good riddance.

"Damn." Charlie frowned.

"Why damn?" Ruthie strummed lightly on her guitar, trying to replicate a melody Kaitlyn had played earlier on the piano.

"I kinda—you know." He glanced between Kaitlyn and Ruthie. "I wanted to get to know her."

"Why?" I asked, the question unplanned. So was the scowl I wore.

Charlie was a nice guy, if not a little cynical and jaded. He was a great drummer, a good friend. I usually liked Charlie.

But I didn't like Charlie right now.

"Because she's Mona-fucking-DaVinci, Abram. How often do you get a chance to converse with a literal fucking genius?" Charlie's attention was on me, so he didn't see Kaitlyn flinch at his use of the F-word.

But because his attention was on me, I made my expression carefully neutral. "What would there be to talk about, Charlie? She's a rocket scientist. Encyclopedic knowledge of Star Trek isn't the same thing."

That earned me a glare from Kaitlyn even though she was fighting a grin. "Hey now, Star Trek is awesome."

"No arguments here." I made *live long and prosper* signs with both my right and left hands. "But you have to admit Kaitlyn, his statement is illogical," I added, doing my best Spock impression, making them all chuckle, and once again successfully hiding my preoccupation with Mona DaVinci and her whereabouts.

I'd been searching for her everywhere for the last two days, except the third floor. Her floor. I had no reason to go up there, and I wouldn't invade her space without an invitation. I'd already invaded her vacation for reasons unclear even to myself.

The house was huge, large enough that you could go all day seeing just two or three of the twenty-seven people currently here until dinner. Everyone ate together at dinner time, except Mona. She hadn't eaten with us yet and her absence had been noticed by more people than just me.

According to Lila, Mona didn't want food to be brought up to her room. Over our meal last night, Charlie had asked Allyn if she needed help making a plate for Mona.

With a bright smile for everyone but me, Allyn had said, "No. No need. She'll come down later and get something if she's hungry. No worries." Then she'd picked up a bowl and in a terrible British accent said, "Oh, what excellent boiled potatoes." Which made a few people laugh.

Taking advantage of the distraction provided by her Mr. Collins reference, Allyn had glared pointedly at me, making me assume two things to be true: Allyn was no longer a fan of mine, and Mona had filled her in on some version of our conversation in the study.

This frustrated me, made me restless, aggravated. I didn't fault Mona for talking to her friend, that made sense. But hiding? Avoiding everyone? Rather than, if she had something to say, seeking me out and telling her side? That struck me as cowardly.

Or maybe she doesn't care.

Maybe she was just as cold and detached as everyone claimed. I didn't know. She didn't give me anything but polite notes and fucking *restraint.*

After dinner, I gave Allyn a wide-berth and I camped out in the kitchen, helping Lila with the dishes, and then reading a book until past 3:00 AM. Mona never came down.

I'd almost convinced myself this urge to seek her out was revenge related. Maybe I really did want to settle a score. If that was the case, if I wanted to get even, then one uncomfortable conversation didn't settle anything.

No, I wasn't finished with her yet.

Except . . . revenge wasn't the reason I'd positioned myself in the library, hoping she'd come down to find a book, or why I'd awoken early the last two mornings to catch her at the pool (Allyn said she still swam laps, usually in the early morning). Knowing she was here but absent was almost as unbearable as it had been the first time, when I'd thought Lisa was my Lisa, and we'd waited for Dr. Steward to arrive in our separate corners of the Chicago house.

Given the murkiness of my motives and how I compulsively sought her out, like a pitiful, lovesick idiot, you might think I'd grow tired of her, of thinking about her, and let it all go. You'd be wrong. If anything, the fact that I couldn't help myself, that she still held this power over me, that I couldn't think straight with her so close, only made me angrier.

"Hey, listen to this." Kaitlyn lifted one of my lyric books, one I didn't remember packing but immediately recognized now that I took the time to scan the front. My hands gripped the arms of my chair reflexively and I readied myself for what she might've found.

"Gone, and she took all her sweet softness with her.

Gone, and emptiness takes a shape.

Gone, and summer is winter.

Gone, and I sleep.

But when she's here, I'm finally awake.

A barren landscape,

Now beauty in her wake."

After Kaitlyn read the poem aloud, silence followed. My friend frowned at the page, and then lifted her gray eyes to mine. They moved over me, searching, thoughtful. But she said nothing.

"Damn, Abram." Charlie hit my shoulder with a drumstick. "That's some beautiful, deep shit. When'd you write that?"

I cleared my throat, glancing at our drummer. "About two years ago." *Two years, four months, eighteen days.*

"How come we didn't use it for this album?" Ruthie reached for the notebook and Kaitlyn handed it over.

I shrugged, standing, and searched for my guitar, wanting to do something other than shrug. I did too much shrugging these days.

"Have you guys seen my guitar?" It wasn't where I remembered leaving it. Strange.

But if I hadn't stood up to search for my guitar, I wouldn't have seen Mona, Allyn, Leo, and a few others walking down the hall toward the kitchen. Stopping short, I stared at them. They were all dressed in snow gear, carrying sleds. Mona had a thick length of rope hanging from her elbow, coiled in a big circle. Leo was struggling under the weight of two large pulleys.

When did she come downstairs? Why now? Did I miss her at breakfast? Was she okay?

Stop wondering about her.

Before I could think or react, Charlie appeared at my shoulder. "It's not here? I swear I saw you put it here by the—oh. Oh, hey!" Charlie jogged forward upon catching sight of the group, placing himself in front of Mona. "Hey. Hey there."

"Hello," she said, stopping. They all stopped.

"I'm Charlie." He held out his hand, grinning down at her, his voice sounding strange (for Charlie).

"I'm Mona."

"I'm so glad to see you." Charlie shuffled closer and grinned down at her in a way I'd never seen him grin at anyone, and I'd known Charlie for going on ten years.

My attention dropped to where she juggled the rope and accepted his handshake with a quick and firm up-down movement. Her arm moved like she was pulling back and his arm followed, his fingers keeping hold of hers.

Flexing my jaw, I lifted my attention from their hands. Charlie was still grinning, and Mona was smiling politely, and I wanted to break his face. I wouldn't do it, but I wanted to break his face, and that was just the way it was.

Leo, God bless Leo, cleared his throat, set down the pulleys, and stepped between them. "You met Mona already, remember? Two nights ago?" When he spoke, I noticed his voice was a little rough, nasally, like he was getting sick or had allergies.

"You were very tired." My drummer continued speaking to Mona, but finally released her hand. He wasn't ceding much room to Leo, leaning over our mutual friend to address his sister. "Where are you going? Outside? Are you having dinner with us tonight?"

My feet moved me toward the group and I nodded at Jenny Vee, Connie Will, and Nicole Mac. The three of them, friends of Leo's, made up the indie rock band, Fin, and seemed to be generally talented, cool, and low-key. Like Kaitlyn and Ruthie, their partners/boyfriends/husbands were supposed to join us yesterday but were stuck in town due to the snow.

And then I looked at Mona.

Her eyes were on me, but her smile had fallen, and she looked pale. Not pale like before, where all the color had suddenly left her face, but pale like she'd been sick for a while. Her eyes were dim, shuddered, bracing, *restrained*, and seeing her this way had my chest tightening. A hot, restive remorse made my stomach twist. I didn't like it.

"I, uh, yes. We're going outside," she said softly, her wary gaze still on me.

"We're going sledding." Leo lifted the two pulleys with effort, finally forcing Charlie to step back. "If you guys want to come, you're welcome. But we only have five sleds and they're all spoken for. You'll need to do some sweet talking if you want to share."

"There's six of you." I glanced at Leo briefly, unable to keep my eyes from moving back to Mona's.

"Allyn and I are sharing." Leo grinned at Mona's friend. She grinned back.

"I'll share with Mona," Charlie said, skipping away quickly, like he was in a rush. "Let me go put on my stuff."

"I don't think so—" Leo didn't finish his thought as he was forced to cover his mouth to catch a sneeze.

Charlie turned and jogged toward the main floor bedrooms, calling back to us, "Come on, man. It'll be fine. She doesn't mind. I'll be right there."

Leo lifted his voice, sniffing. "No, listen. She won't—" he cut himself off, sneezing again, and then making a sound of frustration. Leo glanced at his sister. "Sorry."

She gave him a tight smile. "It's fine. Don't make it a big thing."

"He can share mine," Jenny Vee offered, giving Mona a big grin. "I don't mind."

"He'll share Jenny's and he can deal with it," Leo said firmly.

What is the deal with this sled? I half expected it to be named Rosebud.

I lifted an eyebrow at the exchange, but Connie Will asked Mona before I could, "What's the problem with your sled?"

Mona gave the woman a friendly—but very small—smile, opening her mouth as though to explain, but Leo spoke over her before she could, "Mona built the sled herself, when we were kids, and I broke it. I finally just got it fixed up for her and I don't want it to break again."

The trio said, "Oh . . ." in a chorus.

"It's fine," Mona protested, her eyes darting to me, and then away. "It's really fine. I don't mind. It's just a sled."

"You're telling me you want Charlie to use your sled?" Leo challenged, as though they were talking about something other than just a sled, as though he were referring to Mona herself. "You don't even know Charlie and you want him touching your sled."

Her eyes on the floor, her cheeks turning pink, she whispered, "Can we not make it a big deal?"

Leo gave her an incredulous look, and opened his mouth as though to argue again. Clearly, he saw his sister was uncomfortable. Clearly, she didn't want to talk about it. Clearly, he didn't care.

"What are the pulleys for?" I interrupted, successfully keeping my annoyance with Leo out of my voice.

Again, her eyes flickered to me, and then away, making my next breath painful.

"They're for something Mona set up when we were kids, so we can get the sleds up the hill easier. I'll show you if you want, it's pretty cool." Leo shot a proud grin at his sister, she gave him a quick, closed mouth smile in return.

I stepped forward, lifting my chin toward the stairs ahead of us and addressing Allyn, Mona, and the trio from Fin. "You ladies go ahead, I'll help Leo carry these." And then to Leo, I added, "Wait here a second. I need to let Kaitlyn and Ruthie know we're done for now."

He nodded, rolling his other shoulder. "Go, go. I'll wait here."

I waited another beat before stepping away to tell Kaitlyn and Ruthie the news, wanting to put plenty of space between the group of women and us so Leo and I wouldn't be overheard as we walked.

Ruthie and Kaitlyn seemed fine with the change of plans, and so I quickly returned to help Leo carry his burden.

"You want to get your jacket and stuff first?" Leo picked up the other pulley, sniffing.

"Are you sick?"

Leo shook his head. "No. Just allergies. I'll wait here if you want to get your coat."

I wasn't convinced, Leo looked sick. His face was flushed, he kept sniffing, and his voice sounded raw.

Continuing to inspect my friend, I said, "Nah. My stuff is in the mudroom closet. I've been helping Melvin with the snow."

"Oh. Good. We're headed to the mudroom," he said, using both hands to carry the substantial pulley, laughing as he added, "I think these things are made of lead. Where did she get these?"

"Who?"

"Mona. These are hers."

I nodded, somehow not surprised Mona owned and used seventy-pound pulleys. "What's the big deal with the sled?"

He frowned, pressing his lips together and making a sound of irritation. "I told you, I broke it and—"

"No, no. I mean, what's really going on? What's the deal there? Is it Charlie?"

Leo sighed loudly, tilting his head back and forth, his eyes on his sister's back. "No. Well, yes and no. Charlie has been asking about Mona—a lot—since I told you guys she'd be here."

"Oh." I swallowed this knowledge and the renewed desire to break Charlie's face, and then asked, "So?" hoping I sounded convincingly disinterested.

"He's not Mona's type."

"What's wrong with Charlie?"

"Nothing." He frowned at me, looking confused. "You know I like Charlie."

"Then what's Mona's type?"

Stop asking about her.

Leo's frown intensified. "Her type is no type. She's not . . ." He glanced at me, giving me a face that reminded me of myself when I was worried about my sister. "You know."

"No. What?"

"She's not—she's, you know, asexual."

I almost dropped the pulley, and I turned my face away from Leo so he couldn't see the look on my face. I'd never thought of Leo as dumb, but his sister was as likely to be asexual as Karley Sciortino.

"Your sister told you that?"

Leo huffed again, giving me an irritated side-eye. "Listen, man. I don't want to talk about my sister's sex life, okay? Let's just say, years ago, she told me she didn't believe two people were necessary for getting off during sex, encouraged me to focus on *self-reliance* or some shit like that, and that the modern idea of romantic relationships would soon be considered outdated and irrelevant. She was trying to help me get over a breakup, I think. Anyway, add to that she doesn't like it when people touch her—not even her family—and, yeah, I feel pretty confident in assuming she's asexual."

I nodded thoughtfully, stopping myself from asking *You don't think it might be something else? Like maybe someone hurt her? And how long ago was this conversation? And when did she come downstairs? Is she okay?* even though the urge to question him was overwhelming.

Don't ask about her.

I promised myself I'd stop asking about Mona, but I'd been startled to see her after two full days of self-sequestration. She looked sick. Had she been eating?

Leo paused outside of the door to the mudroom, readjusting the pulley and drawing me out of my thoughts. "I don't want Charlie to get his hopes up is all. It's obvious he's really into her, but she'll shoot him down, 'cause she's always shooting everyone down. And when she does it, it's hard to watch. Brutal."

"Is that why you've never introduced us? You thought I'd make a move and she'd shoot me down?"

He shook his head. "Nah, man. I'm not worried about you. But I've lost friends before. Or acquaintances, I guess. Guys it would have been good to know, keep in touch with. I get it, she's beautiful, unique, interesting. Everyone wants to meet her. That's why I don't talk about her. And I don't want Mona making things bad between me and Charlie."

"Leo, that's bullshit. Mona wouldn't be the one making it bad. It's on him. It's not her job to make your guy friends—or acquaintances—feel good about themselves." I was repeating a general sentiment my sister and her friends had said to me on many, *many* occasions.

Leo smirked, like he thought I was funny, and then he laughed-coughed. "Yeah, you'd be surprised how many guys don't see it that way. But that's why I'm not worried about you. You know better. You've been taught. You have a sister, you know what it's like."

"Not having a sister is a shitty excuse," I mumbled.

"Hey. I agree." Leo's eyebrows lifted high on his forehead, he sniffed again. "But that's the way it is. I'm not saying it's right, I'm just saying you don't make people better by telling them to be better without real life examples, and then it has to be relevant to them, meaningful in some way. Important. Relationships, interacting with someone who has a different point of view, using a mistake as a teaching moment, that's how you make things change. But just saying, 'People should be better. Now, why aren't you a better person? Didn't I just tell you to be better?' That's just lazy."

I laughed. Leo's tangents sometimes reminded me of stand-up routines.

He wasn't finished. "It would be great if stuff worked that way, but it Just. Fucking. Doesn't. It's like saying, 'People shouldn't rob other people. Now why are people still robbing people? Didn't I just say to stop robbing people? Why hasn't this robbery shit magically corrected itself?' Or 'Don't be poor. Now why are you still poor? Didn't I just tell you not to be poor?'" He was laughing too.

"You're comparing being poor to committing a crime?"

"No, man. But, you know, society does. Rich people are good people just because they're rich? Hell. No. I know better. I have a *lifetime* of knowing better. And that's another thing—"

"Okay. Okay. I get it." If I didn't stop him now, he'd be ranting all day while we stood outside the mudroom.

Leo shook his head, smiling at me. "Sorry, sorry. The point is, no. Mona shouldn't let Charlie use her sled. He's a dummy about women, and it'll send the wrong message. She's smarter than he is, she's smarter than all of us, and that means she has more responsibility. That's just the way it is. The greater the gift, the greater the burden."

I could not believe my ears. "Are you fucking kidding me?"

He shrugged, as though to say, *that's just the way it is.*

I scoffed, shaking my head in disgust. "You should win the Brother of the Year Award, really. Nice job."

Leo glared, lowering his voice. "What do you want me to do? I mean, I could talk to him, but then I'll sound like an overprotective older brother and he'll assume I don't like him. I don't want to lose an old friend, I've known Charlie forever. So have you."

"You're an asshole, Leo. And you make no sense."

"Fuck off, Abram. What's the big deal? She should just shut him down now so he's not hoping later. She's going to do it eventually."

Seething at my friend, I walked through the door into the mudroom, too pissed off to say anything else. Charlie was *his* friend. Leo should be the one to step in and set him straight. It shouldn't be Mona's job. Leo, we, all of us weren't even supposed to fucking be here.

At first, I was so frustrated, I didn't notice the other people in the room. I moved to the far wall and set down the pulley, trying to get control of my temper. But as I calmed down—or forced myself to calm down—I glanced around. The women were pulling on their gloves, talking animatedly, laughing. Unsurprisingly, my attention immediately sought and found Mona. Or more correctly, Mona's ass.

She was bent at the waist, adjusting her boot, the coiled rope was next to her on the floor, and her pants were definitely not baggy. They looked like yoga pants, just thicker, and fit her perfectly, though they changed the fit of mine.

I didn't have to use my imagination at all. But I did. Just a little.

Tearing my eyes away before Leo—or anyone else—noticed me staring at the curve of her perfect and gorgeous rounded bottom, I left the pulley by the wall and crossed to the closet to retrieve my coat, gloves, and hat. While I was pulling them on and trying to get control of my blood pressure, Charlie burst through the door.

Upon spotting Mona, who was now standing, her long shirt falling to her thighs, he grinned that grin again and slowly swaggered toward her. I glanced at Leo and found him glaring at me.

On the one hand, I understood his dilemma. Charlie was a good friend, they'd been through a lot together, and Charlie always had his back. On the other hand, just because setting Charlie straight was inconvenient and might be uncomfortable, Leo owed it to Mona, not just because she was his sister, but because it was the right thing to do.

Not thinking about the instinct too much, I crossed to where Mona was standing, not missing how Allyn was glaring at me. This wasn't a surprise. She'd been sending me unfriendly looks since the second day they'd arrived.

Mona's head lifted, her eyes connecting with mine just as I said, "Thanks for letting me share your sled. I'm sure Charlie won't mind using Jenny's."

Mona started, her lashes fluttering, her eyes wide, and she nodded. "No—no problem."

Giving her a flat smile, I nodded, sparing a glance for Allyn. She was still giving me a dirty look.

Sucking in a deep breath, I turned to face Charlie, who was now scowling at me.

Great.

* * *

"What's this for?" Charlie, who was still sending me annoyed side-eyes—which I ignored, he'd get over it—tugged on the rope Mona had just finished threading through the pulley on the top of the hill.

The other pulley had been set in its place at the bottom of the hill. They both hung from sturdy, six-foot poles.

"It's a pulley system. You attach your sled to the rope here, using the hooks welded to the sleds. And then you can pull the rope to send them back up to the top of the hill." She pointed out two metal hooks that had been added unobtrusively to the underside of the five sleds.

Apparently, she hadn't just made one of the sleds. She'd made them all.

The hooks were encased in a small tube of the same metal and were retractable. Since the sleds were on ski rails and the platform sat off the ground, the hooks and their tubes wouldn't interfere with sliding down the hill. The tubes also kept the hooks from inadvertently catching a person or their clothes. The design was smart.

"Huh. Smart." Charlie grinned at her. "So you don't have to carry the sled back up the hill."

"Nice." Nicole said, inspecting her sled.

We were at the crest of a hill overlooking the house, the slope and length were just the right for sledding. Not too steep where going ass over ankles was a concern, not too long where walking back up the hill would make repeated rides not worth the effort.

Mona started back down the hill, stomping her feet as she went and bending over every so often to pack down the snow.

"What are you doing?" Jenny asked. "Do you need help?"

"Making snow stairs, for people to climb instead of struggling with the slope. Even without having to carry the sled back up, as you experienced on the way up here, it can be difficult."

I watched her work for a moment, knowing I'd be down there to help her whether she liked it or not. *But first* . . . I turned to glance at the pulley system she'd set up. Reaching for the rope, I tugged, hard. The poles holding the pulley and rope were extremely sturdy. They didn't budge.

"Why do you need the stairs?" I asked. "Couldn't you use the rope to pull yourself up?"

I felt unfriendly eyes on me, so I looked around. Sure enough, Allyn was watching me through near slits, arms crossed, her mouth pinched.

Glancing at the sky briefly, I decided to ignore her, too.

Keeping her focus on the snow, Mona sighed. "Well, not really. Because if you pull on the up rope, the other side—the down rope— moves in the pulley and you'd end up staying where you are."

"Yeah. True. But if you held on to both ropes, both sides, neither would move. And you could pull yourself up the hill, which would be easier, less energy, and faster than either taking snow stairs or climbing."

Mona glanced up and our eyes met. As I'd come to expect, my next breath was difficult.

I wonder when that's going to stop.

She just looked. Her face blank as she seemed to consider me. Everyone else glanced between us.

"And," I added as another option occurred to me, "if you didn't want to use both ropes like that, you could use the pulley. Someone could stand up here and pull people up using the 'down' side of the rope, while the other person holds onto the 'up' rope."

Mona inhaled slowly, straightening fully, her eyes still holding mine, a glimmer of something behind them. The barest of smiles curved her lips. I countered the compulsion to return her smile by scowling, needing a defensive barrier against the admiring look in her eyes and the faint—but no less impactful—curve of her lips.

She nodded. "You're right. Those are both better options—smarter, simpler options, less time-consuming—than the snow stairs." Dusting the white flakes from her hands, she walked back to where we stood. Specifically, she walked back to where I stood, holding the sled we would share. "We should do one or both of those."

The others agreed and made their way to the set-off point in the center of the hill, lining up to take turns. Jenny made some joke about snow in the pants that had Connie and Nicole jogging ahead.

Mona and I didn't move.

She stood about four feet away. It was still snowing, and a snowflake landed on her cheekbone, melting almost as quickly as it touched her skin. I knew how it felt.

"Thank you."

Steadying myself, keeping my features clear of expression, I gave my eyes back to her. "For what?"

"For being so civil."

"Civil." I tested the word on my tongue and decided I didn't like it. "Civil as in civilized? You think just because people aren't as smart as you, they're incapable of civility?"

Her eyebrows pulled together, and she flinched. "I never—I never thought, nor do I think, that I'm smarter than you."

"Then you're an idiot." I glanced over her head at nothing and I chuckled humorlessly. "What does that make me?"

She made a sound of frustration, taking another half step forward, drawing my eyes back to hers. I was surprised to see a bit of fire behind her gaze, like I'd made her angry.

"Then I rescind my appreciation for your civility, and I thank you instead—and in specific—for sharing my sled. Or, I guess, offering to." Her eyes were whiskey colored today and slightly narrowed, staring at me with what looked like simmering annoyance.

Perversely, I liked that I could get any reaction out of her. I'd been thinking constantly about our conversation in the study two days ago and I'd decided it had been one-sided. She'd barely said anything. She'd made a brave face, let me say my piece, and admitted only that she'd *regretted* it. But she hadn't apologized.

And that fucking note . . .

Just thinking about her admission of regret and that note had me grinding my teeth. I shoved my hands into my coat pockets, a crescendo of anger making me speak without thinking, "Leo should tell Charlie to back off, but I don't think he will."

Mona was quiet for a second, and I heard her take a deep breath. "Okay."

"Charlie isn't a bad guy."

"I didn't think he was."

Returning my attention to her lovely face, I studied the dark circles beneath her eyes, the paleness of her lips. But her cheeks were now pink, probably from the cold. *Has she been eating?* I didn't think so.

Stop wondering about her.

"It's none of my business. . ." I said, unsure what I was talking about. Charlie? Or if she'd been eating? Swallowing the impulse to ask how she was, if she was okay, I worked hard to keep my concern for her buried, shielding it behind the anger I was having trouble holding on to.

"Abram." Mona had also stuck one of her hands in her coat pocket, seemed to be fiddling with something inside. "I'm not interested in Charlie," she said gently.

She'd taken another step forward and it felt too close. Her eyes had turned soft, but also restrained. She looked like she wanted to say more. She didn't.

Kaitlyn had been right. Mona DaVinci was a D minor kind of gal. She was all of those adjectives the interviewers used. Cold, brilliant, calculating, aloof. She was not the sunny, funny girl from Chicago that made me laugh, who was so easy to tease, who made me hot with her brains and body and wit. She was not brave. She was not honest, maybe not even with herself.

"Then you should tell him. Tell him, so he doesn't waste time hoping for more," I said, my voice rough, allowing the cold within me to join the cold without and embracing the numbness of disenchantment. "Try being honest for once. You might like it."

[9]
PARTICLE PHYSICS

Mona

ry being honest for once.

T I couldn't get his parting shot out of my head. *Try being honest . . .* For once.

Even as I checked Leo's temperature and pressed a cold cloth to his forehead, Abram's voice chanted in my head, *be honest, be honest, be honest.*

"That bad?" My brother's unsteady question pulled me out of my musings. He shivered under his covers and his jaw was clamped shut, like he was trying to stop his teeth from reflexively clacking together.

Poor Leo. He'd finally succumbed to his cold about two hours into our sledding adventure and would soon be in a medicine haze. I'd administered a hefty dose of everything we had in hopes it would help him sleep.

Glancing at the readout on the thermometer, I read, "102.4."

"Ugh. This sucks. I just want to die."

Rolling my lips between my teeth to stop my smile, I rolled my eyes at his dramatics. "You're not dying."

"No. But it feels like I am."

Now I did smile, setting aside his thermometer to the side table. On a whim, I placed a kiss on his forehead. "You need to sleep."

As I leaned away, he caught my eyes, ensnared them. Even in his hazy state, my small action seemed to shock the hell out of him.

"Are you feeling okay?" he asked, looking truly alarmed.

"Better than you are." I pressed my cool hand to his cheek. "I'm sorry you're sick, but I'm happy you're not alone and sick."

He coughed, covering his mouth. "I always have friends around, Mona. I'm rarely alone." He had sore-throat voice.

"It's not the same though, is it?" I watched my hand brush hair off my sweet brother's forehead. "It's better with family, I think. You know I'll always love you, no matter what."

Leo frowned, his glassy eyes turning thoughtful. "You love me, huh?"

I smirked at his ridiculous question. "Of course I do."

He shook his head, his frown intensifying, and blurted, "Why don't you like me touching you?"

I stiffened and held perfectly still.

But Leo had more questions. "Was it something I did? I know Lisa had her issues with me, and boarding school. We worked it out and I think we're fine now. But what did I do to you?"

"Nothing," I whispered, straightening to sit upright in my chair, but I didn't completely withdraw. I covered his hand with mine. "You should sleep."

Try being honest for once.

Leo might've been the one who was sick, but Abram's words plagued me.

"There's got to be something, Mona." My brother's eyes, the same color as mine and Lisa's, as my mom's, searched my face. "I'm really sorry, whatever it was."

"It wasn't you," I said without meaning to, wanting to calm him.

It had the opposite effect.

Leo's fingers tightened over mine, his eyes growing wider, suddenly fierce. "Then who was it?"

Try being honest for once.

Swallowing around a knot in my throat that threatened to bring with it a flood of memories, I glanced at the headboard behind him. I told myself for the billionth time that I'd given a meaningless and stupid incident too much power over me, over my relationships with my family, and my friends.

Nothing had happened. I wasn't hurt. I was fine then and I was fine now.

Abram's voice sounded between my ears, demanding, *Try being honest for once.*

I felt my lips curve downward in a frown. "Can we talk about this later?" I slipped my fingers from Leo's, but didn't remove my hand, covering his once again. "When your fever is below 100?"

Leo's forehead twitched, he blinked his eyes, obviously having trouble keeping them open. "If someone hurt you—"

"No one hurt me," I soothed, which I reminded myself was the truth. "But you're going to hurt yourself if you don't sleep."

He didn't believe me, it was written all over his face. "Mona—"

"Go to sleep." I stood, reached for the light on his side table and switched it off. "I'll be back to check on you later."

"Mona."

"Leo. Sleep. Now." I backed away toward the door, punctuating each word with a finger point even though he probably couldn't see me. "And I'll tell you anything you want to know."

"I'll hold you to that."

The shiver of disquiet raced down my spine, causing me to wince, and making me grateful I'd turned off the light. "Sweet dreams, big brother."

He grunted in response and shifted on the bed.

Reaching the door, I stepped backward to close it, and heard him say, "I love you, Mona."

Smiling into the darkness, I answered, "I love you too, Leonardo DaVinci."

He chuckled. I closed the door. I took a deep breath. And, after washing my hands of residual flu-like symptom causing germs, I forced my feet to carry me to the dining room where I knew dinner had already been served.

I craved quiet, but I didn't know if that was because silence had become habitual, or if I actually wished for it. Regardless, I refused to remove myself to my room again, or use Leo's sickness as an excuse to be absent. I could've stayed with him and avoided the crowd under the guise of watching my brother sleep. That would've made me a coward.

After years of wanting to see him, Abram was here, now. At best, he hated me. At worst, he was indifferent toward me. I thought maybe his true feelings fell someplace in between. Everything between us was officially over. Any possibility of a future between us was an asymptote of a curve, approaching zero reaching to infinity but never touching the axis. I was clear on all of that.

But I also recognized these next few days would be my last chance to be near him in any meaningful way. I could avoid him and all the uncomfortable, painful, breath-snatching feelings, or I could experience him and the feelings. Even if he hated me, even if I didn't understand why I continued to feel so strongly about him, even if the only memories I made during this time were agonizing ones, I'd take agonizing over another black hole of nothingness.

And that was honestly the truth.

Walking into the dining room, I scanned the table, my chest seized when I spotted Abram sitting at the head. Next to him were Charlie on the left, and, on his right, the woman Connie Will (from sledding this afternoon) had referred to as Kaitlyn. She'd said they made music together, and they were very, *very* close—whatever that meant. Just thinking about it made my heart beat faster and darkness edge into the corners of my vision.

Indulging myself for a long moment, I let myself devour the image of Abram, tucking it away later for quiet moments, because he was smiling. Sure, he wasn't smiling at me, but that didn't matter. Seeing him happy, smiling, no matter the reason, did wonderful things to my heart. For some reason, his smile made me think of delicious ice cream —rocky road—in a cookie cone, a delectable, decadent, rare treat, best when savored, licked . . .

"Mona! I saved you a seat."

Abram looked up at the sound of Allyn calling my name and our gazes collided, a crash of cymbals between my ears paired with a buzzing, static feedback loop. His smile fell precipitously, but he didn't look away. Peripherally, I was aware of she-called-Kaitlyn turning to look, obviously checking to see what or who had darkened his mood.

Swallowing around another knot, I tore my eyes from his and turned to my friend. Allyn was now waving from her spot at the other head of the table, literally the farthest spot from Abram she could've selected.

I took my place next to her with a *thank you,* and then turned to reintroduce myself to the person I didn't remember meeting at my right and the people across from me.

Once introductions had been made and what I considered appropriate polite chit-chat commenced, I forced myself to take a bite of food. I hadn't been able to eat much since we'd arrived, and I knew lack of sustenance was one of the reasons I didn't feel quite myself now.

"Did you have fun today?" Allyn asked, sounding optimistic.

I gave her a smile that I hoped communicated my gratitude and my remorse. "I'm sorry I haven't been an attentive host."

She covered my hand, not seeming to notice when I flinched. "Oh no, don't apologize. Don't worry about me." Her greenish-blue eyes widened, and she shook her head. "I just want to make sure you're okay. After what you told me—about you and the Captain—if I were you, I would be camped out in my room until the week was over."

We'd decided on *the Captain* for Abram's code name, mostly because of me mistakenly calling him Ahab while he and I had shared the house in Chicago.

"I'm okay," I said automatically.

Try being honest for once.

I frowned, then rubbed my forehead with stiff fingers, Abram's words from earlier still chanting between my ears. "Actually, it's not okay. I'm not okay. I don't understand myself. I can't figure out why I still feel so strongly about a person I knew years ago, and only for one week, and with whom a future is impossible."

"It sounded like an intense week."

"It was intense, kinda. And it wasn't. I mean, we didn't even kiss. Part of me wonders, if I hadn't lied to him, if I didn't feel so guilty, would I still be holding on? Thinking about him all the time? Maybe it's just guilt I'm feeling, and not—"

"Infatuation?"

I was actually thinking more along the lines of love *given the fact that this madness has persisted for over two years, but—*

"Sure, we'll call it infatuation. Maybe I'm infatuated with him because I feel like I owe him? Because I lied?"

"I don't know about that, Mona. If you were going to be infatuated with someone, the Captain is an excellent candidate. I've listened to Redburn's songs on repeat for months now. They're the current sound-track to my life. And Abr—I mean, *the Captain* wrote all those songs. His words—" Allyn sighed, her gaze flickered to the far end of the table, and then back to me. "I'm a little in love with him, and we didn't spend a week together."

Ugh. She likely hadn't meant her statements to be a reminder of how impossible my feelings for Abram were, but that's what she'd done. No doubt, thousands of women—and men for that matter—had sentiments echoing Allyn's. I'd seen it with my parents, admiration to the point of worship based on their music. He was and always would be adored by many.

Musicians aren't monogamous. And I wanted a picket fence, with a lawn, and a rose garden, and children. We would bake pies in the shape of pi. Rock stars don't have rose gardens, and I definitely didn't want an open relationship. I'd seen my sister make this mistake.

And, even if Abram was monogamous, he doesn't want you.

"Maybe it's a combination of things." Allyn bumped my knee with hers beneath the table. "You feel guilty, yes. But maybe you feel so guilty because you truly do like him. And the guilt plus the like creates these super intense feelings that are hard to move past."

Stewing in discontent, I pushed my food around with my fork.

"You never told me," she started, and I felt her gaze on my profile. "What happened on Saturday? When the two of you talked? I want to give you space, and I don't wish to push you about it. But, do you want to discuss it?"

Although I'd told Allyn about my past with Abram—everything in Chicago, how I'd internet-stalked him for a year after, how he'd given me the cold shoulder in the funicular structure after she went inside with Leo, my plan to tell him the truth about impersonating Lisa, etcetera—I hadn't yet filled her in on the outcome of my conversation with Abram the morning after we'd arrived.

"I . . ." I struggled to recall the incident while also forming coherent words. I couldn't.

My first instinct—when Abram and I were in the study on Saturday, and he'd told his side of our twisted story— had been to say sorry. To bleed my apologies all over the place. To rend them from my lips and my hands and my guts and my heart. But as we'd looked at each other, seeing each other for the very first time, I knew with absolute certainty that he didn't want a gushing apology or excuses.

Gushing, pleading apologies and attempts at justification would've made him angrier, more distant, more certain in his disdain and resolute in his dislike. I was desperate to give him what he wanted, whatever that was. But I didn't know what he wanted, and I wondered if he even knew what he wanted.

I suspected not.

Therefore, I'd stood there and listened, doing my best to *not* explain. I hoped that if I gave him space, then he might give me time later.

And on that note, I dropped my fork and fit my hand in the pocket of my snoga pants, where I'd placed the letter. Feeling it there calmed me, and that was good because simply thinking about what Abram had said, how he'd looked at me, made me feel like crying again. I was so tired of crying. I'd just spent two days hiding in my room with the silence, crying, and I wasn't even a crier!

I didn't want to cry anymore.

Allyn gave me a sympathetic look, squeezing my hand harder. "Should I have stayed with you? This afternoon? I saw you and Abram talking, I didn't know what to do. I mean, he looks intimidating in all the band's photos, and he's bigger and scarier in real life, but even though I love him for his music, I will break his nose—no questions asked—if you wanted me to."

"No, no." I laughed at the image of sweet Allyn breaking Abram's nose, even though it was a weird thing to find funny. Maybe I laughed because I appreciated the distraction the image conjured.

It's not that Allyn wasn't capable of it—she totally was, especially if she caught him off-guard—it's just that she was one of those peace-loving sorts, always trying to mediate, see both sides of every issue, and negotiate a cease-fire.

"It was okay. We were fine. Relative to our last interaction, today was fine."

Try being honest for once.

"It *was* fine," I repeated, frowning at Abram's voice in my head arguing the point. Given where we'd ended things in the study on Saturday, our interaction this afternoon felt almost miraculous.

For no reason whatsoever, I found myself glancing down the table, spying on him. He was speaking to the Kaitlyn woman. Their heads were together. They smiled at each other. They looked comfortable and cozy. I felt my stomach tense like I might be sick.

My attention lingered on her for too long, but I couldn't help it. She wasn't particularly pretty—her lips were an unusual shape, her eyebrows thick, black, too pronounced, her eyes a drab shade of gray, and she had a noticeable gap between her two front teeth—but she, taken all together, was strikingly beautiful, and the sight filled me with restive fury.

Her beauty should've been irrelevant. What did it matter if Abram was laughing and smiling with this woman? What did it matter if her rejoining laughter made me want to singe her eyebrows from her face using a hot poker? I wouldn't actually do it. It didn't matter. *It had no mass.*

But somehow, her striking beauty didn't feel irrelevant. It did have mass, and matter, and weight.

Are they dating?

My stomach twisted tighter, hurt.

Do they have an open relationship? Like my parents? Maybe they're just lovers. He probably has several.

"Are you sure you don't want to talk about your conversation with him on Saturday?" Allyn's question yanked me out of my destructive, pointless musings, and I faced her again.

"No, honestly. But I think maybe I should. How about tonight? After dinner."

She nodded. "Sure. We'll have wine."

"Maybe not wine." I didn't need a wine-haze clouding my judgment with potentially hot pokers nearby. "How about tea?"

"Oh, yes. I will make you my winter tea. I should make some for Leo too." She gave me a shy smile and asked reluctantly, "Speaking of, how is Leo?"

I tried not to grin at the way her voice pitched higher at his name.

Yes, Leo was a musician, but he wasn't like all the others. I knew his heart and he craved monogamy. He craved finding that special someone. He was the exception that proved the rule, but he'd made the mistake of only dating musicians . . . *so far.*

Plans. Lots of plans. *Allyn and Leo will marry in the summer, on a vineyard, and I'll be the maid of honor. The table numbers will all be prime numbers, because I'll be planning the wedding.*

Allyn narrowed her eyes, leaning away. "Why are you looking at me like that?"

"Like what?" I mimicked the singsong quality to her voice. "Like, *You and Leo sitting in a tree, K-I-N-E-T-I-C energy?*"

She blushed, making me happy, and her lips twisted to the side, clearly fighting a smile. "I was just asking if he was okay. He seemed really sick."

"He is. You should go take care of him."

"Mona."

"He would love it."

"Mona."

"Give him a sponge bath."

"MONA!"

"What?" I laughed, delighted with the direction and escalation of my teasing.

Allyn cleared her throat and leaned forward, asking primly, "What happed with Charlie?"

"Charlie?" I sat straighter, blinking at the sudden subject change, and glancing back down the table to Charlie.

"Yes. Charlie. He seemed very friendly before we went sledding. I saw you two talking at the top of the hill, right before we all went back inside. What was that about?"

Unfortunately, instead of looking at Charlie, my gaze was drawn to Abram and Kaitlyn again. They were still talking. And laughing. And looking cozy.

Thank goodness Allyn was here to distract me, otherwise I would've spent half of dinner trying not to spy on Abram and Kaitlyn, and the other half spying on Abram and Kaitlyn.

Mortifyingly, Kaitlyn glanced up at just that moment. She caught me staring.

I glanced away quickly, fighting against the embarrassment heating my face and telling myself not to look again.

No. I want to look. I want to see him.

Then she'll see you.

Does it matter?

I couldn't decide.

"Mona?" Allyn prompted.

"Hmm?" I picked up my fork and knife and cut into the tenderloin on my plate, determined to eat more food.

"Did something bad happen with Charlie?"

I shook my head, shoveling steak, polenta with mushrooms, and the rocket, spinach, goat cheese, and cranberry salad into my mouth. Under normal circumstances, I probably would've requested a second serving. But not tonight. Tonight, even mushrooms tasted like unflavored tapioca pudding. *Mush.*

I felt Allyn's eyes on me. I also felt someone else's eyes on me, and I suspected they belonged to she-called-Kaitlyn.

"Hey, you ladies want anything to drink? I'm making cocktails." Bruce—the guy sitting across from me and next to Allyn—leaned forward and glanced between us. "If I may say so, I make an excellent manhattan."

"No thanks," Allyn answered for both of us. "I'm making winter tea later, so cocktails now would be too much, I think."

"Suit yourself," he said, giving her a smile, me a single nod, and stood from the table, taking his plate with him. I decided, even though I didn't know Bruce, I liked him. Anyone who cleared their own plate from the table without being asked was worthy of my respect.

"I like Bruce," Allyn said, watching him go. "Maybe tomorrow I'll take him up on his offer to make me a cocktail. This is the third time he's asked, and he's always so nice about it. I've never had a manhattan."

"Hey now," I said around my last bite of polenta, "what about my poor brother?"

Allyn laughed, giving me a look like she thought I was weird. "I don't like Bruce *that way.* I—" Realizing what she'd just said, Allyn covered her mouth with her hand and stared at me with big eyes.

JACKPOT!

Pointing at her, I shook my head. "No take-backs."

Her hand dropped, she crossed her arms. "Fine. Fine. Now you know the truth. Leo is a cutie pie and I just want to wrap him up in rice paper and eat him up like an egg roll."

"Weird and gross. Nevertheless, I approve." I'd had similar thoughts about Abram, but instead he was ice cream in a cookie cone.

Grinning, finished with my food, and feeling better than I had in days, of course I glanced down the table again and all the good feelings were chased away.

Kaitlyn was shaking her head at something Abram had said and she hit him lightly on the shoulder. He threw his head back, laughing with abandon, his hands over his chest.

Stop looking.

She'll see you and know you're a weirdo. Is that what you want?

Does it matter? He hates you. Look now, because you'll never be this close to him again.

I still couldn't decide, and I still hadn't decided when she caught me spying. Again. But this time? I didn't glance away.

Try being honest for once.

I held her gaze and allowed myself to just be jealous. I'd never been jealous before, but I knew in my bones that's what this horrible feeling was. I felt it oozing out of me, jealousy-radiation coming from my pores and eyes, and then the weirdest thing happened.

Kaitlyn blinked. And then she smiled.

[10]

CIRCUITS AND BIOELECTRICITY

Mona

S he smiled.
Smiled. At me.

And not a mean-person smile, or a villain smile, or even a knowing smile.

It looked genuine, friendly, and—infuriatingly and adorably—cute due to the big gap between her teeth. The next thing I knew, she'd stood from her seat and walked down the length of the table, her eyes never leaving mine. And that's when I got a good look at Abram's Kaitlyn. That's when I regretted eating all my dinner because my stomach now hurt. That's when I wanted to rage against the unfairness of life.

Ladies and gents, this Kaitlyn person was a bombshell. Her boobs were ridiculous, and her waist was ridiculous, and her hips were ridiculous, a comic book rendering come to life. She was Betty Boop with longer hair and an intelligent spark in her eye.

If she were Abram's girlfriend or soon-to-be girlfriend, or one of his lovers, I foresaw a lot of jealousy-fueled snow angels in my future.

"Hi. I'm Kaitlyn Parker." She put her hand in front of me, like she expected me to take it.

I did, giving her a perfunctory shake. "Hello. I'm Mona DaVinci."

Her grin widened and she glanced at the empty seat next to Allyn. "Do you mind if I sit?"

I glanced at Allyn, hoping to see a frown of disdain. But instead of an expression that mirrored mine, Allyn grinned at me, and then turned her sunny smile to Kaitlyn.

"Yes. Come sit down. You and Mona should be friends."

WHAT!?

Now I glared at my *former* friend Allyn, the traitor, and she returned my scowl with a look of innocent confusion. But it was too late, this Kaitlyn person was already on the move, claiming the vacant seat. My fingers closed around the handle of my fork for no reason and I held it under the table. I wasn't going to stab her with it. I wasn't.

I wasn't.

Don't look at me with those judgy eyes!

"Sorry if my hand was sweaty," Kaitlyn said, smiling at us both with her adorable smile. "I'm really nervous. I've wanted to meet you for a while. Can I just say, I really appreciated the testimony you gave in front of Congress this last summer. I was glued to my TV. I feel like what you did made a difference, you seem to have swayed public opinion, and I hope it means things will start moving in the right direction."

I blinked at her, feeling inadequate and tongue-tied and jealous. SO JEALOUS. But rather than continue to scowl, especially since she was being so nice, I worked to keep my face emotionless. This was no easy task considering the direction of my thoughts.

They probably kiss. All the time. They've probably kissed today.

Stop it! You don't even know if they're dating.

Are you kidding? I would date her in a heartbeat. She's stunning and her voice reminds me of how honey tastes.

I blinked, sitting up straighter . . . *where did that thought come from?*

Given all this, I was having trouble pulling a response out of my brain that was anything close to situationally appropriate. I absolutely could not say anything like, *Did you kiss Abram today? How long have you two been together? Does he talk about me? Are you two getting married?*

On that pleasant note, my eyes lowered to her self-professed sweaty hands and that's when I saw it. A ring. But not just any ring. A beautiful, tasteful, HUGE light-blue sapphire engagement ring.

"So, it has come to this," I murmured unthinkingly.

"Pardon me?" The obvious confusion in Kaitlyn's voice forced my eyes back to hers.

"Uh, I mean—" *And thus, I die.* "Um, congratulations." *. . . on your engagement to the man I'm obsessed with. And then the wolves came.* She blinked at me, still confused. I indicated with my chin to her ring finger. "That's a gorgeous engagement ring. A sapphire?" *In this economy?*

"Oh! Thank you." She smiled down at the ring, her eyes turning hazy. But instead of lifting it for me to look at—which is what most women, in my experience, seemed to do—she pulled it closer to herself, like it was precious. "It's an aquamarine."

I nodded, my voice coming out weak as I said with a light chuckle, "As the prophesy foretold." Because I was a dork and I didn't know how to *speak people.* Specifically, I didn't know how to speak to the person who was going to marry Abram. *My* Abram.

MINE!

A surge of possessiveness, such that I was unable to breathe or focus for a few seconds, held me in its grip. It choked me, I was dizzy with it, and I regretted not taking that Bruce guy up on his offer of cocktails. That'll teach me to turn down cocktails.

I was only half paying attention when, with a dreamy quality to her voice, Allyn said, "It's so lovely. Aquamarine is a unique choice for an engagement ring, what made you pick it?"

"There's a reason, but it'll sound cheesy." Kaitlyn grinned at Allyn, and then at me.

"Cheesy? What? No! Pshaw!" I forced a grin along with cheerfulness into my voice, but there must've been something wrong with my face because Allyn's smile fell, her eyes widened, and she was looking at me like my head had been replaced with the genitalia of an animal.

Because, let's face it, genitalia—all genitalia, no matter the animal

—range from distressing to disturbing to horrifying. Human vaginas look like sea creatures that slurp their food—and probably regurgitate half of it—and penises are startling, no matter the situation. If someone made a horror movie entitled, *Dick Pics* and just showed various dick pics? It would be the scariest, most distressing movie ever made.

The *only* species that does reproductive systems visually right are angiosperms (flowering plants). When you're smelling a flower, you're basically smelling a dick. Let that sink in.

"Uh . . ." Kaitlyn blinked at me, her smile wavering, her expression also wavering between perplexed and terrified at my expression.

What could I do? Usually, concealing my thoughts was my super-power, but Abram was my kryptonite. I couldn't hide my emotions on the subject of his engagement. Randomly, selfishly, I didn't want to. And besides, hadn't that been Abram's parting shot/advice?

Try being honest for once.

Honestly, I was (honestly) insanely jealous. Honestly.

I was just about to break things down for her—something like, *Look, Kaitlyn. I'm INTENSELY in love-lust-infatuation with your fiancé. I know it would never work out between us, but I'd like to lock him away from the world in my basement, lick him nightly like an ice cream, and make him the second member of my two-person book club. I think maybe we can't be friends*—when Kaitlyn turned to Allyn.

She said, "The stone is the same color as my fiancé's eyes. See? Cheesy."

And I said, "Look, Kaitlyn—uh, what?" Now I blinked at her, sitting up straight. "What—what—what was that?"

Allyn shook her head at me. "Are you feeling okay?"

I ignored her, patting the table with my hand to get Kaitlyn's attention. "Focus. The eyes? The eyes. What did you say about your fiancé's eyes?"

"That they're—uh—aquamarine?" Her gaze grew shifty, and she looked to Allyn as though seeking help with the cumbersome task of dealing with the crazy person sitting across from her.

Which, since we're all being honest with ourselves, was a fair assessment.

I breathed out. So much air left my body. All the air left my body with that exhale. And I smiled, this time true and genuine. And I laughed.

"Well. That's the best thing I've ever heard. I mean, I think I've never heard anything better than that. Ever. In my whole life."

Kaitlyn nodded, continuing to regard me with cautious bewilderment. "Thank you."

"Kaitlyn's mom is Senator Parker," Allyn said, giving me a searching look. "And Kaitlyn is a composer. She wrote the musical accompaniment for Redburn's 'Hold A Grudge' as well as a few of their other big singles."

Oh!

Ah. I see!

Abram's huge hit, number one single. When Connie Will had said Kaitlyn and Abram made music together, she must've been referring to the literal meaning of "making music."

Kaitlyn and Allyn looked at me expectantly, like they were waiting for me to say or do something else ludicrous. But I wouldn't. Jealousy had dissolved into self-recrimination with a hefty side-dose of confusion. My reaction to Kaitlyn's hypothetical relationship had been strong—stronger than a gamma-ray burst, stronger than my sense of and commitment to rationality—and that was concerning.

Understatement!

Even so, I did my best to locate my composure before responding genuinely, "Congratulations, that's so, so exciting. So happy for you. And Abram. For the song."

"Mona hasn't heard 'Hold A Grudge' yet." Allyn turned to Kaitlyn, confiding in her like they were old friends. "But it's been my favorite since I heard it the first time. You are so talented."

"Thank you, you're very kind," Kaitlyn said to Allyn, sounding sincerely flattered, but then she shifted a penetrating gaze to me. "You haven't heard 'Hold A Grudge'?"

"Who hasn't?" This question came from Jenny Vee, one of the ladies we'd gone sledding with earlier in the day. She was about halfway down the table and her voice carried, probably because she was the lead singer in her band, Fin. "Who hasn't heard 'Hold A Grudge'?"

Yikes!

I shook my head, sitting straighter, patting the table again, this time to get Jenny Vee's attention. "Wait. Wait. No—"

But before I could say anything substantive, Kaitlyn talked over me, "Mona hasn't heard 'Hold A Grudge' yet. She hasn't heard Abram's song."

My now frantic gaze cut back to Kaitlyn. I found her head turned slightly, her stare scrutinizing as it moved over me. Clearly, she was having many thoughts.

Oh no.

"Abram!" This came from Nicole, the third member of Fin. "Where's Ruthie? Since Mona is the last person in the world who hasn't heard the song, you should play it for all of us, before you get tired of singing it on tour."

OH MY GOD!

The fingers holding the fork under the table began to shake, so I covered it with my other hand. A cold sheen of sweat broke out all over my skin. My heart heaved itself into my mouth.

Meanwhile, everyone present erupted in support of this idea, but their encouragement was drowned out by the sound of blood rushing between my ears. Meanwhile, Kaitlyn and I continued our staring contest, her eyes now slightly narrowed, that rascally spark still present, but so was something else. . . *suspicion.*

But then I flinched, closing my eyes, because I heard Abram's deep voice say, "If she wants to hear it, all she has to do is ask."

I swallowed a knot, or many knots, or perhaps all the knots as cheers followed this news. I felt everyone's eyes turn to me even though mine were closed. Beneath the table, I felt a hand close over mine and I didn't flinch this time. It gave me the wherewithal to open my eyes.

Allyn was looking at me, sympathy and worry in her gaze, and she gave me an encouraging smile, seeming to communicate, *You are a badass. I believe in you. You can get through this without making a spectacle of yourself. And then we will cuddle together while you cry.*

Perhaps that wasn't exactly what she sought to communicate, but I felt confident it was close enough.

The room was still a ruckus of excitement and armchair conversation about the likelihood of my never hearing the song.

"How is it possible someone hasn't heard 'Hold A Grudge'?"

"She must be the last person on earth to hear it."

"I hear it ten times a day, no lie."

"They have their instruments, right?"

"I don't think Charlie brought his drums."

"I hope he plays it. It would be cool to hear an acoustic version."

But one comment in particular carried above the others, reaching me from Abram's side of the table. "I guess rocket scientists don't get out much."

For some reason, the statement gave me the bravery I needed to lean forward and lock eyes with Abram, probably because the statement was true.

Try being honest for once.

I didn't get out much, I got out never. And when I got out, I came to Aspen where I could be snowed in and not go out. I'd been living in limbo, in line, waiting in the silence.

Abram, relaxing in his chair, glared at me. His elbows on the armrests, his fingers steepled in front of him. He looked at ease, like a king holding court, and completely indifferent to whatever I might say.

If he doesn't care, then it doesn't matter.

Clearing my throat, and squeezing Allyn's fingers, I lifted my voice above the hubbub and said calmly, "I'd like to hear your song, if you don't mind playing it for me."

* * *

I sat on the periphery of the main floor living room with Lila, slightly separating myself from the larger group on the other side so that, once the song was over, I could make a hasty getaway. Tomorrow, it would begin again, the turbulent rocket ride orbiting Abram. But as of right now, I'd had enough of turbulence, anguish, and making memories.

After Abram had agreed to my request with a nonchalant shrug and a neutral sounding, *sure*, the entire room fell into rapturous excitement, forgetting about me (to my relief). Well, everyone but Kaitlyn forgot about me. While the rest of her companions celebrated, she continued to examine me as though forming various and sundry theories behind her intelligent gray eyes.

Under the guise of helping Lila with the dishes, I quickly excused myself. Allyn followed and wrapped me in a hug once we reached the hallway, which I accepted, telling myself to enjoy the contact. It wasn't uncomfortable, I didn't hate it, and that felt like a win.

Once the hug was over, we helped Lila and Melvin with the dishes, and then Allyn sent me and Lila into the living room to scope out a seat. "I'll be right there, I just want to make the winter tea first. I feel like you're going to need it."

By the time Lila and I arrived, everything had been settled but Abram was nowhere in sight. Jenny Vee informed us that the members of Redburn would be playing "Hold A Grudge" for everyone. But first, Melvin was helping them bring up the drum set from the basement studio, which they were almost finished assembling.

It would be an unplugged, acoustic performance. Nicole Mac from Fin would play Abram's acoustic bass guitar so he could just sing, and everyone present had to agree not to film it or talk about it on social media. In fact, Ruthie went around and confiscated everyone's phones, including mine.

Not that it mattered. Reception up here was always spotty at best, which was why I hadn't called Lisa back to whisper-yell at her yet. Abram had told my sister that he loved me, and she never communicated that fact? UNACCEPTABLE!!

Never mind that you never gave her a chance, did you?

Go away, reason. *You can't sit here.*

"How are you doing?" Allyn handed me a mug from a tray of three, her eyes full of sympathy. I gave my friend a grateful smile, though it was of a small diameter.

"No, thank you." Lila shook her head when Allyn tried to hand her one of the mugs. "I'm not much of a tea person. But thank you, honey! Here, just leave the extra one right there on the coffee table, in case one of you wants another cup."

"Are you sure?" Allyn sat on my other side, warming her hands on her mug.

Lila stood to take the now empty tray. "I'm not much of a tea person, but I think I will have a glass of wine. Can I get either of you anything while I'm up?"

We both shook our heads, saying, "No, thank you," in unison.

Lila turned to leave, and I brought the tea to my nose, sniffing.

"Thank you for the tea." It smelled like peppermint and . . . I lifted an eyebrow at my friend. "Is that whiskey?"

"Yes. It's whiskey." She gave me a pointed look and leaned forward to whisper, "How are you? Are you okay? You were weird around Kaitlyn, and you've been really quiet since everyone pressured you into asking the Captain to play his song."

I shrugged, wanting to be honest, but honestly not knowing how I was feeling. Terrified? Anxious? Cold? Hot? Confused? *All of the above.*

The song title, "Hold A Grudge" had struck me as strangely familiar when Allyn told me about it a few days ago. If memory served, I'd said those exact words to Abram while we were in Chicago. But I'd quickly dismissed the notion that the song might've been about me. I couldn't contemplate it. How conceited would that make me? Thinking Abram had written a song about me, and that song was now number one on billboard charts everywhere.

So I'd said, *Get over yourself, Mona,* and then I had (gotten over myself) and ignored the lingering, nagging suspicion.

However, after Abram's harsh words in the study, I was now terrified to hear the song. Given everything he'd said, the chances of the song being about me—about us—felt more like fifty percent than zero percent. Did that make me conceited?

I had no idea.

These days, I felt like I didn't know much about anything.

Sniffing the tea again, I endeavored to clear my mind of these chaotic thoughts and just enjoy the marriage-aroma of whiskey and peppermint. I decided it was a superior combination of smells. Then I took a sip and tried not to cough.

Allyn's eyes widened, her sympathy for my emotional well-being replaced with concern for my physical. "Are you okay? Did I add too much whiskey?"

Swallowing tea and air and half of my tongue, I shook my head. "No. No, it's perfect." My voice was raspy. She looked unconvinced, so I took another sip—more of a gulp—and smiled. It still burned, but the second swallow had been considerably easier.

"Are you sure?"

"Yes. I'm sure. I feel . . . steadier already."

Her worried eyes conducted another pass of my face. "Let's talk about something else. I asked you earlier, about Charlie. He hasn't come up to you tonight. He backed off, huh?"

My gaze shifted to Charlie just as he lifted his blue eyes from where he was setting up the drum set. He sent me a small smile full of compassion and I lifted my chin, hoping to communicate a silent thanks. "Yes. He did. He's a nice guy, that Charlie."

"I saw you talking to him at the top of the hill while we were sledding, when it was just the two of you. The conversation seemed intense. What did you say?" she asked quietly.

I sighed, meeting her gaze. "He asked what I was doing later, so I told him what I thought—at the time—would probably be the truth."

"Which was what?"

"That I'd be in my room crying."

"What?" Allyn stopped herself just before taking a sip of her tea, which was good. From the way she'd said *what*, I suspected she would've spat tea all over me had she taken the drink.

"I told him I was hung up on someone who hated my guts, and rightfully so, because I'd lied and treated him horribly."

"Oh my." Allyn stared at me, a hand coming to her cheek. "What did he say?"

"He told me it couldn't be *that* bad, that he didn't think anyone could ever hate me. And thus, I told him more truth."

"Oh no." She shook her head, looking distressed.

"Oh yes. I told him I'd pretended to be my sister to keep her out of trouble—I didn't go into too many specifics there, since it's not really my story to tell—and the guy I fell for thought I was Lisa. By the way, this is really good. Is that just whiskey and peppermint tea? Or do I detect honey?" I took another gulp and licked my lips. "Maybe lemon?"

"Mona, you told Charlie all of that?" She sounded dismayed.

"Yes."

"Jeez." Her forehead fell to her fingers and she peered at me with obvious worry. "You didn't tell me about any of this until three days ago, and I'm your best friend. Why did you tell Charlie?"

Movement by the room's entrance drew my attention and I turned my head just in time to see Abram walk in. Almost immediately, his eyes came to my eyes, held for a protracted millisecond, and then he glanced away. Metaphorical swords of self-recrimination and want—so much *want*—speared me, sliced me from sternum to stomach, and I had to hold my breath for several full seconds, wait for the room to right itself, and the world beneath to resume spinning.

Please, please, please, don't let this song be about me.

"Mona, are you sure it was a good idea to tell Charlie?"

"No," I answered, more breath than words. "But I wanted to try being honest. . . for once."

"Okay." Abram called everyone's attention to him, which was unnecessary. As soon as he'd entered the room the energy shifted, changed, seemed to flow from him as a single source. He was the gamma-ray burst and we basked in his overwhelming magnificence.

Or maybe it was just me that felt that way.

Regardless, all eyes were already on Abram before he spoke. "Special thanks to Nicole for playing bass."

He gestured to her and she smiled widely, curtseying to the room as they clapped devotedly. Abram took his place in front of the other three musicians. He sat on a stool set a little apart from everyone else, and then—as though taking their cue from him—the other three sat on their stools.

"We're going to switch it up a little, try something we want to do on the tour." He seemed to be speaking to the other group, the larger assembly comprised mostly of musicians who sat closer to the makeshift stage. "It'll be slower, quieter. You can think of yourselves as our guinea pigs."

"Will we get carrots?" Bruce—the cocktail guy—asked, making a few people laugh.

"I'm not throwing you a carrot or a bone, if that's what you're asking." Abram's response made more people laugh, and harder.

I didn't laugh. My stomach hurt, so I went to drink more tea. Sadly, I found it was empty. Licking my lips, I set the empty cup down and picked up the new one on the table, the one Lila hadn't wanted, and took a gulp of the lukewarm mixture. It was still good, heartening, and I felt myself settle a little. But then, Charlie banged his drumsticks together to mark the beat. Suddenly, they were playing.

The intro.

Every muscle in my body tensed and Abram lifted his eyes to mine. Immediately, completely, utterly I was ensnared, caught. Him, the infinite dimensions of Abram, and all else seemed to fade into a void, even the music. I couldn't look away. I was trapped, so trapped.

And then he opened his mouth, and he sang,

"She falls, I catch her.
She fights, I let her go.
It starts, she stops it.
She has to know. She has to know.

I stand, I kneel, I sit, I chase,
But it's like we haven't moved.
We're still here, with the past between us,
This place
I hate
I'm left to wonder what I haven't proved.

This is new, for me and for you.
Nothing you say, nothing you do
Can make me hold a grudge.

Whispers in the dark, stealing touches, holding my breath.
Replaying moments between us, wanting more, taking less
But when she asked for forgiveness so sweetly,
She has to know, she must know,
I became hers completely.

This is new, for me and for you.
Nothing you say, nothing you do
Can make me hold a grudge.

You tell me to go,
But you have to know, you must know,
If this is a mistake, I'm making it
And if this is my chance, I'm taking it.
I can't regret
Never giving up on you

Nothing you can do
Nothing you can do
Will make me hold a grudge
I'll never give up on you.

[11]

HEAT AND HEAT TRANSFER METHODS

Abram

It wasn't how I wanted her to hear the song, in a room full of people, anger between us.

When I wrote "Hold A Grudge," when we were in Chicago, that night she told me to hold a grudge and I stayed up all night writing poetry about her, I'd imagined myself playing it just for Lisa. I had this fantasy scenario where she'd be the first one to hear it set to music.

But now, staring into *Mona's* captivated and captivating eyes, sharing the finishing note, the last reverberations of Ruthie and Nicole's guitars softly fading, I decided this scenario wasn't so bad either.

We weren't alone. She hadn't been the first to hear the words she'd inspired. But at least, for Mona's first time hearing our song—and I could no longer deny that it was *our* song—I'd been able to sing it directly to her. The words were the same as the version on the radio, but I'd arranged the music in a new way.

She'd inspired that too.

I was still angry. And yet, earlier in the evening, when she'd walked into the dining room and our eyes met, the moment confirmed a nagging suspicion: it wasn't revenge I wanted from Mona DaVinci, it was honesty.

Maybe she wasn't the woman I'd fallen for so foolishly and completely. Maybe she was. I had no idea. She gave me nothing. Her wall built of lies remained a barrier between us, yes. But it was Mona's continued *restraint* and detachment that formed the true impassible chasm.

The applause caught me off guard, stirring me from my reflections. Taking one more look at Mona, as she was now—her lovely eyes misty, unguarded, vulnerable, lips parted, expression open and guile-less—and knowing I'd held her attention rapt, I'd had the entirety of her whole being and focus for the span of our song, it felt like enough.

The group assembled, pressed forward, and their rousing apprecia-tion for the new version demanded my attention. Nearly everyone was on their feet, making noise, and I accepted their praise with gratitude. I was grateful the song, and subsequent singles, had done well. I was grateful for the chance to tour with musicians I respected. But that's not why I wrote music.

As soon as the snow cleared enough for me to leave, I decided I would leave. Whatever I'd hoped to find here, whatever I'd hoped to take from Mona DaVinci, or receive from her, it was never going to happen more or truer than this moment. I felt certain that now, right now, was the most honest she'd been in a while, maybe ever. Perhaps she wasn't capable of more, and—if so—that was heart-breaking.

But it's enough.

Decision made, I gathered a true deep breath, my first one in days, and I turned toward Kaitlyn. She'd stood as soon as the clapping started and gave me a smile that was more smirk than grin as she approached.

"You changed the key. D minor."

"I did." I nodded, my gaze flickering to Mona. She was also stand-ing, her hand fiddling with the waistband of her pants. She pulled out an envelope, her eyes were on it, and she unfolded it with what looked like great care.

"Interesting. *Very* interesting," Kaitlyn said, and I shifted my attention back to my friend, she was stroking her chin, looking in Mona's direction. "I have theories."

More people moved around us, telling me how much they enjoyed the new variation, asking Ruthie if she could convince me to play another song, delaying me from responding to Kaitlyn. I turned more fully away from Mona and answered Jenny Vee's questions about our tour dates, Charlie's concerns about the new arrangement, and Bruce's insistent suggestion that he make me a mixed drink, to which I answered no thank you.

Deflecting requests to play additional songs from the album, I mumbled to Kaitlyn when I got a chance, "You always have theories."

"But these theories are provable, and being snowed in is as close to actions occurring in a vacuum as possible outside of a laboratory setting, which is exciting," she whispered on a rush. "I miss doing 'the science.' Ah! Mona! Hello."

My muscles tensed with the knowledge that she was close, but I kept my back firmly to her.

I'd assumed she'd already left. Asking me to play the song hadn't been her idea, she'd been pressured, that was perfectly clear. But we'd had a moment. A meaningful moment. Our beginning and our end had been hers to define, this had been mine. Poetic justice, a way to force closure, whatever it was, that's what I wanted. Now we were done, now I needed it to be over.

"Hi, Kaitlyn." Mona's voice moved over me like a crashing wave, and I closed my eyes for a beat, frustrated because the sound made me hungry.

"Did you like the song?" Kaitlyn asked, tugging on my bicep to turn me around. "If so, which part did you like best? I like the part where he becomes hers completely."

Shooting my writing partner a look I hoped conveyed the full force of my murderous thoughts, I readied myself for the next several minutes and gave Mona my eyes, but *just* my eyes.

Or, that was the idea. But then, I saw she was still misty, her expression still open, vulnerable with raw hope. I had to swallow. The impact of this image, the sight of this woman as she was now, it struck out, overwhelmed.

"Can I talk to you?" She tilted her head toward the uninhabited part of the large room, her typically staid voice laced with optimism.

I nodded, mesmerized by this version of her and mutely followed where Mona led, walking where she walked, stopping when she stopped. She faced me, lifting her chin, her gaze conducting a cherishing sweep of my features. I held my breath.

"Here," she said, giving me a smile that looked brave and nervous. "This is for you."

I blinked at her, confused. And then I glanced down. There, extended between us, was the envelope she'd been unfolding with care.

"What's this?"

"It's a letter."

A letter.

And just like that, all hope, all anticipation, all madness ended. The spell was broken.

"Another letter?" I sounded bitter. I was bitter. The last thing I needed from Mona was another of her letters. The last one might not have been a memo, but it read like one. I didn't want any more fucking correspondence with a salutation of *Regards* or *Best wishes.*

"Uh, yes. But this one is much—much—wait. What are you doing? Wait."

Crumpling the envelope in a fist, I walked to the fireplace.

"Abram." She was right behind me, at my shoulder, her voice edged with panic. "Wait, what—what—oh my God!"

I tossed it in the fireplace, toward the very back where it was hottest, and turned back to her, prepared to tell her where she could shove her memos. The words expired on my tongue.

Her eyes were big, so big, and her mouth gaped wide open with shock, hurt, and what looked like unfiltered rage. I allowed the sight of her obvious pain and fury to slip past my barrier of indifference, because it surprised me so damn much. Mona was looking at me like I'd tossed *her* into the fire instead of her letter.

Jaw working, up and down, big movements, like she might yell at me. Like she might growl and scream at me instead of the snow this time. But she didn't.

At length, she expelled a short breath, I caught the scent of whiskey and peppermint. Using an extremely low voice that sounded barely controlled, she said, "You, Abram Harris—"

"Fletcher," I corrected, noting that she'd slurred *Harris*.

"*Harris*, preside over a kingdom of lies! You call me a liar, but *you* are the liar." The word *lies* was also slurred. *Is she drunk?*

"I'm the liar?" My glare flickered over her, the bright red flush to her cheeks. She wasn't drunk, she was angry and Mona DaVinci looked scorching hot like this. Eyes flashing, a bundle of restless, ferocious energy. I hated that my body took notice, coming to life, the beat of my pulse encouraging me to do unwise things.

"Yes. Your song? 'Hold a Grudge'? It's a lie. You're a siren selling lies to hapless hopeful sailors, where I am the seaman!"

I stepped closer, shoving my face in hers, heedless of the crowd of people on the other side of the room whose voices I could no longer hear.

"Mona," I said, matching her volume, but lowering my voice an octave, "You can keep your fucking memos. I don't want them."

"It wasn't a *memo*!" she said between clenched teeth, her eyes moving from mine to my mouth.

"Oh, it didn't have a subject line?" I taunted, enjoying this, her reaction, far too much, because—*damn*— at least it was honest.

"It. Was. A. Letter."

"I'm sure you can write another one. But you should know, I'll just burn that one too."

Mona looked like she was choking for a moment, and she lifted both of her hands. I thought she might grab me. I thought maybe she might shake me.

Instead, she pointed at the fire. "You, Abram of rotating last names, are a gamma-ray burst! But not in the strong, blinding and beautiful way. Yes, you're that. But I'm talking about the destructive, horrible, chaotic side of a GRB. And you don't deserve honesty, because when it's given to you, you throw it in a fire. You *destroy* it. Here is my official *I bid you good day, sir.*" She turned, slurring *sir*, and released a low, wrathful low growl.

Without thinking, completely on instinct, I reached for her.

"Mona—"

"I say, good day!" she whisper-yelled, yanking her arm out of my grip while doing an absurd little twirling thing with her hand, almost like a salute, and marched away.

Watching her go, my hands on my hips, I slid my teeth to the side, fire in my lungs. Instead of leaving, which was what I'd expected her to do, she rejoined her friend on the couch, Allyn, who was shooting poison darts of dislike in my direction. *What else is new?*

Mona forcefully sat, grabbed her cup of tea, and glared at me over the rim as she downed the rest of its contents. At her side, Allyn made a short sound of protest, her gaze moving between Mona and the cup, and then to me.

Her friend's eyes were wide, rimmed with worry, maybe a hint of panic. Studying the women, I wrestled with curiosity and the impulse to chase after Mona, and to drag her caveman-style into my room. To ignore the pain and the wrong and seize this rare moment of honesty. She was angry? Fine. Let's take our aggression out on each other in ways that didn't hurt, ways that felt good.

Why couldn't *that* be our last moment?

What would it be like to have Mona DaVinci? I winced slightly at the thought, flashes of carnal imagery an assault. It wasn't the first time I wondered. Would she be cold? Rationing her touches? Requiring that I ration mine? Would she tease me? Make me suffer for her? Would she let me tease her?

These were dangerous thoughts to be having with her sitting there, within reach, still throwing knives with her eyes.

Finished with her tea, she reached for Allyn's. Plucking it from her friend's hand, she spilled a little on the couch. Either she didn't notice or she didn't care, because in the next second she was downing that cup too.

The action felt spiteful, like she hoped to punish me by drinking tea, and I couldn't stop the grim smile at her absurdity. I didn't care if she drank tea. I didn't want to care about her. I'd chased her before, I wasn't chasing her again. She was finished with me? Fine.

"Fine," I said quietly, to no one, but knew at once she'd read my lips. Her gaze narrowed, darker, angrier.

So. Fucking. Hot.

Shaking my head at myself, I exhaled a breath that felt like an inferno leaving my lungs and ripped my eyes from hers. Turning aimlessly in the other direction, I commanded my feet to carry me to the far side of the room.

That's when I finally looked up and remembered we had an audience. Kaitlyn—and presumably everyone else—was looking at me like I was someone different, openly gaping, her eyebrows high on her forehead.

We hadn't been yelling. In fact, Mona had whispered every one of her angry words, but our body language must've been unmistakable. Kaitlyn's attention drifted past me to where Mona and Allyn sat, and a small, mischievous hint of a smile tugged her mouth to one side. She started forward, her eyes cutting to mine, her smile growing.

"I'll be right back," she said gleefully.

"Kaitlyn." I made sure my voice sounded like a warning.

She walked faster. "Or I won't be right back."

Gritting my teeth, suppressing a string of curses, I shook my head and sighed. *Great.* Just great. I couldn't wait for Leo to hear about this.

A hand on my shoulder had me glancing over, following the line of the arm to Bruce's sober expression. "Hey, man. Want that drink now?" He held out a glass. "You look like you need it."

I nodded. I took it. I drank it. "Thanks."

"You bet." He gave me a commiserating non-smile. "Let me make you another."

* * *

I didn't have another drink.

I left.

I needed to cool off, and I knew myself. There wouldn't be any *cooling off* with Mona around. Grabbing the snow shovel in the mudroom and not bothering with my coat, I cleared the slate path between the house and the ski lift house. There wasn't much snow, just a few inches, but it was enough.

Calmer, I returned to the house and removed my boots in the mudroom. I was cold, my teeth were chattering, but my skin still felt hot, too tight. Pulling off my wet sweater, I hung it in the closet and took the stairs up to the main floor, intent on my room and the lyric notebook waiting on my desk.

I had no lines, no clear direction, yet something had to give. Even recording the bursts of nonsense running through my mind would be a relief. I'd just climbed the top stair when I heard a loud groan, like a sound of defeat, coming from the living room, followed by sloppy laughter.

"Oh no! Bruce! You're out." Mona's voice stopped me.

It and the words spoken were very un-Mona like.

Swerving from my original destination, I walked slowly toward the sounds, straining my ears for clues as to what I might see when I arrived. More groaning, glasses clinking, laughter, nothing that would have prepared me for what I found.

I absorbed several things at once: only five people remained in the room, playing cards were scattered all over the coffee table and floor, an empty bottle of vodka and a half-finished bottle of whiskey also sat on the coffee table along with too many shot glasses to count, Charlie and Bruce were in nothing but boxers, Jenny Vee and Allyn in their bras and underwear, and Mona.

Mona.

Mona wore the most—wool socks, yoga pants, plain black bra— but her shirt and sweater were gone.

"Hey ya Abram, old buddy, old pal." Allyn lifted her arm and waved, noticing me first, but promptly lowered it, like it was too heavy. She wasn't giving me the stare down. This was probably because she was intoxicated.

"What the hell is going on?" My eyes moved up and down Mona's body, and everything was right and wrong. Right because I missed seeing her skin. I missed her body. I ached for it. But wrong because no part of her body was mine to miss.

"She wanted to play strip poker," Charlie said, pointing to Mona like they were kids and he didn't want to take the blame for getting caught. But the arm he raised offset his balance and he fell over. Laughing. *Drunk.*

Glaring at my drummer—promising, *I'll take care of you later*—I moved my eyes around the gathered circle.

"Where is everyone?"

"They went to bed after the shots." Bruce held his chin propped up with his palm. His chin kept falling off of it. "Armatures." *Drunk.*

"You mean amateurs?" I asked, incredulous, taking several more steps into the room. I'd only known Bruce for a short while, but I'd never seen him drink past his limit.

"That's what I said. Armchairs." He nodded at himself.

Exhaling a short, disbelieving breath, I studied Mona. She was looking at me, swallowing, a glimmer of nerves in the reflexive movement.

But she'd also lifted her chin to squint at me. "You want to play? Bruce is about to lose his shorts, and then he's out."

I flinched, because every word with an *s* sound had been slurred. Gaping, I looked at her, really looked at *her* and not the skin she'd exposed. She was drunk. Maybe not as gone as the others, but she was close. Sitting upright, she swayed. And the eye squint? She wasn't giving me back my glare, she was trying to keep her eyes focused and open.

"Holy shit," I said, shocked. *Shook.*

"No, we're playing five card stud." Mona shook her head, but then kept shaking it, like she couldn't stop once she'd started.

Closing the rest of the distance and kneeling in front of her, I hesitated for a second, and then I placed my hands on either side of her face to stop the motion. "Stop shaking your head. Where is your shirt?" Not waiting for her to answer, I dropped my hands to the cushion on either side of her thighs and glanced around the room. I didn't see it.

"Where *is* your shirt?" Allyn asked, also searching, yawning. "Didn't you throw it outside?"

"That's right. I did."

I looked back at Mona. Her eyes were on me, hazy but hot, moving over my face.

Lifting her fingers, she smoothed them over my beard, up to my temples, tugging lightly at my hair, sending arcing waves of sensation down my spine. Just as unexpectedly, she leaned closer, her lips inches from mine, and whispered, "I want to lick you like an ice cream and eat the fuck out of your cookie cone."

I started, staring, feeling like I'd just been shocked. A throb of energy pressed against my skin, electrifying. Mona's hair was down, pulled out of its braid, and slipped over her shoulders as she straightened, brushing the tops of her breasts. Gorgeous.

But then, holding my eyes, her fingers still tugging at my hair, she wobbled inelegantly. And I remembered.

She.

Is.

Drunk.

Clearing my throat, I ripped my eyes from hers, catching her wrists and removing her hands. I gulped air, released an unsteady breath, and made up my mind.

"Come on." I stood, not looking at her because doing so would've been unwise. Very unwise. *Extremely unwise.* "Let's get you all to bed." Then, before Mona could react or protest, I turned to Jenny Vee. "Do you know where your clothes are?"

[12]

OSCILLATORY MOTION AND WAVES

Abram

After figuring out just how drunk everyone was—very, but not dangerously—I woke up Melvin and Lila. We put Jenny, Bruce, and Charlie to bed first since they were on the main level.

I asked Melvin to help me get Allyn and Mona upstairs, and Lila to put bottles of water and pain relievers next to each drunk person's bed. I also wanted her to double-check on the ladies, make sure they were all still sleeping alone, and lock everyone's doors—whether they'd been drunk or not—*just to be safe.*

They were both nice about it, which I appreciated.

Giving up on finding anyone's clothes, we wrapped Mona and Allyn in blankets. Melvin carried Allyn up under Lila's supervision, and then they both came downstairs to clean the living room.

"Take Mona up." Melvin pushed me away from the coffee table, where I was stacking shot glasses.

"I can take myself up," she said from where she was crawling around on the ground, trying to pick up playing cards. I had to tear my eyes away from the image of Mona on all fours in just yoga pants and a bra, the blanket we'd wrapped around her forgotten somewhere on the floor.

"Sorry about the mess, Melvin." Mona stretched, her back arching as she reached for a king of hearts.

Kill me now.

"It's fine, sweetie." But then to me, in a quieter voice, he said, "Take her upstairs and we'll clean this."

I gritted my teeth, shook my head, working to sweep away my frustrations and focus. It wasn't just the state of the living room, it was the drunk people who'd made the mess. Mona bending over to reach for playing cards under the table, ass in the air, wasn't helping either.

"Let me get the glasses." My voice was rough. I cleared my throat.

"Don't worry about it." Lila gave me a warm smile as she walked in. "This is honestly no big deal. You should see this place after Kimberly and Troy's parties."

"Who?"

"Exotica and DJ Tang," Melvin answered. "One time we had to replace all the carpets after they left." He amazed me by chuckling, like it was a fond memory. "That was *disgusting.* This is nothing."

I decided I didn't want to know.

"Please." Lila came to me, taking the glasses out of my hands. "You take Mona up. I've already put water and a pain reliever by her bed, and I'll be up to check on her once we get this under control."

When I hesitated, she laughed at me. "Really, it's our job. How would you like it if I tried to record your songs or write your music? Now go."

Heaving a sigh, I reluctantly passed the glasses over to her and nodded, feeling shitty about it. This wasn't how I was raised. It felt wrong to leave them with a mess they hadn't made.

Once I found Mona's blanket, I dropped it over her back and scooped her up.

"Hey. Whoa, wait. Why is the room moving?"

Ignoring her, I turned for the stairs.

She was quiet until we were halfway up the first flight. "What are you doing?"

"Carrying you."

"Why?"

"Because you're drunk and there are many stairs."

"Oh yeah. I guess I am. It's a good thing you're so strong, and have this amazing body, otherwise we'd be shoulder hoofing it."

"Shoulder hoofing?"

"You know, I put my arm around your shoulder, you put your arm around my waist, we try to make it work, but someone is going to fall down the stairs." Her eyes were concentrated on the side of my face. In my peripheral vision I saw her lick her lips. "What do you think about my ice cream idea?"

I stiffened, shoving away thoughts about *that,* and had the where-withal to change the subject. "Why did you take off your shirt before your socks?"

"My feet are cold. Also, I never told you, I love the way you smell."

My steps faltered. I blinked, flexed my jaw.

"I'm sorry." She sounded sorry. "Did that make you feel uncom-fortable? If I'm making you feel uncomfortable, I'll be quiet."

"No. That didn't make me feel uncomfortable."

"Good. Because I need to talk to someone about it, and I've never mentioned it to anyone—the way you smell—because it's not some-thing people talk about, but I always want to talk about it."

"You always want to talk about how I smell?" I paused at the land-ing, lifting her higher and readjusting my hold before taking the next flight.

"Yes. Sometimes, when people ask how I'm doing, I want to say: better if I could sniff Abram."

I rolled my lips between my teeth to keep from laughing, keeping my eyes forward.

She wasn't finished. "It's like how chocolate, the really good kind, melts in your mouth. That's what you do, smelling you, does to my body. I am chocolate, and your smell is the mouth in this analogy, and I just . . . melt."

I swallowed. "Maybe you shouldn't talk."

"Why? Am I making you uncomfort—"

"No. But you might not remember any of this tomorrow. I don't want you to say anything you'll regret."

"Well, I will remember it tomorrow, so you don't have to worry about that. And, as for regretting it, I don't think I will. I mean, I'll be cosmically embarrassed, *that's for sure*, but I'll take it like a woman."

"Take it like a woman?" I smiled at the way she'd modified the *take it like a man* turn of phrase.

"Yes. I'll accept responsibility, apologize, be sensitive to your concerns, work to modify my behavior in the future, and suggest we try to find a way forward with minimal awkwardness. You know, take it like a woman."

"What would *take it like a man* look like? In comparison?"

She shrugged, sighed, rested her head against my shoulder. "I don't know. I guess, pretend it didn't happen? Put on a brave face? Take you out for a beer?"

I scoffed. "That's what you think of men?"

"What's wrong with beer and bravery? I think very highly of men. Well, of some men. I think highly of you, and Poe, and Leo, and Dr. Goldblatt, and Melvin, and you."

"You already said me."

"But I think very highly of you, so you deserve to be mentioned twice." She paused, seemed to be contemplating the issue, and then asked, "Do you want me to take you out for a beer instead? Because I can take it like a man. We could arm wrestle! FEATS OF STRENGTH!" She shoved an arm into the air.

"Shh. Mona, people are asleep." Again, I pressed my lips together so I wouldn't laugh.

"Sorry. And sorry if I'm making you uncomfortable."

We reached her floor. I could've set her down and sent her on her way, watched her from a distance to make sure she made it into her room.

Instead, I carried her. I was enjoying her honesty, even if it was fueled by whiskey. "You're not going to say anything that will make me feel uncomfortable, so you don't need to worry about that."

"I bet I can."

"I doubt it." I used her feet to push her door open and stepped inside.

"How much do you want to bet?"

"Nothing, because I'll win." Glancing around at the huge space, I decided setting her on the window seat made the most sense. It wasn't as close as the bed. But it wasn't *the bed.*

"Oh. I'm thinking of something right now and it'll take you from zero to the speed of light on the uncomfortable Richter scale."

"The Richter scale measures earthquakes." I paused in front of the window seat, looking at her in my arms, liking her there, the weight of her, and didn't put her down like I should.

"Yes." She smiled up at me, sighing languidly like she was relaxed and enjoying herself. "But this will rock your world so much, it'll send it hurtling through space *at the speed of light.*"

Smirking, I shook my head once. "Nope." It was time to go.

"Do you want to hear it?" she whispered, like the question was the beginning of a secret.

"I do, very much," I whispered in return, bending to place her on the window seat and preparing to leave. "But I don't want you to say anything that you'll regret when you're sober, and I don't think—"

"I loved you."

I stopped.

I'd just set her down, was currently crouching in front of her, poised to straighten, stand, and leave, and I stopped. I couldn't move.

I looked at her and I wondered how she could believe the words she was saying even as I grasped at them, willing them to be true. My heart shoved itself against my ribcage and the suddenness and pain of it made anything other than complete stillness impossible.

She smiled at me, her gaze tracing my features like she was memorizing them, or remembering them. "See?" she asked softly, lightly, the word a little slurred. "Now you're uncomfortable. I win. Yay."

I shook my head, dazed. When I managed that small movement, I tried speaking. "I'm not uncomfortable." My voice was hoarse.

"You are." Her golden-brown eyes inspected me, still cloudy with liquor, but no less intelligent or assessing. "And if that didn't make you uncomfortable, this definitely will. I'm still in love with you. I'm so very, very much in love with you."

I closed my eyes, wondering if this was a dream. Maybe I was the one who was drunk. Maybe she wasn't here, and this was me wishing.

"Either I'm in love with you, or I'm in love with my guilty feelings. I don't know. I've never been in love, so I have no baseline comparison. Six days! All it took was six days. Nothing about this makes sense. But it has to be love, because how else could it survive two-years of no contact? How else!? It won't go away. And I win. I win at this game." Her confused agony compelled my eyes open.

Did she know what she was saying? What was love to Mona DaVinci? What did it look like? Did it open and stretch in front of her like a cavern, with no way around, no alternate course? Just through and through, into the unknown, the absence of it only coming into focus when the breadth of it was revealed?

"I love you," she repeated, firmer this time, but somehow awkward. "And that—if me saying so makes you uncomfortable, I understand." *Still drunk*, her clumsiness of speech a sobering reminder. *She's still drunk, and these are just words absent evidence or action.*

I shook my head, scattering the hope. Thinking about this now, taking her seriously was foolishness. I'd been a fool for her once. If I could help it, I wanted to avoid being a fool for her again . . . *if I can help it.*

With another deep inhale, I stood. "I'm still not uncomfortable."

She lifted her hands as though to reach for me. "Okay, how about if I said—"

"Mona." I caught her fingers before they made contact, pressed them between my palms. "Please stop talking. You are drunk and you don't want to say these things."

"I do." She stood and I backed away, letting her go and bringing my hands to my hips. Her voice was still a whisper as she insisted, "I do want to say them, I want to shout them. They burn me up with the heat of plasma, molecules of transcendent temperatures boiling inside me."

"Mona—"

"You burned that letter, and I guess I know why. You thought it was going to be more tepid and polite requests. But it wasn't. It was the opposite of polite." It was unclear whether she was speaking to me or herself. She pushed her fingers into her hair, gripping her scalp. "It was all these hot feelings. I'm suffocating, choking on air, because it doesn't smell like you. And now that you're here, I'm still choking, because you hate me, and I don't blame you. I hate me too."

These are still just words.

I took another step away, stalling, needing to clear my throat before speaking. "I don't . . . I don't hate you."

"You should." She glanced up suddenly, her stare glassy but fierce. "You should."

"And you should go to sleep." I lifted my hands, palms out, hoping she would surrender. Talking about this now, while she was drunk, was pointless.

It was pointless, and yet my heart beat frantically, like it was true.

Her eyes followed me as I took another step backward, and then another, this new, unexpected connection between us stretching, the growing distance necessary, but painful. Would it last the night? *God, I hope so.* But I wasn't counting on it.

Mona watched my shuffling movements toward the door. I told myself the deliberateness of my steps was about being gentle, easing out of her room. It wasn't about reluctance, or hungrily admiring her disheveled beauty.

But before I made it fully to the door, she darted forward. "Since I've already said too much, and you're not uncomfortable, can I ask for one more thing? And if it makes you feel uncomfortable, then—"

"Mona." I stopped, clearing my throat, my attention tracing the lines of her body in the low light. I needed to leave. *Now.* "Nothing you say, or ask, will make me feel uncomfortable. Ever."

"But you don't want me to talk." She was fidgety, her stare searching.

"Only because I realize you're drunk, and this isn't you."

"This is me." Pressing her lips together, her forehead wrinkled, like she was suddenly in deep thought. "Or, rather, a part of me I don't like."

That struck me, and before I could stop myself, I asked, "Why?"

"You mean, why don't I like the part of myself that vocalized my problems and angst, and then vomited them all over the person I've victimized? You know, I think it's probably because it makes me a total—"

"You didn't victimize me."

"I did. And if you don't think I did, then I should make you a diagram and write you a proof that proves it. I could, you know."

I didn't want to smile at her threat, but I couldn't help myself. "You're overthinking this."

"Yeah, probably. But that doesn't make it any less true. Why don't you hate me? After everything I've done, you should hate me. I hate that you don't hate me."

Swallowing several versions of the truth, I settled on, "You're very difficult to hate."

"But my actions demand it." She hit the palm of one hand with the fist of the other. "If the world knew what I did to you, if social media caught wind of it, I'd be crucified and they'd be right. And then they'd call you weak for not hating me and wanting me crucified."

"Maybe that's more telling of the problem with social media than with you."

"What? How does that make any sense?"

"Love doesn't have to make sense," I said, thoughtlessly, stupidly, foolishly.

Dammit.

She let out a little breath, like I'd surprised her, and then she swayed. Instinctively, I reached for her, holding her steady. Mona's eyes grew hazier as her gaze moved between mine.

I couldn't think. I worked to shut down the part of myself that was anticipating the morning, and the new confrontation, and everything that—hopefully honesty—would come after. She was drunk. I had questions and I had a list of demands, but those would have to wait, when her confessions weren't tainted by intoxication.

And then her attention dropped to my lips, and she made no attempt to disguise what she was thinking, what she wanted.

Oh hell no.

I wasn't doing this now. Nope. *Is that what this was about?*

I let her go. I stepped away and crossed my arms, clearing my throat of the choking anger.

Fuck her.

I should have fucking known better. I should've fucking *known!*

She wanted me, that much was painfully clear. What had she said earlier? *I want to lick you like an ice cream and eat the fuck out of your cookie cone. . .*

Fine. Alright. Okay. I got it. I understood what was going on here. If she'd proposed sex while sober, before pretending to have feelings for me, at least it would've been honest. But this? Telling me she loved me, she still loved me, and then this? Why had I expected more?

Just leave the room.

I didn't. Like a fool, I didn't.

"You wanted something?" I asked, working to keep my voice free of bitterness. I knew, beyond a shadow of a doubt, what she would ask for. But perversely, I needed to hear her say it. This would be my escape hatch from hope. This would be all the proof I needed.

"I did?" Her gaze was still on my mouth, and she'd leaned forward as I stepped away.

I did not reach out to steady her this time. "You did. You said you wanted to ask for one more thing?"

She blinked, her eyes completely losing focus for a second. She frowned her cute frown and my temper spiked. After tonight, I never wanted to see her again.

"Oh, yes!" She tried to snap, failed, and waved an index finger through the air. "I remember."

"What is it?"

"I'm only asking you this because you've claimed it's impossible for me to make you feel uncomfortable at present, and when I'm drunk, I'm selfish and have no filter."

"Mona, what is it?"

"Can I listen to your heart?"

I started, blinked, confused. "What?"

"Can I listen to your heartbeat? Obviously, it's fine to say no. It's incredibly fine. In fact, I expect you to say no. But, since I've already confessed to plasma levels of being hot for you, and still in love with you, I figured I might as well make it a trifecta of selfishness and mortification—a trifecta squared? An exponential trifecta? A tripod of shame? I don't know, fill in the blank—and just ask for what I really want."

What? "You want to . . . listen to my heartbeat? That's what you want?"

"I do." She nodded, her eyes earnest and eager. "I want to lie next to you." She redirected her focus to the left side of my chest, and she swallowed, gazing at the spot with naked longing. "I want to place my ear right there." Mona lifted her hand and stopped just short of touching me, her breath coming faster, making her voice softer. "And I want to listen to your heart. I want it more than I want to breathe, if I'm being honest. Which I am being honest, as we've established."

I stared at her.

I stared at her, and stared at her, and stared at her. I stared at her and I worked to keep my balance, because the floor and the earth moved beneath my feet. The cavern opened and stretched in front of me. I stared at her and I was afraid, because I knew.

My whole life, from this point forward, I would be a fool for Mona DaVinci.

[13]

ATOMIC PHYSICS

Abram

"Have you slept?"

Startled, my head snapped up and my neck protested, stars flaring in my vision. I winced.

"You haven't slept." Kaitlyn sounded concerned, and when she came into focus, she looked concerned. "Are you okay?"

"Fine," I said, my voice gravelly, and tested my neck. Slowly, I stretched it. Once I was sure it was fine, I stood from the desk, blinked at the room, at the sunlight filtering in through the windows, and I stretched my back.

Kaitlyn wore a frown of intense concern and I realized at once what was bothering her. "I only had the one drink, okay? I didn't get drunk."

My friend's forehead cleared of concern, obviously she'd been thinking I was hungover. "Sorry. I don't mean to hover. But when you left and didn't say where you were going . . ."

"No need to say sorry." I twisted at the waist, waving away her apology. Kaitlyn had seen the tail end of my downward spiral. She'd been a major source of support for me, helping me climb out of the hole I'd dug for myself. She'd seen me drunk. And when I was drunk, I was disorderly. "Do you know what time it is?"

Her attention moved between me and the open notebook on the desk. "It's just past seven. Have you been up all night writing?"

I nodded, yawning, abruptly feeling the lack of sleep. "I had no idea."

"What?"

"That is was so late."

"You mean early." She smiled, but then it vanished, and she leaned a shoulder against the doorframe. "I'm glad you've been writing."

"Me too." I glanced at the lines I'd been working on for the last hour. Or maybe for the last several hours.

"Abram," she said softly, but there was a note of concern. "Do you want to talk about it?"

"Talk about what?"

"About Mona."

Without looking up, I sighed, and then I laughed, shaking my head. "I don't know where to start."

I felt her eyes move over me before she asked, "Start with when you met her originally. Did Leo introduce you?"

I continued shaking my head. "No. Leo didn't—doesn't—know."

How Leo would react to the news of Mona and me—our past or the potential for our future—was anyone's guess. I'd seen him lose his shit with an acquaintance of ours who'd said that Lisa was "fucking hot." But then I'd also witnessed yesterday how he'd worried about Charlie's interest in Mona, like Charlie was the one who needed protecting.

The sound of the door closing brought my eyes up and I watched Kaitlyn march over to one of the leather armchairs by the window. She motioned to the other. "Please. Sit."

I lifted an eyebrow at her. "Is this a therapy session?"

"No," she said, sitting. "It's a *I'm worried about my friend, Abram* session."

"Really?" I shoved my hands in my pockets, taking my time, strolling to the chair across from her. "Shouldn't you be happy? I'm writing again."

"When was the last time you wrote like this? Staying up all night?"

she asked, challenge in her voice. "Was it, perhaps, the last time you saw Mona?"

That earned her a frown. "How did you . . ."

"You said to me once that your ex had messed with your head, made you think you were crazy. But you'd never been more inspired—or written so much in such a short time—than when you had been with her."

"It's not what you think. Mona didn't—" I huffed, pulling a hand through my hair and scratching the crown of my head. I'd taken it out of its binding at some point last night and now it was driving me crazy, getting in my face. "She didn't do anything—"

"You forget, I was there."

That stopped me. We stared at each other.

Her gray eyes looked silver this morning, in the sunlight reflecting off the snow. "I was there to see the after, the crater left by meteor-Mona, if you will."

My jaw working, I slid my teeth to the side and finally sat in the chair across from her. "You seemed to like her just fine last night."

"Oh, I do like her. I still like her, as an impressive person, as a genius astrophysicist, a public figure. But is she good enough for my friend?" Kaitlyn shrugged.

I'd never spoken to *anyone* about Mona other than Kaitlyn. Even then, I'd spoken in generalities. I'd never given her a name, or told our story.

"Fine. I'll allow it. What do you want to say? You think I should steer clear?"

She shrugged again, this time with her shoulders, her face, and her hands folded in her lap. "I honestly have no idea. If you want my advice, you're going to have to tell me the whole story, not just vague bits and pieces."

I chuckled. "You know, just now, you sounded like how Senator Parker does when she's confronting a bullshitter."

"Well, she is my mom. And you are a bullshitter. Therefore . . ." Again, she shrugged with her shoulders, her face, and her hands, but she also grinned. "Come on, Abram. Talk about it. Talk about Mona. Tell me the whole story."

I hesitated, glancing over her head, stalling. Being the object of an elaborate prank, or hoax, during which I'd made a total fool of myself, wasn't something I wanted to advertise. That said, I knew Kaitlyn's concern for me came from a genuine place, which was probably why it was so disarming.

"For the record, I think she's completely crazy."

My eyes cut back to her and I frowned. "She's not—"

"Crazy about you. Crazy weird. All the good crazies."

"You think she's crazy about me?"

"Yes. After you burned whatever was in that envelope last night and left, I sat with her and Allyn. She kept looking for you. And during dinner, when I walked over, I think she'd assumed you and I were together and engaged."

"She did?"

"Yes. The woman was practically seething with jealousy." Kaitlyn widened her eyes, as though still struck by the memory. "I thought she might do me harm."

I was tired, so it didn't occur to me to hide my smile.

"Really, Abram? That pleases you?"

Now I tried to hide my smile. "No. . ."

She lifted her eyebrows.

"Okay, yes. Obviously not the part about her wanting to harm you. But, the fact that she was jealous? I'm not going to lie, I like that."

Kaitlyn tried to look disgusted, but the effect was ruined by the amused curve of her mouth. "It doesn't matter what I think of Mona. What do you think of Mona?"

Studying my friend, I realized what she said wasn't precisely true. "It does matter what you think of Mona, actually."

"What? Why?"

"Because I trust you. I trust your judgment."

Her lips twisted to the side as she studied me in return. "I'll love her just as long as she treats you like the prince you are and recognizes that your heart requires no tenderizing. It's tender enough."

Shaking my head at my friend, I rolled my eyes.

"Don't you roll your eyes at me. You write *poetry* for barnacle's sake. You can't tell me you're not tender. You're like veal, or foie gras, but without the sketchy ethics issues." She leaned forward. "What's the deal? How did you two meet? How did this thing start between you?"

I gathered a deep breath, debating where to start. "It's a convoluted story, and long."

She grinned. "My favorite kind."

* * *

I knew this already, but Kaitlyn Parker was a great listener. She'd asked a few questions when she needed clarification, but otherwise just listened, her features showing only interest.

However, I'd underestimated how much her excellent listening skills would compel me to reveal, which turned out to be everything. Or maybe it was the lack of sleep. Whatever it was, I held nothing back. Once I started, I couldn't stop.

"Wait. What?" Kaitlyn's forehead wrinkled and she gave her head a subtle shake, like she was certain she'd heard me wrong. "She wanted to listen to your heartbeat?"

"Yes."

Her gaze thoughtful, she shifted her eyes to some spot over my shoulder. "That was—is—not what I expected her to ask for."

"Me neither." I leaned forward, resting my elbows on my knees.

My friend's attention returned to me, sharpened, and she nudged my foot with hers. "What happened next?"

I sighed. "I left."

Kaitlyn stared at me, waiting.

I gave her a tight smile.

"You left."

"Yes."

"Without a word?"

"Yes."

Her gray eyes moved between mine, searching. "And then you wrote poetry all night."

"Yes." I studied my left hand, flexing it.

"And now here we are."

"Yep."

She nudged my foot again, more of a kick this time. "What's the plan?"

I exhaled a light laugh, my face falling to my hands. "You know I'm not big on plans. I have no idea."

We were quiet for a minute, separating to steep in our own thoughts. Except, I had no thoughts left. They'd all been transcribed to the pages of the notebook still laying on the desk behind me.

But I was tired.

"You want advice?" she asked, interrupting the silence.

I nodded, rubbing my eyes. "Yes."

"Okay, I'll give you my advice. But first, I need to . . ."

I peeked at her from between my fingers. Her eyes were on me and felt sharp, intent.

"What? What is it?" I let my hands drop and leaned back in the chair.

She inhaled a deep breath, giving me the sense she was preparing herself for an unpleasant task. "But first, I need to provide content to my advice."

"Okay. Shoot."

"You told me once that, before your ex, you used to write lyrics, poetry all the time. It was a compulsion for you, yes?" Her words were blunt, direct, and I expected no less.

I nodded, setting my elbow on the arm of the chair and placing my thumb under my chin, my fingers along the side of my face.

"But then, you broke up."

"As I explained, we didn't break up, and I shouldn't have called her my ex. I didn't have another word, a better word for what—it wasn't—we weren't—"

"Whatever. You obviously thought of her that way at the time, clearly. The issue is the writing. Before her, you wrote. With her, you wrote lyrics that eventually became four hit singles and an album that is on its way to triple platinum. After her, you didn't write. Not at all."

She paused here, as though to let her words sink in, and then she added, "Yes, you revised what you'd already written. You also got yourself arrested a few times, before we met, and made some question-able life choices. As time heals all wounds, those days post meteor-

Mona are behind you. But now—" Kaitlyn gestured to the notebook on the desk, punctuating the movement with a truncated head nod. "You're writing again."

"Yes." I was too tired to figure out where she was going with this.

"That's great. I know you missed it. I know it's been a struggle. And I hope all these new poems become number one hits, or I hope they never get turned into songs at all. Whatever you want, whatever makes *you* happy. But . . ." She trailed off again.

Her gaze seemed to waver, grow uncertain, like she already regretted the next words out of her mouth.

"What? Just say it."

"But what happens when this week ends?"

Gnawing my bottom lip, I met my friend's somber stare, her words echoing in the room, in my head, and in my heart. *What happens when this week ends?*

I was no longer looking at Kaitlyn. I was looking beyond her, into the future, something I rarely—if ever—did.

"Abram," she started gently, "it's Tuesday. We're leaving early Thursday."

Thursday.

Shit. I broke into a cold sweat.

It's too soon. We need more time.

A thought occurred to me. "If the snow lets us." I brought her back into focus. "We might be trapped here for several more days."

"Look outside." Kaitlyn shook her head, her gaze full of sympathy. "The sun is shining. Check the forecast. No snow for the next four days. If Melvin can plow the mountain road, Martin and the rest of the furloughed significant others trapped in Aspen will probably arrive today. We're leaving Thursday, at o'dark thirty. I think the plane leaves at six. You *have* to be in Seattle for Friday's concert. You and the band have been practicing for *months*, you're at the top of your game, the show is sold out."

I made no sign of agreement, even though she was telling me things I already knew to be true. Also true, Mona had finally been honest and I couldn't leave. Not now. Not yet.

She sighed. It was also full of sympathy. "Now that I've provided context, do you still want my advice?"

Staring at her, undecided, I continued gnawing on my lip.

"Abram?"

"If you're going to tell me to let her go, or that it's impossible, or that the timing makes it impossible, then no. I don't want your advice."

Her lips curved and her eyes warmed from stark to compassionate. "That's not my advice."

"Fine." My knee started to bounce. "Let's hear it."

"I think . . ." Kaitlyn sucked in another deep breath, held it.

I wished she'd stop trailing off her sentences. "Yes?"

"I think you should kiss her."

I blinked, confused, and waited for my friend to continue. When she didn't, I felt my face morph into a scowl. "That's it? That's your advice?"

"Yep."

"That's the plan?"

"Yep. I think that's the plan."

I rubbed my eyes tiredly. "I stayed up another hour, telling you everything, spilling my guts, for you to tell me to do something I haven't been able to stop thinking about in over two years?"

"Exactly."

Laughing weakly, I shook my head. "What? Why exactly?"

"My God, man. Kiss the woman. Kiss her senseless. Kiss her and mean it." She waited, looking at me like she expected me to have an ah-ha moment. When I didn't, she made a short sound of exasperation, adding, "You haven't kissed her and it's been over *two years*. Make a plan to kiss her, and then *do it.*"

Maybe I was missing the obvious here, maybe I was too tired to be having this conversation. Whatever. I was so tired, my eyelids felt like paper.

"Never mind." God, I was tired. "I just want to sleep."

"Yes. You sleep. And then, you wake up, you find Mona, and you kiss her."

"Sure." I stood, swayed, and then stumbled to the bed.

"I'm serious, Abram. Follow the plan." Kaitlyn bumped me out of the way with her hip, pulling down my covers.

"I don't understand you, Kaitlyn. You're nuts, and your plan makes no sense."

"Flatterer. Here, let me tuck you in."

I practically fell into the bed. "I can tuck myself in."

"Do you need any warm milk? Should I leave a night-light on?" she fussed, sounding alarmingly like my mother.

"Go away."

"Fine. I will. Do you mind if I take your notebook? Check out the new lyrics?"

I hesitated.

"You know what? Never mind." Kaitlyn held up her hands, palms out. "I'll look later. But in the meantime, kiss her. Kiss the hell out of her. And then we'll move on to the next phase of the plan."

"Which is?" I asked around a yawn, dizzy, sleep irresistible.

"Securing an official clarification of expectations, with roles defined."

"Expectations? Roles?"

"Exclusive. Not exclusive. Boyfriend. Girlfriend."

I liked the sound of exclusive. Maybe her plan wasn't so bad.

"And then," she said, her words punctuated by the sound of the curtain being drawn, "phase three is—"

"How many phases are there?"

"The phases continue until you reach your goal, whatever that is." Her hands were back, and I felt her righting my covers, tucking me in with perfunctory movements. "Hopefully, the goal is happiness, for both of you."

Without thinking, I muttered, "I think I'd die happy if we made it to phase one."

Kaitlyn chuckled. It sounded farther away. I couldn't say for certain because I was already half asleep.

"Then you better draw up a will before phase four."

"What's that?" My words sounded slurred even to me.

"I'll give you a hint, it rhymes with trucking."

My eyes flew open and I groaned, glaring at my friend where she stood holding the doorknob. "Great. Thanks. Now I'll never sleep."

"And rucking. And mucking. And sucking. Actually, it involves sucking—"

I threw a pillow at her.

[14]
FLUID STATICS

Mona

U pon waking, the first thought that popped into my head—the instant my eyes opened—was, *Did I tell Abram last night that I wanted to lick him like an ice cream and eat the fuck out of his cookie cone?*

Or did I dream that?

Staring at the ceiling, studying the vaulted beams of exposed wood, I realized that, no. It hadn't been a dream. And furthermore, the statement hadn't been the most shocking proposal I'd made.

Am I making you uncomfortable?

I loved you.

I'm still in love with you.

I'm so very, very much in love with you.

I'm suffocating, choking on air, because it doesn't smell like you.

Can I listen to your heart?

A rush of mortification—so intense it made me groan out loud—crashed over me. It was a nuclear blast of embarrassment, befitting the gamma-ray burst that was Abram (Harris) Fletcher's death grip on my psyche. Because I could, I ducked under my covers and squeezed my eyes shut, wishing for the wolves to actually come.

I don't know how long I stayed like that, replaying the evening over and over. The moment our eyes met across the dining room, how awful I'd been to Kaitlyn, how beautiful and meaningful his song had been, how brave and foolish it made me—*stupid bravery!*—and how he'd thrown the letter I'd been carrying around for years into the fire.

Into. The. *Fire.*

I'd been so angry. So angry. The closest I'd ever come to that kind of anger was the last time I'd been with Abram, when he'd forfeited the pool race in Chicago. I didn't get angry like that. I simmered, but I never struck out.

But Abram makes me SO ANGRY!

The rest of the evening—the drunken game of strip poker, Abram finding me, the disappointment in his eyes, my sloppy confessions, him leaving without a word after I'd asked to listen to his heart, me crying myself to sleep—made me sad.

Therefore, instead, I focused on the lost letter. I was tired of being sad, so sad. Between madness and sadness, I chose the former.

Tossing the mess of covers from my body, I stood and frowned at my surroundings. He'd been here, in this room, just a few hours ago. When my heart fluttered a little, achy, wistful, I told it to cease and desist. It didn't listen.

Therefore, I left. I rushed through getting dressed, intent on spending some quality cold time in the snow, and marched out of my room. I'd have to see him at some point, hopefully when I was too tired and numb to care that I'd revealed too much of myself, or that he'd repaid my honesty by burning my love letter, and later walking out on me.

I was almost to the mudroom when I heard Leo call my name. "Wait, Mona! Wait."

I turned toward the sound of his voice, and then twisted completely around when I saw he was jogging toward me.

"Leo. Should you be out of bed?" I felt his forehead as soon as he reached my location. He was still warm. "Why are you up?"

"I need to talk to you." His words and his expression were grim.

"Okay. Fine. Let's go back to your room."

Frowning his stern frown, his gaze traveled over me. "Where are you going?"

"Outside. For a walk."

"Here, I'll come down with you."

"You're not going outside, you still have a fever."

He gave me a half-eyeroll. "We can talk in the mudroom."

"Okay. If you're sure you—"

Leo nodded and brusquely walked past, leading the way.

I chalked his abruptness up to still being sick, so when we reached the lower room and he closed the door, I was surprised to see how annoyed he was.

"You know," he started, gritting his teeth, and then exhaled a humorless laugh. "Abram is a good friend of mine. I mean, a really good friend. He and I have been through a lot, and he's always been there for me."

Standing straighter, I flinched back a little, realizing that Leo must've heard what happened last night after Abram played his song. No one had asked me what was going on with Abram, not even Kaitlyn when she came over and sat with Allyn and I on the couch. She'd talked about satellite internet delivery and a non-profit organization that helped provide internet connectivity to underserved areas. You know, the normal stuff women talk about when they hang out.

I'd been thankful for her company and for her lack of Abram-related questions at the time, grateful for the distraction, even though I hadn't been totally distracted. I kept looking for Abram, hoping he'd come back, and unsure of what I would do if or when he did.

Everyone else kept their distance until Nicole suggested shots. Then, we'd all become fast friends. There was no greater bonding agent between strangers than alcohol.

But now I could see, even though Leo's friends hadn't asked me about Abram, they'd obviously asked him.

And Leo was pissed.

"Leo, I—"

"I get it, okay? I should've checked with you first before bringing everyone here. I knew you were going to be here, and I shouldn't have invited a house party."

"It's fine. It's honestly not a big deal. The house is huge, and I—"

"Why Abram?" he demanded, stone-jawed, his feverish eyes flinty. "Why him? He's my oldest friend."

I reared back. "Did—did Abram say something—"

"No. He's asleep. I haven't talked to him yet. Kaitlyn said he was up all night, so he's sleeping now. God, Mona." Leo growled, shaking his head and turning away to pace. "I really don't want to lose his friendship, okay? Can you understand that?"

"Yes. Of course." My instinct was to soothe my brother, especially since he was sick, but I didn't understand precisely why he was so agitated, so I tried again for clarification. "I don't understand why you would lose Abram as a friend, or why you think you're going to. Because we argued?"

I didn't add that, if Abram hadn't walked away from our nutty family already, after what Lisa and I had done, I couldn't fathom what would make him walk away now.

"Because!" He rushed forward, his eyes wide. "He's into you, okay? I heard what happened, and it was obvious to everyone—and everyone was there to see it."

That had me searching the walls around him, hunting for the puzzle pieces I was missing. "Wait. Wait a minute. You're worried about losing Abram as a friend because you think he's 'into' me?"

"Yes," he spat, gritting his teeth, his hands coming to his waist. "Could you avoid him? Please? Just until I get a chance to smooth things over? Or . . . just don't make it worse."

I stared at my brother, my stomach lifting quickly to my throat, and then dropping slowly to my feet with the comprehension of what he was saying.

A short, stunned exhale pushed itself out of my chest. It tasted sour, and I said and thought at the same time, "I can't believe you."

Leo glanced at me, his eyebrows suspending high on his forehead. "What? What can't you believe? That I don't want to lose a good friend?"

"How good of a friend could he possibly be if he let this—supposed feelings for me—impact your friendship?"

Gritting his teeth, he angled his chin, his eyelids drooping to administer a glare.

I wasn't finished. "If Allyn liked you, and you didn't like her—"

He perked up. "You think Allyn likes me?"

"Shut it, Leo. And listen," I whispered harshly.

He snapped his mouth closed and rocked back on his heels, looking feverish and exhausted and confused. And since he looked feverish and exhausted, I worked to harness my temper at his confusion.

I'd walked down here on a cloud of anger, clutching it close, because the only other option had been sorrow. Had I made mistakes with Abram? Yes. Did Leo deserve to lose his friend because of my mistakes? No. Obviously not.

But, dammit. "I'm your sister," I whispered, less harsh, searching my brother's gaze for some spark of understanding. "I would never do anything to hurt you, or Lisa. Or Mom and Dad. I'm your family. I want that to mean something."

He swallowed with what looked like effort and sighed. "It does, Mona. But—" he stopped himself, shaking his head as though to clear it. "Abram isn't the first, okay?"

"What does that mean?"

"It means I lose friends whenever they meet you. They meet you. They fall fucking crazy stupid for you. You shoot them down. They don't want to know me." He didn't sound angry. In fact, he sounded calm-ish, reasonable. He made it all sound so reasonable, and like it was my fault. "I don't want to lose any more friends, okay? Friends are how you make it in this business. It's all about who you know."

My eyes stung. So did my nose. So did my heart, and I asked the first question that popped into my mind. "Would you rather lose a sister?"

Again, he rocked back like I'd surprised him. Again, he looked confused. He struggled. I could see he struggled to respond, and it occurred to me that, had he been well, without a fever, he probably wouldn't be saying or thinking any of this. The temptation to soothe him, to apologize, to promise to avoid Abram—if that's what Leo wanted—surfaced once more.

But the words wouldn't leave my mouth.

Don't be too smart. Don't admit you're smart. Don't think you're smart. Be brilliant. Make some mistakes. Give your opinion. Don't make any mistakes. Stop trying to be perfect. Don't talk so much. Talk more. Don't be too nice. Be nice. Smile. Don't smile so much. Act like a man. Act like a woman. Be assertive. Don't be emotional. Be sensitive. Not too assertive. Be nice to my friends. Don't lead them on. Let them down gently.

I was so tired of walking a tightrope, at work, here, with my family, with everyone. Enough. I'd had *enough*.

Turning from my brother, I pulled on my hat and opened the door leading outside. I shut it. I didn't look back.

* * *

Four hours in the snow, making snow angels, listening to silence, and staring at the sky was just the kind of numbness I'd needed. But now I was freezing my nipples off and needed to pee.

Trudging through the snow, debating what to do with the rest of my day, and deciding something hot was in order, I made it back to the house just after two in the afternoon. I left all my snow clothes in the mudroom closet, my gaze lingering on the sweater I recognized as the one Abram wore last night while he sang "Hold a Grudge."

I hadn't been prepared last night to face the music (pun intended), but I was ready now. Tired and resigned, I was prepared. In fact, I was at peek detachment (i.e. preparedness).

Finished stripping off my outer layer, I swung by the kitchen to grab a bite to eat, and then I climbed the stairs to my room. The basement had a saltwater pool and a hot tub, and both of those options sounded absolutely divine. The idea of a few laps followed by a warm soak sped my movements, and after changing and wrapping myself in a bathrobe, it was back down the stairs, to the basement, past the studio, and to the pool.

The pool was a simple rectangle, and the space in which it was located ran the entire length of the house. It was a long, narrow room that smelled like salt, chlorine, and water. With lounge chairs at one end, the pool and then the hot tub until about three-fourths of the way down, a little shed-type structure at the far end and that's it, every sound echoed.

The shed was set away from the wall and housed a bathroom. Why the original owners had opted for a shed instead of a built-in closet and bathroom, I had no idea. Maybe they wanted to give the illusion of being outside? The walls were painted light blue, like the sky, so that was a distinct possibility.

Leaving my bathrobe on a lounge chair, and after grabbing some goggles from the shed, I walked to the water's edge and dipped my toe in the water. The temperature wasn't particularly hot, I estimated close to 302 degrees Kelvin (84 Fahrenheit/29 Celsius for all the non-physics nerds in the room). But it felt wonderfully warm given how cold my body was after the snow.

Using the pool steps, I submerged myself, my bikini shorts, and my swim shirt, pushing my hair out of the way as I surfaced and wiping my eyes. I'd just turned my attention to the googles when I heard the door to the pool room open. Glancing up from the water, I did a double take, and then my muscles spasmed. I dropped the goggles.

It was . . .

He was—

"Abram."

His deep brown eyes were on me and his shirt was nowhere and those seemed like the two most relevant facts at the moment. Yes, he wore a bathing suit. But his chest—*my God, his chest.*

What looked like a single tattoo covered one side of his torso—the left side—disappearing into his shorts, swirling over his shoulder and down the entirety of his arm. A full sleeve, gorgeous ocean waves in black and gray and vivid blue.

A small, stunned, panting breath escaped me, and I backed up a step. Tangentially, I realized my mouth was hanging open, my eyes were approaching circular, and it was a good thing I was in the pool because I might have been drooling. And his shoulders? HIS SHOUL-

DERS??! No one was prepared for the reality of his shoulders, least of all me.

His gorgeousness felt like an attack. I felt *personally attacked*. He wasn't Hallmark handsome, he was Turkish TV show handsome.

WHAT IS EVEN HAPPENING?!

"Hey," he said, and my eyes cut to his.

He wore a small smile on his lips and in his eyes, and I snapped my mouth shut, swallowing the thirst. But there was so much thirst. So much. So. Much. I was in very real danger of choking on my thirst.

As Abram made it to the pool, walking down the steps and toward me in fluid, unhurried movements, I realized I was not prepared. I mean, I'd been prepared for talking to him, or hearing him talk while I listened thoughtfully, contritely, and apologized for my drunken honesty-vomit. If we'd come across each other in the hall, as an example, or taken our discussion to the study again, I would've been more prepared than an Eagle Scout.

But now?

No.

No.

It was impossible to be prepared because it was impossible to be mindful when one's brain is addled by metric tons of lust. My lust was so huge, so substantial and unwieldy, it probably had its own gravitational field.

The water pushed me, swirled as he approached, the sound of gentle, lapping waves echoing in the cavernous, relatively bare room. And when he was just a few short decimeters away, he stopped. And then he waited.

And then he asked, "Aren't you going to say hi?"

"Hi," I said, the greeting weak, because apparently his body made me a weak woman. *Gravitational lust was a weak force. Good to know.*

His smile widened, his eyes that familiar shade of amber I remembered from Chicago, sparkly and twinkly and hitting me right in the nostalgia amblagada (which was the lesser known, fictional counterpart to the medulla amblagada).

With one more look, he dunked himself under the water briefly, returning to a standing position, but now fully wet. He was so beautiful, it hurt. It hurt so bad.

This is the worst.

I had a nagging suspicion that he was doing this on purpose, that this was payback for the night in Chicago when I'd shown up to the pool wearing a string bikini. He'd looked like he wanted to strangle me. If that's what this was, I applauded him, because his payback plan was a raging success.

And if he'd felt even half as turned on as I felt now? He deserved a standing ovation.

I swallowed, telling my eyes not to look at the droplets rolling down his sculpted chest, or pooling at his sternum. He wiped his beard and eyes and lips, and returned his eyes to mine, like they belonged to me.

"What do you remember?" The question was softly spoken, and he was closer now.

I didn't remember that happening—him moving closer—which made me wonder how long I'd been staring at him, but I did manage to say, "Everything."

"Everything?" He lifted an eyebrow, studying me, his voice low.

"Yes."

"Are you sure?" With this question he drifted closer.

"Yes." I nodded, sobriety finally penetrating the lust fog, because I did remember. With the memory came embarrassment. "I'm sorry."

"You're sorry?"

"Yes."

"For what?"

"For making the mess in the living room. And for—uh—if what I said made you feel uncomfortable last night, I'm sorry."

He nodded slowly, his hands moving back and forth under the surface of the pool, like he was caressing the water. I was now jealous of the water.

"It didn't make me uncomfortable," he said at length, his tone deep and thoughtful, and then asked, "So you're not sorry for what you said."

"No. I'm not sorry for what I said," I responded immediately, telling the truth even though I could feel the heat of mortification climbing up my neck. "I take full responsibility for my actions and my words. I am to blame."

Yesterday, he'd asked me to be honest, *for once*. This was me being honest, for twice. Once last night, again today. No one could claim I wasn't an overachiever at accepting responsibility.

"Even the part where you said you loved me?" The question sounded equal parts curious and taunting. Or maybe not taunting. Maybe . . . defiant?

I angled my chin. "Yes."

He angled his chin in a movement that mirrored mine. "That you're still in love with me?"

"Yes." My voice cracked, I cleared my throat, ignoring the fluttering in my stomach, and repeated more firmly, "Yes." *Ugh. This is hard. So hard.*

"I see." His chin lowered, his lush amber irises seemed to warm, maybe with amusement? "How about the part where you asked to listen to my heart?"

I winced a little and, unable to hold his gaze any longer, I stepped away and dropped my eyes to the floor of the pool. I spotted my goggles. "Yep. I remember that, and I'm not sorry I said it, because it was true. And you wanted honesty. As such, there you go. I remember all of it. Thanks."

Why was he doing this? Was he trying to torment me? What was the point?

"What about us kissing?"

My head whipped up. "What?"

What! WHAT!?! I missed us kissing? If I missed us kissing, I was going to be SO ANGR—

"Calm down." He moved closer, giving me a full smile now, looking like he was trying not to laugh. "I'm joking. We didn't kiss."

A gush of air escaped me, my shoulders slumping, my forehead coming to my hand. *Thank God.* But also, *darn.*

Abram's eyes were on me. I felt them. I also felt the water push and swirl again. Between my fingers I saw he'd come closer.

"Mona."

"Yes?" I shivered. The way he said my name, it was the auditory equivalent to being stroked.

"Will you be brave with me?"

My eyes stung, I shook my head, and I continued to be honest. "I'm so tired of being brave."

That seemed to give him pause. His hand came to my arm, curled around it gently, and smoothed down to my elbow, his palm hot against my chilled skin. Other than shaking his hand that first day, was this the first time we'd touched since Chicago? It felt like . . . it felt indescribable. A terrifying relief was the closest description I could summon.

Abram tugged on my arm, bringing me closer, his other hand sliding against my cheek and lifting my chin. My fingers fell away from my face. I braced myself. I felt like I might crack, splinter from the hum of uncertainty and anticipation.

I don't know what I expected, but when our eyes locked, his were an odd combination of kind and covetous. "Then will you let me know you?"

I pressed my lips together to keep my chin from wobbling. "Why? To what purpose?"

The question seemed to amuse him. "I need someone to listen to my heart." His face inched closer. "And it only wants to beat for you."

Wha—

Bah!

Argra!

DAMN POET!

It was no use. I couldn't stop the tears. Wherever fear meets hope, that's where I was. I wanted to believe him. I wanted it so very, very badly. But he'd been intensely angry with me just days ago. *Too fast. This is all happening too fast. And I know better. He is a wildly famous musician! You will be just one of his many consorts!!*

"Are you going to hurt me?" I blurted, knowing I sounded broken. Gripping his wrist, I gave myself permission to enjoy the strength of him, the solid sturdiness, even if it ultimately turned out to be a lie. "Because if this is payback, you win. You win. Consider me punished. I surrender."

His eyes grew impossibly soft, concern etched itself between his eyebrows. "No."

No.

What he really should have said was, *Not yet.* Because, eventually, he was going to leave, or I was going to leave, and it was going to hurt.

"I don't understand what's happening. You said—" I sniffled, shaking my head, blinking against hot tears, "You said you regretted it. You said you weren't—that you didn't know me, and that you didn't—"

"Shh. Don't cry. Please don't cry."

Abram brought his other hand to my opposite cheek and pressed his forehead against mine, our stomachs, hips, and legs brushing, warm accidental touches that set my pulse racing. I couldn't think.

"Mona, I *don't* know you, not really. You keep everyone at an arm's length. But you've given me glimpses, scraps, and they've only made me hungry for more."

His right hand slid down my jaw to my neck, curling around the back of it; his left hand smoothed over my shoulder, to my arm, and gripped my waist, pulling me to him evocatively; one of his legs moved against mine, bracketing it, and he angled his body such that all those accidental touches now felt powerfully purposeful.

I felt myself shake with the effort to hold still, but not because I wanted to push him again. For once, for the very first time, I was surrounded and overwhelmed by another person and my instinct was to draw him closer, ever nearer, sink into him, merge our bodies together, accept his strength and cocoon myself within.

Abram's nose nuzzled mine, his lips brushed my lips with the faintest of touches, and he whispered, "Let me in."

[15]

FLUID DYNAMICS

Abram

S he was shaking.

The plan had been to find her and kiss the hell out of her. But she was cold, and shaking, and crying, and it wrecked me.

I made a new plan. I wrapped my arms around her, my intention was to hold her for as long as she'd allow, but Mona surprised me by lifting her chin and pressing her lips to mine.

Fuck. . . YES.

Without inhaling, my lungs filled, and I heard a single note between my ears, perfectly pitched, traveling down my spine and heating every nerve ending with carnal, electric *want*. I'd wanted this for so long, it seemed there'd never been a time I hadn't thought about it, fantasized about this moment with her.

Her hands gripped my sides, her nails digging into me, anchoring me, as though to ensure that—should I withdraw—I wouldn't leave unscathed. As punishment? I found I didn't care, or couldn't, because her lips parted and I wanted *in*.

My tongue swept inside. She moaned, sucking, swallowing, her mouth slick and soft and fiery hot. I moved instinctively, walking her backward, charging forward as though I could enter her this way, gain access to the furtive parts of her through strength and force. And she, rather than stumble backward, jumped slightly and wrapped her legs around my waist.

Fuck, I was hard. My mouth alternately devoured and sipped her. *So hard.* My body selfishly sought relief as her back met with the wall of the pool. I rocked against the apex of her legs, spreading her wider, and she tilted her head back to gasp, shivering again.

But then her mouth immediately returned, fused to mine, and she tilted her pelvis—up and down—using me, rubbing herself on my cock through the layers of our bathing suits.

This is insane.

A spark turned inferno. My skin hindered me. I grew frustrated by the constraints of my body. It only imprisoned, subjugated and diminished this transcendent craving, reducing the wonder of it to something merely carnal, physical.

Her breath hitched and she broke away to suck in air while her body chased friction, bouncing clumsily, riding the length of my shaft as sparks and flares and bursts of hot promise ignited at the base of my spine.

But I wasn't inside her, and I wanted *in*, every barrier removed. I wanted inside her, all her secret places. I wanted her open, exposed, bare, and hot, and wet, and panting . . . and I pictured her that way. Even with my hands on her now, even with her clothed pussy sliding over my dick encased in my board shorts, I saw her naked, reclined, reaching for me, wanting *me* to be *inside*. That's what I saw. Not this imperfect, clumsy, hurried grasping.

This is insane.

A corner of my mind told me that this wasn't part of the plan. I'd hoped for a sweet moment, a step toward something lasting. Not this lascivious spiral we'd been sucked into, humping like mindless animals.

But maybe that's what we were.

Everything about this—how she grabbed me, how hot I burned, her nails digging into my back and sides, scratching, biting at my mouth, how I rocked against her greedy strokes, held her confined, reached my hand beneath her swim shirt to grab and pinch and twist one of the softest parts of her body—was animalistic and base, depraved and instinctual. On a physical level, it felt fucking amazing. But . . .

Is this what you want?

She blinked at me, like she was startled, and I realized I'd said the words out loud to her, a question meant for myself.

I flexed my muscles, tensing, thrusting against her open legs. She shuddered.

I repeated, "Is this what you want? For us?" I massaged her breast, circling the peek mercilessly with my thumb. "You wanna fuck?"

Her eyes dazed, a puff of breath leaving her, she whimpered, and she said, "No," like it cost her, like she wasn't sure.

But a no is always a no.

I swallowed, torn between relief and brutal frustration, and relaxed my hold. We were both breathing hard, and the effort required to remove my hands from her glorious skin felt like slicing my body in half. But I did. Reminding myself that I wanted *in* helped, made stepping away easier as her legs slipped from around my waist. I backed away, my hands on my hips. I wanted to conquer and be conquered, to be broken and reassembled using her pieces.

I retreated. For now.

Looking at her from across the pool, watching her suck in air, gripping the edge, her gaze still dazed and hot and conflicted, I knew taking Mona now wouldn't do a damn thing other than make us feel good—really fucking good—for one moment. I didn't want one of her moments, I wanted all of them. I wanted an invasion, not a visit.

"What are you thinking?" she asked abruptly, her searching eyes moving over me.

I cleared my throat. "I probably shouldn't say."

That made her frown, so I quickly added, "It involves you being very naked."

Her frown cleared, and the side of her mouth twitched. "Very naked? As opposed to just a little naked?"

I wasn't ready to smile, because my dick hated me, and I spoke to stall, just for the sake of speaking. "Yep. My cousin's friend was a lingerie model at some ridiculous shop in the Northeast, and one time she told me there are stages of naked."

Mona's eyebrows pulled together, but not in a frown. "Stages of naked? What stage is fully naked? I mean, with no clothes?" She sounded curious.

"Stage five."

Her eyes moved up and to the right, to some spot over my head. "Then what's stage one?"

Sexy lingerie.

I cleared my throat again and shook my head, needing to clear it. "I'll tell you later."

"Why? Is it bad?"

"No."

"Will I hate it?"

"I hope not."

That made her smile. "I think I figured it out."

I laughed, shaking my head again. Her smile widened and she wrapped her arms around herself, like she was cold. We needed to get out of this pool. Surreptitiously, I tucked my erection up and to the side, into the waist of my shorts, and tried not to wince at the action. I didn't want it tenting my wet suit. She'd already felt it, so I didn't think Mona needed to see how she affected that part of me.

Also, I didn't need my dick leading the way.

"Come on." I waded toward her gingerly, cock throbbing from how I'd concealed it, my hand outstretched, my voice rough. "Let's go."

She glanced between me and my fingers, stepping forward to grab them. "Why?"

"You're still cold."

"I don't feel cold," she muttered.

"Your skin is cold." It was. Her fingers were chilled where they tangled with mine. "Let's go warm you up." Tugging, I led her to the pool steps, careful to stay in front of her just in case my erection slid free of the waistband.

"Where are we going? The hot tub?"

My steps faltered and my balls ached. "Hot tub?" *What the hell?* Was that my voice?

"Yes. Right over there."

I swallowed around the thick band of lust and glanced at the hot tub, but only allowed myself a glance. Otherwise, I wouldn't be able to get the resultant image of Mona out of my brain, and tonight's lyrics would be brought to you by the words horny, hot, and tub. For an unknown reason, I felt like punching something.

"Bad idea," I rasped.

She studied me, her gaze beautifully earnest. "If you don't like the one in here, I have one in my room too."

Oh God. "What?" And what the fuck is wrong with my voice?

"It's actually on the balcony, not in the room."

My body quickly pocketed this information, hoarding the knowledge for later, just in case we were to find ourselves in her room and struggling with boredom. By the end of the day tomorrow. *Torture.*

"I was thinking more like hot tea, or hot chocolate." I made my voice deeper to disguise the strain of speaking while my brain fought a losing battle against my imagination. "Something warm to drink."

"That sounds great. I guess I am a little cold," she said, her lips now a shade of purple. "If I'm cold, I love anything hot."

"Me too," I said, my voice rough.

Something hot would be more than appreciated, it would be necessary, especially after the cold shower I was about to take.

*   *   *

As she dried off, I wrapped my towel firmly around my waist, and then walked Mona to her room, relieved to find she'd brought a huge bathrobe to cover herself, and not just because she was cold.

We agreed to meet in the kitchen, drink something hot, and talk.

I didn't care what we talked about, I just needed to hear her speak, about anything. I suspected the last time we'd had a meaningful, genuine conversation was after I'd taken her to Anderson's Bookshop in Chicago. Now I wanted to know how much of that dinner conversation had been the real her, and how much had been Mona pretending to be Lisa.

I wanted to believe she'd been 100 percent herself, but I didn't *know.*

Mona was already in the kitchen by the time I'd arrived, pulling spices out of the cabinet. She looked up as I walked in.

"Hi," she said, swallowed, and gave me a small smile.

"Hey," I said, giving her a much larger one, and crossed to her.

I watched her carefully as I approached, how she reached for and gripped the counter behind her, how she tensed, but also lifted her chin, her eyes on my mouth.

She wanted to be kissed? Wonderful. In fact, *fantastic.*

Bending my neck, I gently slid our noses together—she'd liked that in the pool—and pressed my body and my lips to hers. *Soft. So soft. Velvet and satin and heat.*

A tension I didn't know I'd been carrying relaxed, and my mind quieted. Kissing her, I wanted more, but I also calmed. A new kind of restlessness surfaced. Anticipation.

The goalposts were moving: Talking without anger. Honesty. Forgiveness. Touching. Kissing. *What's next?* I couldn't wait to find out.

Immediately, she also relaxed, lips parting, and she sighed. Mona's arms encircled my neck, and I kissed her again, this time catching her bottom lip lightly between my teeth. I licked it, loving how slippery and hot and delicious she tasted.

She moaned—arching, pressing, straining—a hitching breath, a needy sound, and I knew it was time to back off.

Removing my hands from her body, I placed them on the counter behind her. But I wasn't ready to cede our closeness. Lowering my face to her neck, I whispered, "What are you making?"

"Hot chocolate," she whispered in return, tilting her head to the side, exposing her soft neck to me, her hands sliding to my biceps. "Do you want some? Or do you want tea?"

"Which do you prefer?" Unable to help myself, I placed a hungry kiss where her graceful shoulder met her equally graceful neck, inhaling something mild, and sweet like cream. "You smell good."

"It's just soap." She was still whispering, and every time I spoke against her skin her body arched in a lithe, reflexive movement. She continued, "And I love both tea and hot chocolate. But I have to be in the mood for hot chocolate, and I am, so I'm making it."

"I'll have what you're having." I placed one more kiss just under her jaw, and then pushed myself away. She smelled too good, she felt too good, she tasted sublime. I could've spent all day with my nose in her neck, her body flexing and rubbing against mine. But the frenzy between us, the urge to touch and be touched, didn't need to be stoked. We needed space, and conversation.

Gathering a steadying breath, I turned from her, closed my eyes to gather myself, and reluctantly crossed to the stools at the end of the island.

Place granite between you. Good idea.

The stool creaked under my weight and I watched Mona move around the kitchen, a little wrinkle between her eyebrows. She pulled out a can opener and a can of sweetened condensed milk, setting both in front of me.

"Will you open that, please?"

"Sure." I was happy to. "What's this for?"

"For the hot chocolate." Mona placed a saucepan on the gas range, the burner clicking three times before catching.

"You use sweetened condensed milk?"

"Yes. I also use unsweetened cocoa powder, which is why I use the sweet milk. This isn't my favorite hot chocolate recipe, but we have all the ingredients, so . . . "

"You have hot chocolate recipes?" I grinned. "What's wrong with the powdered stuff?"

"Nothing. But I like to make the good stuff."

I finished opening the can and pushed it toward her. "You make the good stuff every time?"

She grabbed the can and scraped out the thick liquid with a spatula. "Yes."

"Fancy," I teased.

Her eyes lifted, connected with mine, and she promptly returned to her task. "I rarely have hot chocolate, so I want to make it count."

Considering this, I watched her place the ingredients into the saucepan—the milk, the cocoa, cinnamon, cardamom, orange zest, a pinch of salt—and a thought occurred to me.

I hadn't decided whether or not to share the thought when she said, "You look like you want to say something."

"I was just thinking." I tugged on my beard, just under my bottom lip. "I'm not saying this is the case, but maybe you only like having hot chocolate so rarely because you only drink the kind that requires a lot of work and cleanup."

She stood at the range, stirring the mixture with a whisk, splitting her attention between me and the hot chocolate. "It's not that much work."

I moved my eyes to the orange and the zester and the measuring spoons and the spices. "Not everything worth having requires a struggle. Sometimes, things that are easy are also very, very good."

Her lips quirked to the side. "You say that, but just wait until you drink this." She nodded to herself. "Then you'll be singing a different tune. Struggle can sometimes make the end result so much better."

"The end result is the end result. A struggle doesn't change it."

"Ha! I disagree."

I leaned my elbow on the countertop, placing my thumb beneath my chin and pressing my index finger along my bottom lip. "How so?"

"Because then you know you've earned it."

My eyebrows jumped. "Does everything have to be earned?"

Mona kept her eyes on the saucepan, and it seemed like she was working to keep her features free of telling expression. "Not everything. Just most things."

"Really."

"In my experience," she said quietly, her lips thinning.

I blinked at her, because a great deal of Mona DaVinci had just come into focus, and this clarity had me asking, "You expect people to earn a place with you? To prove themselves?"

Her frown was immediate, and she looked confused as her gaze searched mine. "What?"

"You expect people to struggle? To earn a place?"

Now she reared back, looking genuinely perplexed by my conclusion. "No. Of course not."

"Then what did you mean? 'In your experience'?"

"Just that—" she shrugged, stirring the hot chocolate faster "—I don't want anyone to give me something I don't deserve. I want to feel like I've earned what I have, then I know it's mine." She sighed, and then huffed a laugh devoid of humor. "And, believe me, I understand the irony of my statement. Here I am, in my parents' mansion, surrounded by luxury I had nothing to do with."

I want to feel like I've earned what I have.

Huh. . . *well, damn.*

A conversation I'd had with Melvin the evening Mona had arrived resurfaced in my memory, felt pertinent to the conversation she and I were having now. Suddenly, it was difficult to breathe.

Mona brought her own food. She made her own bed. She cleaned up after herself.

"Did you pay for your own college?" I asked.

Mona gave me a funny look. "Yes. Kind of. I had a scholarship."

"And now? Grad school?"

"Yes. I have grants, and scholarships."

"What about living expenses?" I was being tactless, but now that the suspicion surfaced, I needed to know. "Who pays those?"

Mona closed one eye, scrunching her face, and peeked at me through the other. "I do. Why?"

Of course.

"What did you get your brother for his birthday?"

She swallowed. "A few things."

"And what did he get you?"

Her lips thinned again. She didn't answer.

I stood. "And your parents? Did you get them anything?"

She shrugged.

"And they sent nothing, right?"

Mona tucked her lips between her teeth and when she lifted her eyes to mine, they were cool, aloof. "What's your point?"

The urge to wrap her in a hug had my feet moving before I'd told them to and I gave myself a mental kick for having it backward. Mona didn't expect anything from anyone. She'd saved her sister, because that's who she was.

Which meant what for us?

Did she think she needed to earn me? Conversations, interactions between us—both here and in Chicago—reframed themselves, and one in particular struck me as important.

"When we were in the pool, in Chicago," I started carefully, trailing my fingers on the kitchen counter as I moved slowly closer, absorbing every shift and change behind her gaze. "When we raced."

Mona straightened her spine, her attention darting over every part of me except my eyes. "What about it?"

"What were you trying to earn?" Her anger at me, when I'd forfeited the race, had never made sense. I stopped swimming because I didn't want to fight with her, and also because seeing her in that bikini had been torture.

Currently, Mona pressed her lips together, swallowed again, and when she spoke her voice was gravelly, quiet. "If you remember, the bet was that whoever won got to stay and do laps, and the other person had to leave. I wanted to earn the right to stay and swim laps."

"But that wasn't the reason why you were angry. What were you really trying to earn?" I'd made it to where she stood, still stirring the hot chocolate, but I didn't touch her.

She huffed another laugh, this one sounded nervous. "It was—I was being silly." She turned off the stove, wiped her hands on a towel, her movements fidgety.

"Tell me."

"You want honesty," she said, and I got the sense she was talking to herself, reminding herself. "If you want to know the truth, fine. I made a secret bet with myself too. That if I won the race, then I'd, uh—" she crossed to a cabinet, finishing her sentence with her back turned while she pulled mugs down for the hot chocolate "—I'd tell you the truth, right then, about who I was and why I was there."

I flinched, stunned, blinking rapidly, feeling like I'd been slapped. Holding my breath for a moment so I couldn't—*so I won't*—yell, *are you fucking kidding me right now?*

Instead, I waited. I stalled. I tried to think of as many words as possible that rhymed with *regret*—which ironically included *bet*—and then I switched to the word *resentment.*

I waited until the edges of my vision cleared, and then I did my best to match my volume to hers, since what I really wanted—what I really fucking wanted—was to rage. "But you didn't. You didn't tell me."

How different would things be now if I'd just finished that damn race? She'd been winning. She was so fast and fierce, and it had turned me on to the point of torment. I hadn't wanted to fight with her any more. I'd wanted to lift her to the edge of the pool, pull the tie on that flimsy bikini, and taste her, make her come with my mouth and fingers, right there. And then I'd—

Stop.

Back up.

Take a deep breath.

Shit.

There was no hiding from that night. I'd dreamt about her and that night many, many times; and we did many, *many* things in those dreams; but none of those things included fighting.

"I didn't tell you because I didn't win. You forfeited and I didn't earn the right to tell you," she said, making it sound entirely reasonable in retrospect. But at the time, she'd been angry. She'd been furious.

I didn't earn the right. . . My bones ached, my breath became shallow with the effort. What happened to her to make her this way? Make her think she wasn't deserving? That she needed to earn the right to tell the truth and take what she wanted? And what would've happened if I'd pushed her?

What if I'd kissed her? What if I had lifted her to the edge and untied the bikini? What if I hadn't been patient?

And what does this mean for us, now?

Mona's shoulders were stiff, and she seemed to take a few deep breaths before returning to the range and to me. She didn't look at me. She served the hot chocolate and handed me my cup first.

"Thank you," I said quietly, my fury slowly morphing to frustration, and then to grief.

Looking at her now, at her lovely face, so deserving of every beautiful, wonderful thing, I couldn't help but think back to real Lisa, not

Mona-as-Lisa, and what she'd told me about making other people happy.

They have to do that for themselves, she'd said. Was she right? I had no idea. I hoped not.

Setting aside my mug, I took Mona's cup from her hand, drawing her hesitant and beautiful gaze to mine. I wrapped her in my arms and placed a lingering kiss on her neck. I held her tightly and I stroked her back.

"You deserve everything," I whispered.

Instead of relaxing, she held me tighter.

I hoped Lisa was wrong. I hoped, if you love someone enough, it was possible to show them what they deserved, and be their source of happiness.

[16]

ATOMIC MASSES

Mona

I awoke to the sound of a heartbeat, and I smiled.

Blinking open my eyes, I carefully lifted my head from Abram's chest, doing my best to make as little noise or movement as possible while propping my chin on my palm and gazing down at him. He was divine. And he was 100 percent asleep.

What time did he come to bed?

After hot chocolate, the conversation had become much lighter and easier. I hypothesized Abram was trying to stay away from heavy topics after grilling me about whether I paid for my own school and whether my family reciprocated birthday gifts. They didn't, but I honestly didn't mind. I was a hard person to buy gifts for—as my sister and my mom's personal assistant in charge of shopping had told me countless times—and I appreciated the fact that they didn't send me things just to send me something.

It was fine. I was fine.

And I was grateful he'd dropped the topic. I'd wanted to spend time with him, get to know him, not discuss my family.

We'd talked about so many things, including how I didn't like cereal, or anything that grows soggy, and that my favorite element on the periodic table was sodium. Then, he'd made a periodic table Chuck Norris joke, and I'd laughed with more gusto than I'd expected, surprising myself. Which led him to telling his entire arsenal of Chuck Norris jokes for at least a half hour. I laughed so hard my face hurt.

Lila came in at that point to start dinner and Abram asked her if she could make ours to go. That earned him a look from me.

"What?" he'd asked, drinking the rest of his hot chocolate, his gorgeous brown eyes dancing.

"If we're both missing, people are going to notice."

"Let them notice." He placed a soft kiss on my forehead, followed by another on my cheek, and then the corner of my mouth, his beard brushing against my face. *Holy particle accelerator, Batman.* My stomach fluttered mercilessly.

And then he'd followed up the kissy-face treatment with, "I only want to be with you."

He was too good with the words. *Damn poet.*

I glanced at Lila, who was trying not to be too obvious about watching us. Regardless, I felt myself smile.

We had our meal in the solarium on the second floor, just the two of us, but I made a point to leave a note for Allyn under her door. I wanted to give her a heads up. She'd integrated with the group just fine, genuinely seemed to be having a good time, but still. I'd been the one to invite her. I worried I was being a bad friend leaving her alone for dinner again.

Abram proved to be an excellent distraction from my worries. I didn't typically mind quiet. I've never been one of those people who felt compelled to always fill it, and Abram didn't seem to be either. But, between the two of us, there was no break in conversation, no spots of silence. Every void was filled, every empty place occupied, and it didn't occur to either of us to check the time until I suppressed my second yawn.

"It's late," he said, and my stomach dropped as he showed me the time on his phone. "And as much as I want to keep you up all night talking, you need to sleep."

"What about you? Don't you need to sleep? You should sleep. We could both sleep." We'd been sitting on the couch under the lemon tree, facing each other, holding hands over the back of the couch. It was SO AWESOME!!!!

I thought I was already melty and relaxed, but his small, sexy grin liquified me. "Mona DaVinci, do you want to sleep with me?"

I tried not to smile, but I failed so hard. "Honestly? Yes. Sleeping with you in Chicago, in the theater room, is one of my fondest memories." At this point, after the day we'd had, confessing these small truths didn't feel brave anymore. With every confession, he made me feel less and less self-conscious, always confessing something in return.

I almost forgot that we were doomed. *Doomed like a dying star.*

"It's my heartbeat, isn't it? That's what you're after."

Yes. It's you're heart I want. "Yes. It is. And your body. I really love your body."

"I really love your body," he said, like it was an easy and natural thing for two people to admit to each other, making my own heart do a wonderful and painful flip-flop. "But I need to write before I can sleep."

"Okay." I nodded tiredly. "I can stay up for a while longer. If you don't mind the company, I can read while you write. I finished the books I brought, but I have two journals I need to read before I leave."

Abram's gaze dropped suddenly and so did his smile. Before I could ask him about it, he said, "How about you go to sleep, and when I'm finished, I'll come up and lie down with you? No pressure."

I was already nodding enthusiastically before he'd finished. "Sounds great!"

And that's what we'd done. He'd tucked me in with a toe-curling kiss, and then left. But now he was here.

As I looked at him, sleeping so deeply, I realized, in addition to still wearing his jeans and long sleeve T-shirt, he was lying above the covers. Smiling at his strangeness, I took a moment to study his face, working to memorize every detail. I then placed my head on his chest again and listened to his heart.

I'm going to miss this. A lot.

Sadness abruptly weighed down on me, felt as tangible as the blanket covering my body, and I squeezed my eyes shut. The Abram chant sounded between my ears, telling me to be honest, telling me this was fleeting, telling me to be cautious, reminding me that I was leaving on Sunday.

I tried to reason with my reason, asking myself, *What is the harm in staying a little longer? Will listening to the cadence of his heart now make leaving him later more difficult?*

YES!

Absolutely. Yes.

Dammit.

Allowing myself to linger, to grow used to this closeness, would just make everything worse in the long run. I needed to get up. I needed to keep living my normal life. I couldn't pause it, like I'd done the last time, because reentry into reality would feel impossible and I'd crash.

If I were smart, I'd start distancing myself now.

. . . Just another ten minutes.

My heart squeezed and I held my breath. Yesterday had been wonderful, and I would treasure it and whatever time we had left. *Always.* But smart Mona was right. And unfortunately, smart Mona was also the primary decision maker.

With great care, I lifted away from Abram's glorious heart and body, and rolled out of the bed. The effort required made my pulse hammer between my ears. Standing, I hurriedly turned back to Abram and covered him with the blanket, I didn't want him to be cold.

And then I walked quietly to the bathroom and began going through the motions of my normal day.

* * *

I left Abram a note on the side table. On the envelope I wrote, "DO NOT BURN," hoping it would make him laugh. Though I was still a little sore about him burning my letter, and I sorta mourned the loss of it, I recognized now that I'd dodged a bullet.

My first draft of the new letter read,

~~Abram,~~

~~Dear Abram,~~

My dearest Abram,

I hope you ~~slept well~~ had sweet dreams. When you wake up, ~~and if you feel inclined, please~~ come find me. I'll be in the solarium reading until the afternoon, and then I think I'll go outside and take advantage of the sun and the snow. I'll be by the sledding slope. Maybe I'll build a snow fort! But ~~I'm happy to modify my plans if you'd prefer to do something else~~ I'm up for anything ~~if you want to spend the day together.~~

~~Regards,~~

Missing you.

Love, Mona

The final version didn't have all the strikeouts, obviously, and it struck me as reckless. I'd fretted over the word *love* for far too long, but eventually committed to it. It felt like the truth, so it stayed.

I didn't see anyone as I walked down the stairs and halls leading to the kitchen, but I did hear conversation coming from the living room. I wasn't avoiding anyone, but I was hungry, so I decided to stop by the kitchen first, eat, and then seek out Allyn.

As it turns out, the two activities weren't mutually exclusive. Allyn was sitting at the kitchen table next to Leo, and the way they seemed to be so entirely engrossed in each other, and whatever they were talking about, made me smile. Even though I was still annoyed with my brother about our conversation yesterday, I wished him nothing but the best, and Allyn was *the best.*

"Hey, Mona." Kaitlyn's greeting had me turning toward her voice.

"Oh. Hi, Kaitlyn. How are you?" I hadn't spotted her when I first walked in. She was standing by the refrigerator, holding a carton of half-and-half.

"Great!" she said, her smile bright. "I don't think you've met Martin yet?" Lifting her chin, she gestured to a man, another person I hadn't immediately noticed upon entering the kitchen.

He was on the same stool Abram had sat on yesterday while I made hot chocolate, and the first thing I noticed about him was that his eyes were the most startling shade of blue-green. *Like an aquamarine.*

"Oh, hey there. I'm Mona, Leo's sister." I walked forward and extended my hand. He glanced at it impassively, took it, gave it a perfunctory shake, and let it go.

"You're Mona DaVinci," he said in a way that made me feel like he was contradicting me. "That would make Leo *your* brother."

I lifted an eyebrow at him. His lips curved at my confusion, and said bluntly, "We were just talking about this before you came in. In newspaper headlines about the two of you, it always reads something like, 'Mona DaVinci *and brother* are spotted having breakfast at blah blah blah.'"

"It's true!" Leo chimed in cheerfully from his spot at the kitchen table, his eyes full of pride. "Some of my friends call me *and brother.*"

That made Allyn laugh, Kaitlyn shake her head, and Martin smile.

I rolled my eyes at Leo, relieved to see he seemed mostly recovered from his cold, and that he didn't appear to be upset with me about our tense conversation yesterday.

"I'm Martin Sandeke," he added, giving me an assessing look, so I'm sure he didn't miss the recognition flicker behind my eyes.

"You're Martin Sandeke?"

He nodded, his expression bracing.

I glanced at Kaitlyn, recalling our conversation about how her fiancé had started a non-profit organization for helping rural areas gain easier access to the internet.

And suddenly, all is revealed.

Before I could stop myself, I blurted, "Your dad is an asshole."

I knew Denver Sandeke. He was the CEO and majority stakeholder in Sandeke Telecom Systems, the country's largest telecom company and arguably its largest unapologetic monopoly. He'd worked to block any binding measures on net neutrality. He'd also lobbied heavily against the launching of low cost, low maintenance satellites that would serve the dual purpose of providing inexpensive internet service to underserved areas AND helping scientists with space exploration.

Suffice it to say, I loathed him.

Leo and Allyn gasped, but Martin grinned, and then he laughed.

Kaitlyn also didn't seem surprised by my statement either, shrugging and lifting a hand in the air toward me. "Yes. Yes, he is." To

Martin she said, "I told you that you two would get along." And then to herself she mumbled, "You're basically the same person."

Even though Martin didn't seem upset, a rush of embarrassment crested on my cheeks and over my ears. I apologized, profusely, but he continued to be delighted by my outburst. Eventually, he changed the subject to my opinion on anti-laser masquerades, and then drilled me on what we (physicists) knew about merging neutron stars, seeming intensely fascinated by the subject.

Soon, I forgot that I'd made an idiot of myself, and settled into the conversation. Kaitlyn set a cup of coffee down in front of me, along with sugar and the carton of half-and-half, and two hours later I was stunned to discover so much time had passed.

This? Discussing subjects about which I was an expert? This was easy. So easy. This was the center of my rocket. Perhaps I'm pointing out the obvious, but I was always perplexed by people who found this part of me impressive. It's easy to do something when you find it effortless. I mean, that's the definition of easy.

"We should do a double date," Kaitlyn announced to Martin during an extremely short pause in the conversation, like she'd been biding her time to make the proclamation. "The four of us should go out the next time Mona is in New York."

Martin's eyes narrowed on his fiancée. "You're sneaky."

"I am." She grinned.

"What? Why are you sneaky?" I picked up my mug to take a drink and discovered it was empty. Clearly, drinking without thinking was becoming a habit of mine.

"Martin doesn't like Abram," Kaitlyn said. Just like that. Like she was saying, *Martin doesn't like tacos*, which—for the record—seemed equally nuts to me.

"What?" I asked, ignoring the fact for a second that Abram and I would never be double-dating with anyone, and focusing on the impossibility that anyone wouldn't like Abram.

He slid his blue eyes to me. "We don't have anything in common," he said, and I got the sense that this was Martin Sandeke trying to be tactful.

"You both have penises." Kaitlyn hit him on the shoulder lightly and I was suddenly very glad my coffee cup had been empty.

Martin also looked like he was trying not to laugh, and he leaned closer to his fiancée, lowering his voice, "Other than that, we have nothing in common."

Kaitlyn leaned around Martin and focused her attention on me. "I've been trying to get these two to hang out for over a year. Now that Abram is leaving on tour, it'll never happen."

"That's not the only reason it'll never happen." Martin said, *not* under his breath, making me quirk an eyebrow at him.

"What's the other reason?"

Martin glanced at me, his expression frank (I had a feeling his expression was always frank), and said, "Kaitlyn's pregnant."

My mouth dropped open and I asked unthinkingly, "Is the baby Abram's?"

WHAT? MONA! YOU DOOFUS!!

Kaitlyn sucked in a breath, and then tossed her head back to laugh, hitting the counter with her palm.

Martin's lips twisted, like he also thought my question was funny (but maybe also not funny), and he shook his head. "No."

"Oh." Again, embarrassment climbed up my face and I glanced around the kitchen, hoping Leo and Allyn hadn't overheard my stupidity. They weren't anywhere and must've left at some point without me noticing. "I'm sorry. That was, that was—"

"It's fine." Kaitlyn grinned at me, wiping her eyes. "I needed that laugh. Thanks for that." She sniffled, still chuckling.

"Uh, I guess, uh, I don't understand then." I glanced between the two of them. "What does Kaitlyn being pregnant have to do with Martin not hanging out with Abram?"

Martin straightened on his stool, his eyes flickering over me. "We'll have the baby. I'm not going to have time to hang out with anyone, especially not some rock star with groupies all over him, and—"

Kaitlyn elbowed Martin, sending him a stern look. "You know he's not like that."

Martin scoffed. "*All* men are like that."

Her eyes hardened, and she challenged, "Really? Are you like that?"

I couldn't help it, I watched this interaction with interest, hanging on every word. I suddenly wished for popcorn, or a large houseplant to hide behind.

"Of course not, not for a long time and never again. You know how excited I am about the baby, *our* baby. I can't wait. You know better than to ask that. Which one of us is the one pushing for the house? So we'll have a yard?"

Her expression seemed to soften, a small smile curving her lips, but then he added quietly, "But I *was* like that. And your friend Abram is about to travel the world with a fucking harem."

She flinched and said firmly, "Abram has changed." Her gaze darted to me, then away.

"Come on, he's never going to settle down. Remember when you asked him where he wanted to live after the tour? If he was coming back to New York? He said he had no idea, that he had no plans. He just did that underwear modeling thing, soon there will be posters of the guy *in his underwear* everywhere. That's not a guy who's changed. That's a guy who is just getting started."

Underwear modeling?

Martin's words made my heart do strange things in my chest, but my brain seemed to be nodding along, like it wasn't surprised by any of this. *Yep, yep, yep. I agree.*

"You don't know him." Kaitlyn sounded angry.

"So you keep saying," Martin mumbled, clearly disbelieving, and clearly just—in general—disliking Abram.

For the first time since I'd met her, Kaitlyn's face was devoid of humor, and she was staring at Martin like she wanted to singe his eyebrows off with a hot poker.

And that was my cue to leave.

"Well." I stood, making a show out of looking at the clock over the ovens. "It was nice talking with you."

Martin lifted his chin in my direction, and I detected a glimmer of something like devious satisfaction behind his eyes. "You too, Mona."

I looked at Kaitlyn—just briefly—and gave her a tight smile. She seemed to be experiencing many emotions, and I had no doubt that as soon as I left the kitchen, she was going to have a few choice words for her fiancé.

* * *

I marched around in the snow, stomping it down for no reason other than to feel it crunch and compress under my boots. I was extremely agitated. But I didn't have a right to be. Therefore, I stomped.

Maybe I'll start an avalanche and it can match the avalanche of feelings IN MY HEART!!

I sighed, glaring at the horizon, talking myself back from the edge.

Drama llama green isn't a good shade on you, Mona. It brings out your pores.

Try as I might, and despite how exhausted and cold I eventually became, I couldn't escape the agitation caused by accepting my fate. We, Abram and I, were a red giant. A dying star. And that was that.

I sat on the snow, breathing hard from my last bout of stomping, and drew my legs up. Resting my elbows on my knees and clasping my gloved hands together lightly, I stared at the cloudless blue sky.

You know what? I can do this.

Abram and I had a few days left before Sunday. It was only Wednesday. We could fill these hours with a lifetime of memories. Not every happily ever after lasts forever. Why couldn't ours be days instead of years?

I can do this.

I'd had sexual contact with men without being in a relationship. In fact, I'd never been in a romantic, committed relationship, so this—with Abram—should be easy. I'd done it before. Why not with Abram? It made so much sense.

I'm going to do this.

But just like those encounters, what I needed from Abram was his explicit consent. Of course, first I would define my expectations and boundaries, he would define his expectations and boundaries, and then we'd enter into our brief arrangement fully informed. Perfect!

Consent was good. Consent saved people heartache. It removed doubt and disorder and hopefully would dispel this nebulous agitation.

Good. This is good. Good plan.

Movement in the corner of my vision caught my attention and I turned my head. As though I'd conjured him, Abram was there, walking toward me, his hands in his jacket pockets, a lazy smile on his face.

Goodness. I sighed.

I watched him come, enjoying every movement of his body, every moment of his approach. I took a greedy snapshot, saving the image for later, when I needed it.

"Hey there," he said, his voice still sounding sandpapery with sleep. Abram sat next to me in the snow and immediately leaned close to give me a kiss, his hand fisting in my coat to tug and hold me closer.

When our mouths met, he tasted like mint, and his beard tickled my cold face, and warm lips were soon replaced with hot tongue, and that's when my body decided to climb onto his lap. Lifting to one knee, I straddled him, grabbing the front of his coat like he'd done with mine, tugging and holding him closer.

Yeah. We made out in the snow. I felt him grow hard beneath me, through underwear and snow pants and maybe leggings. It frustrated me. Unlike my bathing suit, there were too many layers to yield any real friction or satisfaction. But his mouth made up for the constraints of my clothes, the heat of it moving from my lips to my jaw to my neck to my ear, increasing the temperature of my entire body, my breath hitching, my mind frenzied.

And then, just like he'd done in the pool and in the kitchen yesterday, he stopped. He breathed against my neck for several seconds, sending ticklish shivers racing along my clothed skin, and his hands were gripping me through my puffy coat. Even with the fabric and feathers between his fingers and my body, I felt the strength of him, of them, how he held me.

"Thank you for the note," he said, his voice strained.

He was still hard, pressing against my inner thigh. The man's self-control was impressive, and frustrating.

"You didn't burn it?" I took a deep breath, inhaling his delectable scent, and then leaned back to look at his face.

Abram was smiling. "You told me not to. You wrote *DO NOT BURN* on the outside of the envelope."

Delighted with his grin, without considering my words I said, "I missed your smile. It's infinite-dimensional." That wasn't even the right way to express the concept, but my ability to form words, coherent, intelligent phrases, didn't feel necessary at present.

His smile grew, and he laughed. "Infinite-dimensional?"

"Oh yes. Thank you for it." I moved my arms to twist around his neck. "And I missed it, a lot. Your smiles in photos—and even when I first arrived—they weren't. But this one, up close, and without meanness, definitely is."

"My smiles were mean?"

"Yes. Since we're talking about it, I also remember you being funnier," I teased.

"What?" He continued to grin at me, sounding mock-offended.

"You're not a very funny person anymore."

"How can you say I'm not funny? You were *begging* me yesterday to stop telling jokes."

"Yes, but those were Chuck Norris jokes. Those are universally funny." Now I was laughing.

Abram flashed his teeth, making a face like a snarl. "Is this a mean smile? How can a smile be mean?"

"I don't know, but it's something you've perfected. Mean smiles, no jokes, broody eyebrows. You're like an arthouse movie but without the nudity."

He laughed, *hard,* at that, and so did I, loving his face right now. I decided I loved his face best when he laughed.

Eventually, tilting his head to the side, he said, "Well, I can fix that."

"Good. Because, like I said, I really miss your smile. And you—"

"I meant the nudity."

I barked a laugh, and his answering chuckle sounded low and sinister.

"Very funny," I said, shaking my head at him. "Now you're a comedian."

He smiled, just a small one, but my heart lifted at the sight. Though it was small, it looked meaningful, intentional, like a gift just for me. My breath caught and, again, I sighed.

"Am I smiling?" he asked, his eyes on my lips. "Is it mean?"

"No," I responded, dazed. "It's a good one." It was the best. I took another greedy snapshot, saving the image for later.

When I needed it.

[17]

SELECTED RADIOACTIVE ISOTOPES

Mona

We made snow angels. Together. It was fun. His were huge. He'd also brought food with him in a bag I hadn't noticed earlier. My Abram-tunnel vision was apparently a strong force.

Abram spread out a picnic of hot broccoli and cheese soup, warm, crusty sourdough bread, and hot tea laced with the barest hint of whiskey. He warned me before drinking it, pointing out that he'd brought un-spiked tea as well. I was freezing, so I'd had the winter tea.

We spent several hours in the snow, having *the best* time while I struggled to find just the right moment to bring up my proposal. My *fling* proposal, to be precise. But whenever a break in conversation occurred, I swallowed the words, bargaining with myself, reasoning that I could do it later.

Ten more minutes.

But then the perfect moment presented itself. We'd just finished the picnic and were packing up, quietly working side by side. Our previous conversation had just wrapped up—about his sister and how she was engaged and getting married soon—and I had my chance.

And so, sucking in a breath for bravery, I asked, "Do you think you'll ever want to get married?"

Ah. Comet balls!

That wasn't asking him about a fling. That was literally *the opposite* of asking him about a fling.

He smiled a small smile, his attention on his hands as they packed the bag. "To be honest, I've never really thought about it."

I nodded, my blood rushing between my ears. I couldn't think. How could I save this conversation and redirect it toward fling territory?

Abram added, "I read an article about you once where the interviewer asked that same question." He lifted his eyes, they ensnared mine. "You said, 'Irrelevant. Next question.'"

"Oh. Ha!" I tried to laugh lightly, but it sounded forced. "They always ask me that, and it irritates me, because no one asks any of my male colleagues. It's always, 'What will you do when you have kids?' and I'm like, 'The same thing I do every night, Pinky. Try to take over the world.'"

He grinned at me, shaking his head like I was *too much* of something wonderful. "I loved that cartoon."

"I would judge you if you didn't." Returning his smile, I gave into the urge to grab his coat and pull him forward for a quick kiss. Because I could.

But when I went to lean away, I discovered he'd caught my jacket again and I couldn't move.

Staring at me, his gorgeous brown eyes serious and searching, he said, "Mona, I want to see you again."

A spike of blissful happiness was followed quickly by a spike of dread. I blinked, bracing myself, it was now or never.

Here we go.

"Of course." I nodded, my throat full of fire. "Actually, yes. I want to talk to you about that. I'm—" I uncurled his fingers from my coat "—I'm glad you brought it up."

"Good." His tone was firm. "I wanted to bring it up yesterday, but I didn't want to ruin our time together. Mona . . ." Abram opened his mouth, closed it, opened it again, his gaze felt both eager and restrained. "Mona, I leave tomorrow morning. We have to be at the airport by 4:30 AM."

. . . *Oh.*

Abram's face, less than two decimeters away, blurred, my vision becoming gray, cloudy. I wasn't crying or close to it. I'd cried my quota for the last ten years over the past week. If I cried today, I would no longer be able to label myself "not a crier," and that felt like an essential part of my identity.

But, given this news of his imminent departure, I probably would cry at some point. *And then I'll have to call myself a crier. I won't be "not a crier" anymore.*

. . .

Okay. That's fine. I'll just be a crier.

I made a mental note to invest in Kleenex.

"Mona?"

My name coming from Abram's lips brought him back into focus. Apparently, I was nodding for some reason.

"Of course." I continued nodding. Then I stood, studied the ground where we'd had our picnic for any left items, and then turned toward the house.

"Mona, talk to me." He was right there, walking at my side while I swallowed reflexively and worked to paste a convincing smile on my face.

"Yes. We should definitely meet up again," I said, trying to force a little cheerfulness into my tone.

He must've suspected something was off because I felt intensity behind his eyes as he continued to watch my profile. "What's wrong?"

"Nothing."

"Mona. Honesty."

"Nothing. Not really." Now I shook my head. "It's just, I don't know why I thought I would have more time with you before you had to leave."

His hand on my arm brought me to a stop and he tugged, encouraging me to face him. "I wish we had more time too. But we'll see each other. I'll have breaks during the tour. I can come visit you."

"In Geneva?"

Abram frowned, his fingers flexing on my arm. "What?"

"I'll be in Geneva until at least June. Maybe longer."

He stared at me, blinking several times. "Geneva, as in Switzerland?"

"Specifically, at CERN, at the European Laboratory for Particle Physics."

I studied him while he absorbed this news, noted how his eyes lost focus and they darted around at nothing.

"I didn't realize that," he said quietly, like he was talking to himself.

"I didn't tell you. Or, I mean, it didn't occur to me to tell you, meaning we've only really been on speaking terms for about thirty-six hours and I honestly thought for some inexplicable reason that you would be here through Sunday. So . . ."

He stared at me. I stared at him. We were surrounded by a mountain of snow, but it felt like—instead of surrounding us—it stood between us.

But we can have tonight. We can—

"Mona."

"Hmm?"

The muscle at his jaw flexed, his stare now determined. "We'll make it work."

I nodded, but the nod was a lie, so I stopped nodding and turned back to the house. His hand on my arm slid down to my gloved fingers, squeezing them.

We walked in silence, holding hands, for a while, reaching the house, removing our wet boots and outer layers in the mudroom. The silence continued as we walked up the stairs, each footstep sounding like the seconds ticking on a clock.

We made a detour to the kitchen where we dropped off the picnic stuff. Lila was putting the finishing touches on dinner and shooed us away when we tried to clean our dishes. She was so nice. I liked Lila.

Eventually, too soon, we reached my door. I placed my hand on the door handle, Abram at my shoulder, his hands in his pockets. I didn't turn the handle.

I'd never experienced the sensation of time running out. Yes, I'd had projects with due dates—big ones—and deadlines. But it never felt like this. That whole "sands through the hourglass" thing made so much more sense to me now. Each grain of sand was a moment, a final moment.

The meal we'd shared was probably our last meal, together. Holding hands as we walked through the snow would be the last time we held hands. This would be the last time I opened my door with him standing next to me. Tonight he would come inside my room, we would be together, and the final—the very last—moment would follow.

And that would be the end.

Give me another minute. I just want one more minute.

Keeping my eyes forward, I said, "You should come inside."

"Yes." His answer was immediate. "Yes. I'll come in."

I opened the door. I walked inside. He followed. He closed the door. I turned on him. I grabbed him. I kissed him.

He kissed me back.

Smart Mona reminded me that we hadn't yet discussed expecta-tions and boundaries. He hadn't consented. But, you know what? Neither had I. At no point had I consented to feeling like my heart was being ripped out of my body, that tomorrow didn't matter because he would be gone. Thinking about the day after that, and the day after that, and the day after that felt overwhelming, like attempting to comprehend the vastness of space.

It stretched on, forever. There was a hypothetical end, to the universe, to me, to all this pain and longing and damn *yearning*, but it remained just that. Hypothetical. Beyond my reach or understanding. I couldn't fathom it.

But I could fathom now.

"Mona, what are you doing?" He caught my hands as I reached for the button of his pants, so I redirected them under his shirt, to the hard, glorious planes of his stomach and chest and back. He felt so good, hot, hard, necessary.

"I want you." I kissed his neck, his jaw. "Don't you want me?"

Time moving. Always away, always forward. Once lost, lost forever.

"There's no rush," he said, but his hands moved under my shirt too, lifting it, rushing to palm me through the fabric of my bra. "We can—" I felt his Adam's apple move with a swallow, his fingers pulled down the cup, massaged me, he groaned, "—take our time. This isn't goodbye."

This isn't goodbye.

My throat closed at the words. This was goodbye. In the morning, he'd be gone. His tour was twelve months. He'd be surrounded by women who desired him for his talent and body, and maybe even for his glorious heart. They would be gorgeous, and clever, and tempting, and probably lovely, good people.

Monogamy isn't for musicians. They will feed his voracious creative soul.

"Wait." Abram caught my hands again, lifting his mouth. "Wait. Mona. Stop."

I did. I stopped. I dropped my chin to my chest and I took a deep, bracing breath.

"What is going on?"

"I told you, I want you."

"No. You're frantic."

"I frantically want you." I pulled my hands out of his grip and turned away, pacing to the window and opening it. "It's stuffy in here," I mumbled.

He watched me as I breathed in the cool air, saying nothing.

He watched me as I turned and walked to the bed, saying nothing.

He watched me as I sat on it, folding and refolding my hands, and he said, "You don't believe me."

"About what?"

"This isn't goodbye."

"It is goodbye." My voice was robotic, because if any situation deserved a divorce of emotion from facts, it was this conversation.

"Oh? Really? You don't want to see me after this?" He sounded so hurt.

I rubbed my chest, because the hurt in his voice echoed in the chambers of my heart. "I would love to see you after this. I would love to see you any time you want to see me."

He seemed to pause here, as though trying to parse through what I'd just said, as though it were a riddle.

Eventually, he demanded, "Then why do you think this is goodbye?"

"Because—"

"Because you'll be in Geneva? That's not an issue. Distance won't be an issue. We'll make it work."

I covered my face, rubbed my eyes, and then dropped my hands. "Because monogamy isn't for musicians."

The room fell eerily silent, almost like he'd disappeared from it. Or maybe I'd disappeared.

Even if I was speaking to an empty room, I felt compelled to say, "A year is a long time. I know . . . I know what tours are like. I went on several with my parents. Lisa and I always got along with my dad's friends. They'd take care of us backstage. One woman, Vivviane, taught us how to braid our hair into crowns."

I lifted my eyes to Abram. He was still watching me, but his expression teetered between anguished and bracing. I suspected he already understood where I was going with this story.

Even so, I continued, "It wasn't until I was eleven and my mom visited me at a science summer camp with one of *her* friends that I added one and one together, and I realized one plus one makes several more than two. After meeting her boyfriend, after she confirmed who and what he was, so many other things made sense— about the women I'd seen with my father when he'd taken us on tour, about why my parents never seemed to both be home at the same time, about the women who sometimes spent the week with us in Chicago, to keep my father company, while my mother was out of town."

"Mona—"

"They've been open with us about it, and I don't judge them for their lifestyle. In fact, they've always made a point to be sex positive with us, which I've appreciated. Sex should be fun. It should be equally beneficial for both parties. Reciprocation is a must. Clear consent, communication of expectations ahead of time, and safe words are essential. And, on that note, what's your safe word?"

Abram's forehead wrinkled, his dazed expression telling me he was having trouble keeping up. "You want to know my safe word."

"Yes. I do."

"Why?" he demanded, the anguish in his stare replaced with suspicion.

I was glad he'd burned my letter, *the letter*.

In addition to brimming with hot feelings, it also contained the hopes I'd had for our future. Ever since I'd driven through that neighborhood with him—his parents' neighborhood—the recollection of those pretty houses with picket fences, and US flags, and gardens, and toys in the front yard had become the centerpiece of my imagined future.

My childhood had been so chaotic, and those houses, each looking so similar, exuded order and consistency. If he'd read the letter I'd been carrying with me for over two years, full of impossible dreams, then I wouldn't have been able to say the words that were on the tip of my tongue. He would've known what I really wanted.

"I'd like to have sex with you," I said, folding my arms. "And if you want to have sex with me—no pressure—we should talk about it, before we do it, make sure we're both on the same page, you know?"

Abram, staring at me, his lips slightly parted, stood as though a statue for a count of four seconds. I know because I counted. And then a little puff of air left his parted lips, one of disbelief.

"You want to have sex with me," he repeated, not a question, more like restating my take-out order, to confirm.

"That's right. I'd like a fling. But, obviously, I'd like your consent first."

Something behind his eyes shifted, grew darker. It reminded me of the sky when a sudden storm gathers, the light changes, the mood shifts.

He was angry. I'd made him angry.

Confirming this, through clenched teeth, he said, "I do not consent to a f—" he stopped himself, like he'd been about to say something he didn't want to. Breathing out, he finished, "To a *fling*."

I likewise gritted my teeth, a cloud of fury encased my brain. "Well. Fine. Fine. Okay then."

"Mona—" He took a step forward.

I lifted a hand to stop him. "No. That's, I mean. That's it then. Right?"

"No!" He began pacing in front of me, pushing his hands through his hair, loosening it from the tie that held it back "Stop trying to put us in a fucking box!"

"Oh? You want space?"

"Mona—"

"I get it. You want to fly, right? You need freedom. For your creativity. For your—"

"Mona!" he snapped. Actually, he exploded, my name sounding like a command. "Shut. Up."

I closed my mouth, pressing my lips together, and moving my eyes to the wall behind him. He crossed to me, knelt in front of me, covered my hands with his, and I flinched at the contact.

He noticed, his eyes flashing hurt, but he didn't pull them away. "Listen to me. Listen. I'm in love with you."

I scoffed, shaking my head, shifting my gaze to a spot beyond him. "You said yourself, you don't know me."

"I don't want anyone but you."

"That's kind of you to say. Thank you." I gave him a tight smile but not my eyes, removing one of my hands to pat his. "And, as we've established, I also want you."

He exhaled, it sounded beyond frustrated. "No. I'm not—this isn't —*goddamnit!*" His hands moved to my arms and I finally looked at him. His eyes were wild, his voice a deep growl. "Listen and believe me. I've done that. I've tried that. Maybe it works for some people. I hated it." He shook his head firmly. "When you left, and all I could think of was you, all I wanted was you, but I thought I was crazy, I tried filling the hollowed out spaces with women. With alcohol. With violence and aggression. With anything that might distract me from the blinding absence of *you*."

Ugh!

My eyes were stinging, and my emotions were banging at the door with a battering ram. *Let us in! We want to hurt you!*

"Abram—"

"What I'm telling you is this—" His fingers flexed and he bent his head, forcing me to maintain eye-contact. The courage and determination within his gaze stole my breath, it seemed endless, boundless, immeasurable. "I am not built that way. Being sober isn't hard. Keeping my temper comes naturally unless it comes to you asking me to consent to a *fling*. I haven't been with anyone in over a year, and I don't miss it. I don't miss women. I don't crave women. I've never craved women. I crave *you*. There is no substitute, there is no additional accessory required. But if you don't feel this way about me, if you don't, you have to tell me. Now. Right now."

It was no use. Feelings bashed through the last barrier, pitchforks in hand, and punched smart Mona in the face. She was down for the count, leaving stupid Mona to throw herself into Abram's arms. I bawled. He caught me, cradled me, brought me to his lap on the floor, stroked my hair, kissed my face, held me close. He was so warm.

"I love you," he said. "Trust me," he said.

What else could I do?

I did.

* * *

I looked around the empty room, my gaze focusing on dust dancing in a beam of sunlight. A reminder.

There was so much, in life, in the world around us, that we rarely had a chance to see, but it didn't make those things any less real. We might experience and have access to the by-product, but rarely the thing itself.

Invisible forces, energy, quarks, radiation, dust dancing in a sunbeam, Abram.

Abram wasn't here. I couldn't see him. But I could remember his words, his smile, his touch, the sound of his heart. When I left Aspen, I would download and listen to his music. He was real.

Nodding at the truth of this, and trying to find comfort in it, I fought against the rising wave of tears. I took several deep breaths, blinking my eyes, and promising myself I wouldn't cry. *I won't cry*, not until I made it to the bathroom for a box of tissues. And then I would cry like crying was my job.

Tossing my legs over the side of the bed, I paused to drape a blanket along my shoulders, smelling it because it smelled like him. And that's when I spotted an envelope on the side table.

The outside read, *Do not burn*, but it wasn't my handwriting. My heart leapt, and then fell, and then recovered enough to settle some-place in the vicinity of my throat. He hadn't woken me when he left. We'd lain together, talking, holding each other, sometimes kissing, until I'd fallen asleep.

And when I awoke, he was gone.

I snatched the envelope and stared at the blank ink on the white paper, the remarkably elegant cursive, and I opened it, feeling greedy for even a small portion of him.

Within was a piece of lined white paper that looked like it had been ripped out of a notebook. I unfolded the paper, taking care to press the crease neatly open, and I read the words.

Thoughts come easiest in the night.
In a room of light,
I see only the absence of you.
Darkness, though I cannot see,
Embraces me.
I'm blinded, yet my view is clear.
It feels possible that you are near, present, here.
So when you view your evening sky
Reach out to the night and there I'll be.
This is not goodbye.

—Yours always, Abram

ABOUT THE AUTHOR

Penny Reid is the *New York Times*, *Wall Street Journal*, and *USA Today* Bestselling Author of the Winston Brothers, Knitting in the City, Rugby, Dear Professor, and Hypothesis series. She used to spend her days writing federal grant proposals as a biomedical researcher, but now she just writes books. She's also a full time mom to three diminutive adults, wife, daughter, knitter, crocheter, sewer, general crafter, and thought ninja.

Come find me -
Mailing List: http://pennyreid.ninja/newsletter/
Goodreads: http://www.goodreads.com/ReidRomance
Email: pennreid@gmail.com ...hey, you! Email me ;-)

OTHER BOOKS BY PENNY REID

Knitting in the City Series

(Contemporary Romantic Comedy)

Neanderthal Seeks Human: A Smart Romance (#1)

Neanderthal Marries Human: A Smarter Romance (#1.5)

Friends without Benefits: An Unrequited Romance (#2)

Love Hacked: A Reluctant Romance (#3)

Beauty and the Mustache: A Philosophical Romance (#4)

Ninja at First Sight (#4.75)

Happily Ever Ninja: A Married Romance (#5)

Dating-ish: A Humanoid Romance (#6)

Marriage of Inconvenience: (#7)

Neanderthal Seeks Extra Yarns (#8)

Knitting in the City Coloring Book (#9)

Winston Brothers Series

(Contemporary Romantic Comedy, spinoff of *Beauty and the Mustache*)

Beauty and the Mustache (#0.5)

Truth or Beard (#1)

Grin and Beard It (#2)

Beard Science (#3)

Beard in Mind (#4)

Dr. Strange Beard (#5)

Beard with Me (#5.5, coming 2019)

Beard Necessities (#6, coming 2019)

Hypothesis Series

(New Adult Romantic Comedy)

Elements of Chemistry: <u>ATTRACTION</u>, <u>HEAT</u>, and <u>CAPTURE</u> (#1)

Laws of Physics: <u>MOTION</u>, <u>SPACE</u>, and <u>TIME</u> (#2)

Fundamentals of Biology: STRUCTURE, EVOLUTION, and GROWTH (#3, coming 2021)

Irish Players (Rugby) Series – by L.H. Cosway and Penny Reid

(Contemporary Sports Romance)

The Hooker and the Hermit (#1)

The Pixie and the Player (#2)

The Cad and the Co-ed (#3)

The Varlet and the Voyeur (#4)

Dear Professor Series

(New Adult Romantic Comedy)

Kissing Tolstoy (#1)

Kissing Galileo (#2, read for FREE in Penny's newsletter 2018-2019)

Ideal Man Series

(Contemporary Romance Series of Jane Austen Re-Tellings)

Pride and Dad Jokes (#1, coming 2019)

Man Buns and Sensibility (#2, TBD)

Sense and Manscaping (#3, TBD)

Persuasion and Man Hands (#4, TBD)

Mantuary Abbey (#5, TBD)

Mancave Park (#6, TBD)

Emmanuel (#7, TBD)

CPSIA information can be obtained
at www.ICGtesting.com
Printed in the USA
BVHW082121260219
541209BV00003BB/3/P